CHANGES COME HARD

SAVANNAH TAYLOR

Dedicated to my horse, Chica

Foreword

Hello!

I can't wait for you to get started with *Changes Come Hard*. I knew Carmen and Lander needed a second book, if only because of the trauma Lander endured. There was no way he could make a night-and-day switch and have it stick. His changes will come after struggling with himself in ways he never planned on. But change... true change will only come when he sees the effect this struggling has on Carmen. His love for her is the only thing that can save them.

I hope you enjoy this wonderful story.

Savannah

*let's keep in touch! Sign up for my newsletter here...
https://sendfox.com/lp/1w9yz6

Chapter One

This was no East Coast, New York City snowstorm. Carmen wrapped a wool throw tighter around her shoulders. A fire crackled behind her, warming one side, while the chill of winter pushed straight through the glass panes and sent shivers up her arms. The snow had dropped another few inches in the time it had taken her to shower and dress for the evening. That made over twelve inches in less than twenty-four hours. Even power and cell service were out. Thank goodness for a large wood-burning fireplace.

"We're headed out for the day, Carmen."

She turned from the window to see two farm hands, Jake and Chance. Jake with brown hair and Chance with blond. Although they weren't related, they had the same dark brown eyes. They were both young, with Chance being twenty-four and Jake just turning nineteen. They waited patiently for her to answer as if they were ready to complete another task should she ask. But the cattle were fed and watered and huddled safely in their shelters. The horse stalls were cleaned, and the animals were cared for. The pathways and roads to Cedar Lodge had been plowed, and the firewood was stacked. Everything was in order for the night.

"Thank you," she said, genuinely grateful for their help. "Goodnight."

"Goodnight," they both replied. Jake held his hat in front of him, and Chance touched the brim of his hat as he left.

"Oh, wait." She turned from the window suddenly. "Did those propane tanks get delivered to Lander? With the cell service down, I haven't been able to contact him." Her pulse quickened as a hundred possibilities crowded her mind. Visions of the man she loved shivering and sick, trapped or hurt. If only cell service would return. It had been two days, and she was barely hanging on.

"It's a wonder he was ever able to get service in the high country," Chance said.

"We did, ma'am," Jake answered, always the one to give a direct answer. In the days and weeks that Lander had been away, she'd relied heavily on him. "I loaded them myself onto the sled, and Asher took them out to him along with the supplies he paid for. Lumber, tarps, and water barrels being among them."

Carmen sighed, finding a bit of relief from her anxiety.

"You loaded the supply sled with tanks for Lander?" Chance asked, turning to Jake. "Full propane tanks? Two days ago?"

"Of course," Jake responded. "He needed them for heat. That little cabin of his doesn't have a working fireplace. He should have gotten them right before this storm, thank goodness—" Jake stopped suddenly, analyzing Chance's face. "Is there something you need to tell me?"

"I..." Chance glanced at Carmen and then turned back to Jake. "I removed the tanks."

"You what?" Carmen's shock had her thoughts spinning. "Why would you do that?"

Chance lifted his hands in defense. "When they were loading up supplies and said it was going to Lander, I assumed they needed to be removed. Why would he be using propane in the high country? I—I thought they were needed here, so I placed them with the rest of the tanks in the supply shed."

Jake took a deep breath, wiping one hand across his face. Then he looked at Carmen.

She was sure her heart was going to beat clean through her chest. And that imagination? It ignited with all the possibilities of horror and anguish. Her eyes strayed to the window where night had fallen and still, the storm continued to rage.

"Now hold on, Carmen," Jake said. He placed his hand on her arm as if to steady her. As if he feared she would bolt out the door and run all the way to Lander's cabin.

And he wasn't exactly wrong.

In fact, she was already plotting the best ways of getting out to him. Her chest was crushed with the sudden need to make sure he was okay. Never mind that it was dark out and the storm had piled a ridiculous amount of snow across the entire region. This was Lander! He was living in a pathetic shack, and if he was depending on those propane tanks for heat...

She took a deep breath, and another followed quickly on its heels.

"Look at me." Jake placed his hand on her other arm, holding her in front of him and waiting until her eyes settled on his. "Lander isn't helpless, and if he's the man I believe he is, he wouldn't just sit around hoping we got the tanks to him. Right? He'd have a backup plan."

"Right," Carmen said, dropping her head with an exhale. Jake was young, but right now, she was grateful for his strength. "You're right." She swallowed down her panic and steadied herself, glancing from Jake to Chance. "I just wish I could talk to him. How long do you think the power will be out?"

"Usually, it's a few days in a storm like this one," Chance said. There was sympathy in his eyes, but also a hardness she knew she needed. This wasn't a place for panic. She was hunkered down in the middle of the Bridger-Teton wilderness of Wyoming. Self-sufficiency and courage were the values people lived on. Even Chance and Jake hadn't thought twice about traveling home in such a storm. It was life for them. Just another winter day.

"Thanks, both of you," Carmen said, mustering more confidence in her expression than she felt inside. But faking it was just going to have to work for a while until she had more experience. "I'll be fine."

"How's Maddie handling all this?" Jake asked. His gaze scanned the quiet cabin.

Carmen managed a smile. "She'd doing good, but she came down with a cold and went to bed early. I'm sure she'll be feeling better tomorrow." After visiting from New York City, her quiet, book-loving friend had changed all her plans and asked to stay. She said the wind of Wyoming spoke to her and she needed to be surrounded by its melody for a little longer. But Carmen suspected her friend would never leave. Once the grandeur of the Tetons sunk under your skin, there was no other remedy for such an obsession.

"I'm sorry to hear it."

Carmen's gaze lifted from her musings to settle on Jake again. He was looking down the hall now. Maddie's bedroom was the first door on the right, and he knew that. Carmen had suspected Jake admired her friend, but now she could see it clearly on his face. He undoubtedly had at least a small crush. But if he wanted to surpass all Maddie's book-boyfriend expectations, it was going to take some work.

"She'll be okay," Carmen repeated, giving him a quick smile as his eyes returned to her.

"Of course, she will," he said with a grin and a whisper of rouge on his cheeks. "Asher said he'll be clearing the roads at midnight, and we'll be back in the early morning to clear them again."

"Yes, thank you." Carmen followed them, holding on to the door as they left. "Goodnight."

Once she closed the door, the cabin was silent. With all the deep snow pressed against the sides of the wood logs and piled on top of the roof, it acted as a muffler to the world. She could feel its heavy presence even from indoors. In a small way, it was comforting, like the protection of a cave in the mountains.

Usually, she would have the caretaker with her. Annette, a seasoned woman with a gentle spirit and a strong work ethic. But she'd gone to visit some family in southern Arizona. A great time for it, really. Getting the sunshine in before a long Wyoming winter. Then there was her cook, Dusty. He was a burly man with tatted arms and a joyful smile. But he'd made a change of careers, settling close to the nursing home that housed his parents. He'd opened up a corner bakery, and by the last report, it was doing very well.

Carmen stood in front of the fire, watching the blaze

smolder away. It had been burning most of the day and now generated heat waves that distorted the lines of the metal grate. Its warmth was soothing, but her mind hadn't calmed. After talking to Jake and Chance, she was only worrying more about Lander and how he could possibly keep warm and safe in this storm. She'd heard others talking about the early winter storm and how fierce it was. Only mid-October. Apparently, big winter storms like this one didn't hit until late November or even December.

What if Lander was caught off guard? When she'd spoken to him last, he sounded like he was working more on preparing spaces for his cattle than he was working on his own shelter. And now, with him not receiving the propane for his two portable heaters...

Carmen cringed and began pacing, trying to force her thoughts in a positive direction. She reminded herself that Lander had been on his own since he was only fifteen. He knew how to survive in the wilderness and had done it before. He was going to be fine.

Still, she bit her lip and forced herself to settle in for the night. She pulled the softest chair closest to the fire and wrapped herself in a heavy alpaca blanket. The flames of the fire flickered and leapt above glowing orange embers, making her eyelids grow heavy.

Her cell phone rang, and she jumped. Finally! She raced to the counter where it sat vibrating against the granite. Lander's name was on the screen, and she answered before the second ring.

"Hello?"

Wind howled through the phone. She pulled it back a few inches, but there was no answer.

"Hello?" she asked louder.

"Jake!" Lander's voice bellowed into the phone. "I need your help! The storm came on too strong. The front was so powerful, it knocked down most of the south wall of my cabin. There's nowhere for me to go for shelter, but I can't leave my cows."

Panic exploded in Carmen's chest. "Lander?" She'd tried to yell, but her voice was shaking.

"Can you hear me?" Lander shouted. "Can you get Asher and the boys and bring the sleds out?"

"Lander, this is Carmen!"she shouted. But there was no answer. The sound of the wind flickered and cut out.

"Lander!" She looked at the screen of her phone to see the call had ended. Cell reception was down again. She pressed call again and again, but there was no dial tone. Nothing.

She stared wide-eyed across the cabin, picturing Lander at that moment. She'd gone out to the cabin with him once before he'd begun repairs. It was practically uninhabitable. To imagine him attempting to shelter there through a storm like this one was terrifying. Especially with one wall knocked down.

There was a sudden gust of wind and the wood logs of the cabin creaked against it.

What was she going to do? She couldn't call anyone and the soonest they'd return was at midnight when Asher plowed the roads. That was four hours away, and Lander sounded desperate. He needed help now.

"Is everything all right?"

Carmen whipped around to find Maddie's green eyes blinking back sleep. Her short, brown hair was mussed but still managed to look cute. She had a blanket wrapped around her, and her cheeks were red with fever.

"Were you shouting?" Maddie said, yawning and rubbing her eyes.

"Oh, Maddie, I'm sorry I woke you." Carmen crossed her arms around herself, realizing what she had to do. "Lander's in trouble, and I don't think it can wait until Asher returns. I'm going to go out there."

"What?" Maddie's eyes opened completely for the first time. "Now? You can't be serious, Carmen."

"I can take Dax and bring the propane tanks out to Lander." Carmen's knees began to shake, and she took a deep breath. "Then at least he'll have heat. And Dax is a great horse. He knows the way, and you can tell Asher when he gets here. Have him get his brothers and Jake and head up with the sleds and some tools. Whatever they might need to help build up a cabin wall."

"No, Carmen. This is crazy." Maddie grabbed Carmen's arm, but her grip was weak and tired. "Just wait until Asher gets here. He'll know what to do."

"I already know what to do, Maddie." Carmen gave her friend a hug, and she could feel the heat from her fevered skin. "I'm sorry to ask you to do this when you're sick, but —" Carmen's voice faltered, and she took a quick breath, chasing off the emotions before they could build. "If I don't go out there, he might not make it. It's not that far. With Dax, I can be there in an hour. Okay? Just send the guys behind me and it'll be fine."

Maddie still looked unhappy with the idea, but Carmen was happy enough that she didn't argue. She hurried through the cabin and grabbed her pack before she could think too much about it. Gathering food and emergency supplies, she shoved them all inside, zipping it up. She dragged Maddie to her chair and guided her into a comfortable spot. "Here,"

Carmen said, pulling the blankets up around her. "Just set the alarm on your phone for 11:30 and flicker the porch lights when you see his truck. He'll come up to see what's wrong."

"And if he doesn't notice?" Maddie was eyeing Carmen with a tired mixture of irritation and fear.

Carmen looked down at her phone, but the reception was still out. "He'll notice," she assured. Before her friend had the chance to talk her out of it, she slipped on her snow pants, a heavy sub-zero coat, and tall snow boots and headed for the barn. Maddie looked like she was already half asleep as she raised her hand in a goodbye gesture. Thoughts of her friend sleeping through her alarm had Carmen breathing harder. She closed her eyes and whispered out a quick prayer, knowing that God was the master of the storm. It might not be in his plans to stop the snow completely, but perhaps he could shelter her enough to make it through and give Maddie a nudge if needed.

Amen.

The moment she opened the door and stepped onto the deck, wind thrashed at her body. Snow caked into her eyes and hair and the chill took her breath away. She pulled her hood up, providing a little cover, and trudged down the snow-covered steps. Her hands cramped from the cold. She reached into her pockets to find her snow gloves and slipped her hands quickly inside. They provided much-welcome protection, and she hurried to the barn, sliding the heavy doors open just enough to squeeze through. Snow swirled into the opening with her, shooting into the dry barn until she pulled them shut again. The noise of the storm whistled through the small cracks and spaces in the wood planks.

All three horses nickered at her, their sounds each a

different pitch from low and hollow to high and firm. It was a beautiful sort of melody, and she was grateful for their calm strength. Horses seemed to only fear small things, like snakes or plastic bags. A big, powerful storm? It was nothing.

"Okay, Dax," Carmen said, patting the other two horses as she made her way to the last stall. "Lander needs our help. You ready to do this?"

Dax was a big, black Appaloosa gelding. His rump was doused in white, like paint had been splattered across it. A beautiful animal that she'd loved since she was a little girl, even if she'd spent most of her adult life away from Cedar Lodge. Now, the lodge belonged to her. She intended to make a good future out of it. But that future was nothing without the man she loved. She needed to get to Lander.

When Dax was saddled and loaded with emergency gear, blankets, and propane, she opened the back door of the barn. The snow hadn't eased one bit. In fact, it howled stronger than before.

"It's just a little snow," Carmen said. She stepped into the saddle and pointed Dax straight toward the high country of the Bridger-Teton wilderness.

Chapter Two

The ride was torturously slow, but Carmen feared pushing Dax too hard. With each step, it seemed the snow grew deeper until it nearly touched the big horse's belly. With his nose tucked against the wind and his ears down, the strong Appaloosa plowed ahead. As long as they didn't rush, she knew he had plenty of strength for the journey. The bigger concern was keeping track of their location. Everything was white, and the trees were caked in snow. It covered the natural landmarks so completely that her only guide was the clearings between the forested areas.

She hoped that wolves hunkered down in storms. The thought of the neighboring pack tracking them during their journey was enough to have chills tingling at the back of her neck. But she kept her focus on leading Dax up the mountain, glad when she was able to spot the lookout that Lander had brought her to once. It was at the edge of a sheer cliff with a view of Cedar Lodge. At least, it did when the sky was clear. Now there was nothing to see but snow and clouds. But to miss the cliff would be a deadly mistake.

Turning the big horse up the mountain, she let him slow as he navigated the larger boulders. Most of them were still visible and left a lump of snow protruding far above the rest, but others were smaller and required a readjustment of his foot placement. He paused at nearly every step, tapping his foot down until he was sure. It seemed he understood where they were going, even though he'd only been there once. Carmen was glad the big horse at least had that memory.

Her memories from that day rushed in as she shivered against the storm and rubbed Dax's neck encouragingly. She'd chased after Lander when she learned he'd left Cedar Lodge. Riding Dax, she'd charged up the mountain and confronted him. Her anger she remembered well, as it had been searing on her skin like fire. She'd been hardly able to hold back her frustration at him, and her words had come sharply from her lips. But the moment he confessed his feelings for her, it all crumbled away. As easily as dust in the wind, it was gone and all that remained was an overwhelming need for him. It had broken her apart in the best way.

Suddenly her heart throbbed, feeling raw. Unprotected and vulnerable. Carmen brought her hand to her chest, pressing against the sudden ache. The snow stung her cheeks, but she no longer felt it. All she could feel was her fear that something had happened to him. She wanted to kick Dax's sides, to urge him on until he couldn't go any faster. But that would be a mistake. Getting there carefully was the only way to go in conditions like these, especially when she was alone. So, she held the reins loosely and let him have his head. He had a better feel for the land around them than she did; that much was obvious.

It hit her slowly, the moment they were back where

they'd been before. She sat up in the saddle, looking around at the curve of the land and the way it sloped down in front of her. Snow flew into her eyes, but she shaded them with her gloved hand and looked out on a thick forest to her right and a meadow at the bottom of the hill. A tiny cabin huddled at the base against the trees. There was no light in the windows and no smoke coming from the chimney. Only silence and stillness.

"Dax, there it is!" She shouted, squeezing her legs ever so gently. She couldn't help it. The big horse's steps quickened, and he lifted his head in the direction of the cabin. Whinnying floated above the wind and then the chugging rhythm of a mule's bray, signaling that at least Lander's animals knew of her arrival. But there was no sign of Lander.

Carmen searched desperately, squinting against the snow as she scanned the cabin and barn and then the trees. Had he gone somewhere else for shelter?

Dax stumbled, and she quickly pulled back on the reins. He pranced a bit, finding his footing again. As much as her heart was racing, she let him continue as slowly as he needed. It was agonizing waiting, but there was no other option.

When they finally managed to reach the cabin, she swung out of the saddle and led Dax under the trees and into a shed. Lander's horse and Mule stood watching with their ears perked. She tied Dax up and headed back to the cabin.

"Lander!" She shouted, with the storm billowing in her ears. The side of the cabin that faced down the mountain had a large piece missing, like it had caved in. It must have been what Lander was trying to say when he called. She walked toward it with her adrenaline pumping so hard she felt ready to pass out.

Stepping into the hole in the side, she ducked her head and entered the dark room. There was no change in temperature aside from a small amount of protection from the wind. "Lander?" She called, quieter now. As she went farther into the building, the storm was mostly blocked, which was more than she'd expected. But she didn't see any sign of the cowboy. It looked like she'd entered the living area with a small kitchen at the back. She continued down a dark hall to find two-bedroom doors on either side.

Pushing one open, she glanced in to see it wasn't furnished. Just a wood floor and a window on one wall. There was no closet to speak of, just a space cut out of the wall where she assumed one could push a dresser. She hurried across the hall and opened the last door. "Lander?"

Something moved on the floor, and she jumped, covering her mouth with one glove before she could scream. A sleeping bag was bundled with blankets, and she dropped to her knees. Snow rained down from atop her hood and onto Lander's sleeping face. His eyes flickered and then opened.

He shot up, propping his elbows behind him and blinking quickly. Reaching up, he rubbed his eyes and looked at her again. "Carmen?" His voice was quiet and his face a bit ragged. But then, he was living without most amenities. He frowned. "What are you doing here? Where's Jake?"

Carmen's heart fell. All she wanted to do was throw her arms around his neck and cry, but he looked less than happy to see her. She steadied her frazzled emotions and sat on the floor. Maybe he just needed an explanation. It clearly had been a difficult couple of days. "When you called tonight," she began, "you called my phone instead of Jake's." She watched his face, waiting for a sigh of relief and perhaps a light chuckle. But his expression was stony. "Cell reception cut out before I could talk to you, and there wasn't going to be anyone back at Cedar Lodge until maybe midnight."

He squeezed his eyes shut and brought one hand to his forehead, pinching the skin between his eyebrows. "Hold on, now," he began. His voice sounded stronger, but not much happier. His hand dropped away, and his turquoise eyes found her again. "You came out here in a blizzard, in the middle of the night, alone?"

"No, of course not." She lifted her chin a fraction. "I have Dax."

Now there was a laugh, but it wasn't the cheerful kind. "Carmen." He paused, shaking his head as if he was too upset to continue. But after a deep breath, he managed it. "I don't even know where to start. This is so dangerous. I"—he glanced across her face, looking deeply into her eyes—"I don't want you here. We might not have cell service for a week, and if the storm doesn't let up, the trip back to Cedar Lodge will be impossible, even for Dax." He shook his head. "I don't have enough supplies for food and heat and—"

"Stop." Carmen didn't mean for her voice to come out as harshly as it did, but her mounting worries from that night had quickly turned into aggression. She took a quick breath. "Look, I understand. I left Maddie with instructions to send Asher and the boys right behind me with anything you might need to build up your cabin again." She gestured behind them. "Strapped to Dax are blankets and emergency kits and supplies." Her eyes narrowed. "I'm sorry if you don't want me here, but that's a little irrelevant at the moment, wouldn't you say? I'm here. So, let's just get a heater running and get some sleep."

She stood as briskly as she could in her winter gear, but just as quickly, Lander was on his feet beside her.

"I only meant that it's dangerous, and you're safer at Cedar Lodge." He ran one hand through his dark, wavy hair. It had gotten longer now so that it reached the base of his neck. It was a good look on him. And with how close together they were, she couldn't help letting her gaze linger on the beautiful turquoise of his eyes.

Still, there was something she needed to set straight. She took a step back, and from the tilt of his head, she could see that he took notice.

Good.

"Let me just clear this up, Lander Casey." A bit of fire stirred in her chest as she thought through his words again. She tried to keep it off her face, but as she watched the apprehension grow on his, she knew she was failing. After a steady breath, she continued. "I'm not beholden to anyone but myself. If I want to ride into a storm and check on my —friend..."

She stumbled on the word, wanting to use something so much stronger. Boyfriend, at the very least. But even saying that right now seemed a little presumptive. After all, he said he didn't even want her there. He was still standing exactly sixteen inches away from her quick calculation, and that was sixteen inches too far. What he needed to do was wrap her in his arms as tightly as his strength would allow, and even that wouldn't be enough. Not after she'd wrestled with the mind-numbing fears that he might not have made it in the storm. Now, not only did he make it, but he was scolding her for coming.

The fire in her chest grew.

"Well, if I want to, then I will," she said firmly. "You have nothing to say about it." Her eyes smoldered with frustration. "Is that clear?"

Something melted in his gaze, a change that had the fire in her chest turn to something else completely. Desire coursed through her veins. It was nearly impossible to keep from reaching for him.

"Carmen," he said, lifting his hands and sweeping the hood back from her head. Her auburn hair tumbled forward, and his hand trailed along one side of her face gently, brushing it back. "Of course, I respect your freedom, but there's just one thing wrong." His eyes gazed into hers passionately. "You have no right to treat my entire reason for living so carelessly."

He set one hand on her cheek. It was cold. Alarmingly cold. But for the moment, she couldn't even concentrate on that. His face was coming closer. So slowly, her lips burned at the thought of his kiss. What was she angry about, again? She couldn't remember. She only closed her eyes as their lips met. His hand trailed from her face to her neck so tenderly, but his lips were freezing.

She moved in close to him and brought her hands to his face if only to warm him. Her thoughts weren't on their kiss, as intoxicating as his lips were. She only thought of the slight tremor she could feel running through his body. As much as she wanted to draw out this moment, there was a very real possibility that he was already progressing through stages of hypothermia.

Pulling back from him, she unzipped her coat quickly and wrapped it around him. He frowned and looked like he would take it off, but he appeared disoriented as if he didn't know where the coat had come from. She pulled the hood over his head and looked seriously into his eyes. "Stay right here," she demanded, glancing at the two large indoor heaters in the corner of the room. All they needed was propane.

Running out of the house, she half-jumped through the hole in the wall. The wind had calmed, but now the snow was piling up fast. Dax nickered, and she patted his rump, loosening the bungee cord that connected the propane tanks. But they were heavier than she realized, and the bungee cord zipped out of her hands. She caught the tank in front of her while the one opposite Dax *thunked* to the ground. The big horse sidestepped quickly, leaving Carmen holding a heavy propane tank and stumbling backward.

She fell into Lander's bare arms. With a gasp, she jumped up to see he only wore a thin T-shirt and his jeans. "Lander!" she shouted, not getting any reaction out of him. He was looking at the propane tank as if he didn't know what to do with it.

She grabbed his wrist in one hand and heaved the propane tank in the other, dragging him with her as she hurried back into the house. The tank scraped against the wood floor until they were inside the bedroom again. She closed the door behind them and set the tank down. Grabbing Lander's coat, she slipped his arms through it and reached for her coat next. She draped it across his shoulders and pulled the hood over his head again.

"Don't take that coat off," she said, grabbing his arms firmly. Still, he didn't react to her touch or her voice. Breathing hard, she hurried to the first heater and read the instructions too quickly. Taking a breath, she slowed her thoughts and tried again.

"Hose," she said. "Where—" She twisted the tank she'd brought and saw the hoses that should have been attached weren't there. Had they been on the other tanks in the shed?

Had she brought the wrong ones? She couldn't remember. But maybe Lander had extras.

"Do you have the connecting hose?" She turned to him. He was watching her but didn't look like he'd heard anything. "Lander, do you know where the hose is?" She repeated. Panic swelled in her chest, pressing against her heart. "Do you have something to connect the propane to your heater?"

Lander shook his head. "No, don't turn on the heater. It's so hot in here already." He pulled her jacket from his shoulders and threw it on the floor.

"Stop that," she said, taking her coat and wrapping it around him again. "You're hypothermic, Lander. We need heat or you're going to be in big trouble. We both will be."

He just nodded quietly.

With a groan, she paced around the room. There was a pile of equipment in the corner by the heaters, but nothing that looked like a connection hose. She slid the closet door open along the back wall. Lander's clothes were hung on hangers and folded on one long shelf. At the bottom of the closet, on the floor, were a row of boots and a black hose that had been tossed atop.

She snatched it and hurried back to the tank, connecting the large end to the propane tank, and opening up a side door in the heater. A small, empty tank of propane was inside, and she unscrewed it, setting it aside. Carefully, she connected the small end of the hose and turned on the propane. It hissed away and with one click of the button, the coils in the heater began to change. From cold black, they heated to red and then orange.

"Come over here, Lan—" She turned around to see him lying down, stripped to his T-shirt again. "Lander!" Grabbing the propane and heater both, she dragged them closer and wrapped her arms around him, lifting him to a sitting position. His head lolled to one side, and he groaned in what sounded like a complaint.

Holding him in front of the heater, she sat behind him, wrapping herself around him. She dragged her coat over his legs and used his coat to wrap around them both. "Lander," she repeated, rubbing his cold arms frantically. "Can you talk to me? Lander!"

"What?" he groaned, sounding irritated.

"Tell me what you're doing out here," Carmen said, rubbing the skin of his arms until she felt it warm. "Your, uh..." She couldn't help smiling a bit. "Your cabin looks beautiful. How are your cows?" He sighed, sounding exhausted. She rubbed harder.

"The cows are good." He reached up and pulled the coat tighter around them, and Carmen was sandwiched to his back. But at least he was talking. "I like the isolation, really. Being around other people has never worked out for me. Makes me think I'm going to have to just accept who I am in the future. I'm not a team player. I belong on my own. I just need to make a living for myself. Prove I belong in the high country."

Carmen's rubbing slowed, and she leaned to the side, trying to get a look at his face. "What do you mean by that?" She asked, trying not to let herself feel the stabbing pain in her heart at his words. He was practically delusional, after all. Surely he didn't mean what he was saying.

"I mean I don't plan to go back." He gazed into the heat coils and their orange glow reflected off his skin. "There's a group of 'em out here. Loners. Hermits." He shook his head. "Guys like me. None of 'em have family."

"You don't want a family?" Carmen felt like she should stop him as if she were somehow breaking into his deeper thoughts like the inner pages of a diary. But what if he wasn't delusional? Maybe this was the real Lander.

"No family would want me." He said quietly. He was leaning against her as if he would fall asleep soon. "I should just tell Carmen now before it gets harder. I should tell her there's no future for us."

Carmen's throat seized up, and she swallowed hard. "What?" She asked, leaning in again. But his weight had sagged against her, and his eyes closed. Tears welled in her eyes and trailed down her cheeks, and she wiped at them angrily. Lander wasn't in his right mind. He didn't mean what he said. He was just exhausted and incoherent. But no matter what she told herself, the fear wouldn't leave her.

Fear that he might have just told her the very painful truth.

Chapter Three

"Hello?"

Carmen woke to a voice calling from outside. Sunshine streamed in through the window, and Lander was gone. She lay on the floor in front of the heater with a blanket and her coat piled on top of her. Pushing up, she wiped the sleep from her eyes and slipped her arms through her coat. Still wearing her snow boots and pants, she wandered outside to the sound of voices. She recognized the sound of Lander's voice and realized he was talking to Chance.

Their voices were lowered and hard to hear as she made her way through the deep snow. She paused to listen. After what she'd heard from Lander the night before, she was prepared for anything. Her heart still felt wounded. All she needed was to speak with Lander when he wasn't delirious, and everything would be fine.

"... tried taking the snow machines, but it was no use," Chance was saying. "They were too heavy, and the snow had fallen so fast, it was all powder. There was no surface to travel on."

"I understand," Lander said. "It's no wonder it took all night. It was a shock to see Carmen, but it was also a good thing she came when she did. I don't remember much, but I do remember being cold enough to worry."

"Can't believe she made it out here," Chance replied. "On Dax?"

"Yeah." Lander's voice was strong. There was no tremor or strain, which meant he'd made it through the night just fine.

The sudden surge of relief had the air leaving Carmen's her lungs in one breath. Lander was okay, and they were both safe. She leaned against the cabin and tilted her head back. The sky was a bright, sunny blue, and she gazed up at it. "Thank you," she whispered.

"...take Carmen with you."

Carmen's head whipped around, staring at the corner of the cabin. Her eyes narrowed as Lander's voice continued. She knew she should stop listening in, and she fully intended to walk around the building and show herself. But first, she needed to know what Lander was saying about her. There was a lot she still didn't know about him, and the sooner she found out about his inner workings, the better.

"I have a feeling she'll want to stay, but it's not the life for her out here," Lander said. "At least not yet. Especially in the winter. If I can get it fixed up over the next few months then—"

"Then, what?" Chance's voice cut in. "You think she'll abandon her grandfather's ranch and inheritance and come live out here?"

The silence between them spoke volumes.

Carmen bit her lip, searching her feelings. Would she ever sell Cedar Lodge? She couldn't imagine it, but when she pictured herself with Lander, things got a little muddy. There wasn't a definite no or yes anymore. Just a solid maybe. And now that she knew she'd be interrupting a very uncomfortable situation, she just wanted to retreat to the cabin.

A horse whinnied from the shelter. She needed to hurry before they came around the cabin and spotted her. Slowly, she lifted one foot, taking as large a step as she could manage. She began lowering her big snow boot into the layers of snow.

"I'm just saying that right now isn't the time."

Lander's voice finally replied to Chance, but they sounded like they were moving. She needed to get out of there! She pressed her foot down faster and lifted the other. But then she realized something. Her big footprints in the deep snow would be impossible to hide. Frozen in place, she could hear Lander and Chance coming. She spun around and pumped her arms, running towards them. When they came around the cabin, she almost ran right into them.

"Whoa!" Chance said, holding his hands up as if they might collide. His expression was guarded, but she caught the way he glanced at Lander and then back at her.

Lander's expression, however, was suspicious. He crossed his arms and his gaze flickered behind her. She panicked, hoping he wasn't reading her every movement in the snow. Maybe if she just distracted him.

Now, that was something she didn't mind doing.

With a rather wicked grin, she wrapped her arms around Lander's neck, hugging him tightly. Her heart pounded with adrenaline, but it only made her ruse of running to him more believable. "You're awake," she breathed, pressing her cheek to his briefly before stepping away. What she really wanted to do was kiss him, but with the whirlwind of fears and relief over the past few hours, she was afraid she'd never stop. And that would no doubt embarrass poor Chance. Even her exuberant hug had him taking a few steps back as if he was afraid she might try hugging him next.

She entertained the idea, but instead, just gave him a handshake. "Thanks for coming out," she said, glancing behind him. "Is anyone else with you? How'd you get out here?" She didn't see a horse or snow machine. Just Chance.

"Yeah, actually." Chance gestured behind them. "My brothers and I came out, and once we knew you were both okay, they returned for supplies. Should be back in a few hours and we can get this place fixed up."

"Great," Carmen said, anxious to help. She started walking back with them. "I brought some food out if you're hungry. But I left it in the shelter with Dax last night and I just realized it might have fallen to the ground when I unloaded the propane tanks. Hopefully, he didn't stomp it all to powder during the night."

"He didn't," Lander said.

The way his eyes settled on her was unnerving. She almost didn't remember the topic of conversation.

"I went in this morning and got him unsaddled and brushed down. Gave him a couple of flakes of hay. The food was fine. I left it in the bedroom, but you must not have noticed it this morning."

As Lander spoke, Carmen's thoughts were elsewhere. All she could think of was what he'd said to her the night before, about being so careless with his reason for living. It had her whole body warming. But then he'd gone and changed the conversation absolutely. She needed to talk to him about it as soon as they had a moment alone.

"Carmen?"

Her gaze flickered up from the snow to see both Lander and Chance looking back at her. "Yes?" She said, feeling her cheeks warm. "Sorry, I was thinking. What did you ask?"

"I suppose I didn't ask anything," Lander said, a grin forming on his face. "Just suggested that we go inside and eat. Maybe warm up for a bit."

Chance nodded. "Sounds good to me," he said, walking ahead of them and entering through the broken wall.

Carmen looked into Lander's eyes, preparing herself. If he was having second thoughts about a relationship between them, she needed to know now. She took a breath. "Lander—"

He moved in close, and the words caught in her throat. "I'm sorry," he breathed, so close. "I'm sorry, just..." He glanced across her face as if asking a question, waiting for permission. She glanced across his face. Reaching up, she touched his cheek, and his eyes finally lifted to hers. "Lander," she whispered, hardly able to find her voice. "Is there something going on?" His breath blew in her face, and she watched him struggle to answer. His expression was tortured, and the longer he looked into her eyes, the more devastated he appeared. Whatever anxiety was coursing through him, it was only growing.

"Hey," she whispered, placing both hands on the sides of his face. "It's okay. Just tell me."

His hands came to her sides, but his anguish remained.

Now she was really beginning to worry. It must have shown on her face because, for the first time, he managed to choke back whatever emotion was attacking him. He seemed reluctant, but his hands slid away from her, regardless. He straightened and swallowed hard, taking a long, slow breath.

"I..." He swallowed again. "I think this life is going to take longer to build than I thought. This ranch, this house." With the last word, a look of disgust crossed his face. "It's not something I should ask you to wait for." His lip trembled. He took a quick breath, and his face hardened suddenly. "So, I won't."

He took a step back, and Carmen's heart fractured. She wanted to argue, to scream at him. But the words wouldn't come. There was only shock as she both tried to understand and waited desperately for him to explain.

"I'm not asking you to wait for me," Lander said, his voice steady for once. "You deserve a future with the right man, and honestly, I can't say that man is me."

So, he was telling the truth the night before. He really did mean it. He intended to leave her behind like he'd left Cedar Lodge. If she hadn't raced after him and demanded an answer, maybe she never would have seen him again. The thought was devastating.

And infuriating.

She worked to control her anger, even as the taste of his kiss lingered on her lips. Struggling to understand his reasoning and possibly see into his broken soul, she still only felt anger. It tingled through her relentlessly. She ran one hand through her hair, giving her anger time to cool, and couldn't help noticing the way his eyes followed her. It gave her the tiniest validation that he might not mean what he was saying.

With a slow step forward, she caught the way he eased back. Was he afraid of her? Uncertain, maybe? Did he need to know where she stood? Because she'd be happy to remind him. She took another step, and he didn't move. It was enough encouragement to have her continuing toward him, slowly tangling her hands at the back of his neck and leaning against him. She waited to kiss him, making sure he wouldn't move away. Rejection wasn't something she handled well. Finally, her eyes closed, and her lips brushed his.

The buzz of a snow machine broke the silence. With a quick breath, her eyes flew open. Lander stepped out of her arms, but his eyes were deep in her gaze as the snow machine grew louder. He lifted one hand, and his fingertips touched her lips so gently, her heart raced.

He turned to the oncoming sled, and Carmen's eyes flooded with tears. She was shaking with anticipation and rejection both and suddenly wished she'd never kissed him. She told herself she should leave and never see him again. No phone calls, no contact. Not one more thought of Lander Casey. But as her emotions cooled, she knew that was a lie. She loved him more fiercely than she'd ever loved anything.

Still, she couldn't simply brush the moment aside and meet up with the farmhands. However capable she was, Lander managed to shake apart her strength every time. She fled to the horse shelter and ducked inside, where Dax stood, swishing his tail and munching on the last of his hay. It appeared he'd had a much better morning than her. She leaned against his warm side, closing her eyes.

"I don't know anymore, Dax," she said, rubbing his coat. "I used to be so sure. Like, absolutely positive." He continued munching but paused to lift his nose a few inches off the ground. It was a good enough response. She patted him. "Now I feel like I'm at square one again. All alone."

The men talked in the background, and she picked out their voices as one after the other commented about the cabin. It seemed they hadn't noticed her yet. Maybe Dax was blocking their view; she didn't bother turning her head to find out. Instead, she listened to Chance as he listed everything they'd brought out, and then his two older brothers, William and Asher. They all agreed that they had more than enough material. Lander spoke briefly, thanking them. It hurt just hearing his voice, but Carmen tried to distance herself from the pain. To simply listen in as if she were watching the world instead of living in it. A trick Grandpa Tagen taught her once. Except now, the aching in her chest wasn't so easily brushed aside.

Alone.

Carmen's eyes flew open as she suddenly remembered Maddie fighting a fever all alone back at Cedar Lodge. What if her illness got worse? What if she needed to go to the hospital?

The voices behind her were silenced, and she turned around to see they'd gone into the cabin. Perfect time for her to slip away and head back. The fewer people she had to talk to right now, the better. She was so shaky inside.

"Let's get going, buddy," she said, settling a thick plaid blanket across his back and hoisting a saddle over it. She tightened the cinch and buckled the back strap and then fed the bit gently past his front teeth. Lifting the reins over his head, she stepped into the saddle. Turning him around quickly, she let him go at an eager pace, as he seemed anxious to get back as well. He shook his mane out as they went, something he did when he was excited.

Carmen glanced back once, fearing the sight of Lander looking back at her. But he wasn't there. It had her heart sinking, even though she'd wished for it. She focused again on the path ahead. The sun on the snow was blinding but at least their road was clear. No more searching for the right direction. It was easily found now. Her thoughts wandered often and always in the same direction. She wondered what Lander was doing and what he was thinking and if he would come after her.

She snickered out loud at the thought. Of course, he wouldn't come after her. In fact, he was probably running in the other direction. As much as she wanted to laugh at herself, she found her eyes again wet with tears. This time they trailed down her cheeks and onto her coat, but she didn't bother brushing them away. Who would see, anyway? Maddie was the only one around, and Carmen could use a good, long girl-chat right about now.

When she got to the barn, the tears were still falling. Slow and occasional, but they wouldn't stop. She put away Dax's gear and led him into his stall and then left the barn for the lodge. It was halfway between the two that she stopped, feeling suddenly punched in the stomach with the reality of it all. Had he really ended things? She turned slowly, wanting to look back the way she'd come, hoping somehow to see Lander.

A hand settled on her back, and she jumped so violently, she almost screamed. Spinning around, she saw Jake's face full of concern. Tears streaked her cheeks and gathered in her eyes, and here she was staring into the face of the youngest ranch hand at Cedar Lodge. She'd forgotten all about him. But he didn't seem so young now, not when he quickly brushed her cheeks, wiping her tears. He wrapped his arms around her.

"Are you okay, Carmen?" His voice was soft and deep,

with the strength and confidence of someone sure of himself. But Carmen wasn't sure of anything anymore. She needed to explain, but her mind couldn't come up with the words and her tears only fell harder. Holding on to Jake, she cried into his heavy canvas coat, humiliated and grateful at the same time. If only she could sneak away without uttering a word. If only he could forget this ever happened. But it was too late for that. She'd run back to help Maddie, thinking she was alone, and Jake had been there the whole time. Had he watched her ride up with tears trailing down her cheeks?

The thought had her swallowing away her devastation and working to gather herself. She was still the owner of Cedar Lodge. What kind of confidence would it build to see her falling apart like this? Still, the pain in her chest never eased. Not since Lander had spoken the words. Not since he'd stepped out of her arms.

Turning her head, she laid it on Jake's shoulder, closing her eyes. The overwhelming waves of sadness were calming, but she wasn't ready to let go. Jake was amazing for going with it. He only held her, saying nothing, doing nothing. Just there. It was exactly what she needed. Finally, when her cheeks began to feel warm from embarrassment and her heart began to pound at the apprehension of looking into his face, she took a hesitant step back. Her gaze wandered up to his eyes. She knew her own eyes were swollen and her face likely red, but he smiled back at her all the same.

Before she could explain, he lifted his hand to her arm, holding it gently. His brown eyes were steady, and the set of his mouth was kind. A bit of blond hair peeked out from under his brown suede cowboy hat. He tipped his head slightly. "Is there anything you need my help with tonight, Ms. Rivera?"

The purposeful formality of a title had her mind easing. For such a young man, he had more intuition than most men twice his age. It was tempting to shake her head and run away, but his kindness meant so much. She couldn't leave without letting him know. Stepping forward, she kissed his cheek. "No. Thank you, Jake."

A smile grew on his face, and he nodded. "Goodnight, ma'am."

"Goodnight," Carmen continued to the house, resisting the urge to scan the valley for Lander. He was where he chose to be, and so was she.

Chapter Four

Lander listened as Asher explained the various supplies they'd brought him. With four men and two full sleds of equipment, it would only take a day to patch the cabin wall. But as the ranch hands debated on the best way to get started, Lander's mind wandered back to Carmen. He'd thought of her almost constantly over the past months.

At first, he'd been swimming in a happiness he could only call euphoric. But as he began the real work of patching up the cabin, reality slowly picked away at the edges of his optimism. He'd ignored it at first, reminding himself of the pure heaven it had been with Carmen in his arms, but his fears were persistent. He tried to imagine them together in his little broken cabin out in the high country. But as hard as he tried, he could never picture her there, and he knew why. He knew that a moment of pain was better than years of it. And what Carmen didn't realize was that a relationship with him would be just that. Pain.

His troubles were deeply rooted, having wound their way into his soul at a young age. Hard work had been his lifeline, and it had built up his strength, but it hadn't repaired anything on the inside. When he thought about the kind of man Carmen deserved, and then took a good look at himself, it just didn't match up. How could it? He wasn't accepted in the community like other men were. His past was a juicy bit of gossip that others seemed to enjoy dredging up whenever they saw him. His murdered parents and now his union with a woman who inherited the land where he worked. He hoped starting up his own ranch would change others' opinions of him, but he couldn't be sure it would. How could he ask her to live like that? The topic of gossip and cold shoulders.

A chill shuttered through his body.

Suddenly, her words to him came rushing back. The day she'd pursued him up the mountain. Her faith in him and love for him she'd expressed so freely. So fiercely. The way she whispered I love you was something he'd never forget. She believed in him like no one he'd ever known.

Didn't she have a right to her opinion now? Shouldn't he give her the chance to choose him or not?

Lander turned away from the group with his pulse beginning to rise. The men were gathered around the damaged wall, pointing out sections and pulling away broken bits of wood. How far away was she by now? Had she already made it back to Cedar Lodge? His breath came harder as he anticipated speaking honestly with Carmen. It would be difficult, but if it ended with them having a life together, it was worth it. Part of him wanted to brush the thought aside and get back to work. Be realistic. Build up the cabin and just wait until the next time he saw her. But he knew he needed to be more. If he wanted to be the man Carmen deserved, she needed to see that he could put her above anything else.

He sprang into action, striding toward the shed that acted as a barn and tack room altogether. Saddling his buckskin quickly, he stepped into the stirrup and swung his leg over the saddle. He'd attached spurs to his riding boots and all it took was a gentle tap at the horse's sides. The buckskin knew that spurs meant speed, and he never disappointed. They charged out of the shed and Lander looked back to see he'd caught the attention of the group. "I'll be back," he shouted. Then he held the reins halfway up the buckskin's neck, letting him run as snow flew out behind them like a blizzard.

He hoped she hadn't made it back to the lodge yet. The thought of her arriving home with the ache of their last encounter still pressing on her heart was devastating. It was something she wouldn't show, he knew it. Here he'd gone and laid the weight of his insecurities atop her shoulders, proving his point while trying to avoid it. The chaos inside of him wouldn't still. Why was his mind so dark? Why couldn't it just let him have his happiness and be done with the torment of his childhood?

He groaned aloud, pressing his horse on and on as the trail stretched out in front of them. They raced past the lookout and down into the valley. Cedar Lodge was in sight, and he finally spotted her. She rode slowly into the barn on Dax, and he eased back in the saddle for the first time, giving his horse a much-deserved rest. The buckskin blew a firm breath and shook its long, black mane.

"Sorry, boy." Lander rubbed the gelding's strong shoulder. "You got us here. Thank you."

They walked along the side of the field where the cows

would graze come the spring thaw. For now, they stayed close to the lodge and feeding area. The snow had been stomped down, and there were remnants of their last meal spread about, as well as stains from manure having been raked away.

Something caught Lander's eye, and he tightened his hand on the reins, bringing the buckskin to a stop. He'd nearly reached the barn and could see Carmen stopped halfway to the lodge. It was a moment before he realized she was crying. It pierced through his chest to see her in pain, but what did he think would happen? How he wished he hadn't pushed her away. Were his own thoughts an enemy to their relationship? Here, perfection and happiness beyond his own belief had been offered to him. She saved his life, for goodness' sake. What was he thinking?

He meant to call out to her, but Jake suddenly appeared. By her posture and movements, he could tell she was surprised. But what the young farmhand did next had Lander's hope plunging into devastation. He could only watch as another man comforted Carmen from the pain he'd caused as she leaned against him and cried on his shoulder. As he held her. It seemed forever that they were in each other's arms, but he couldn't blame her. He'd waited too long, and now there was nothing he could do. This moment wasn't his. Perhaps it could have been, but now the tables had turned.

Carmen separated from Jake, and Lander's breath was captive in his throat as they looked into each other's eyes. He watched Carmen lean forward and kiss him. Pain split through his chest, and he felt his cheeks flush with heat. How he wished he'd made the decision to return just a few minutes sooner. But now, he only watched as Carmen walked back toward the lodge. For a moment, her head turned as if she would look in his direction. He froze, waiting for it. Above all, wanting it. But she didn't turn. Maybe she refused to give in to the desire. But whatever the reason, Lander was left alone.

Devastation nearly overwhelmed him, and he dropped his gaze. How could he talk to her now? After another man had come to her aide, what would it mean for him to offer his apologies? He'd been so sure before, but now there was only doubt. The demons that had so easily darkened his world before, now came rushing back.

He'd always admired Jake, even though the boy was nearly a decade younger than him. There was a sense of confidence in the way he went about his work surrounded by hardened cowhands. He'd started bucking hay at the lodge at only fifteen and had always refused alcohol and tobacco when Hal and Ernie would offer it to him. Lander had warned them not to do it, but they never listened, always making a joke of it. He was glad Carmen had fired them on her first day at Cedar Lodge. They didn't deserve to be here. And clearly, neither did Lander. What was he doing but bringing trouble into her life? As much as he hated his dark thoughts, he couldn't argue when they were right.

For a moment he looked back at where Jake had stood. Then he scanned the area until he was looking in the window of Cedar Lodge. He couldn't see inside, but in his mind, he pictured Jake with Carmen. Devastatingly, it seemed to fit together. Maybe it would even be better for her; she just didn't realize it yet. Lander no doubt touched her natural instincts to nurture and care for wounded things. Like the day he'd seen her shoot an attacking wolf and then lament the creature after it had died. She'd knelt next to the animal, stroking its fur.

His horse dug at the snow with one foot impatiently, stretching out its neck to pull at the reins. It woke Lander from his memories. Here he'd come to offer restitution for the pain he'd caused, but maybe God had sent Jake in his place. Maybe He was looking out for Carmen. Lander didn't doubt that God would intervene for her. She was worth all His time.

A lump pressed at his throat and Lander finally turned the buckskin's head around, toward the high country. Toward his future. The animal walked slowly and looked back often as if he didn't understand the purpose of their journey—as if he didn't agree. But Lander felt sure for once that the best future for Carmen would be one without him.

The terrain passed slowly this time, and he didn't urge the horse on. When he got back to the cabin, the men had stripped away all the damaged areas. He didn't speak to them although their eyes followed him. He only cared for his horse and when he emerged from the shed, he got right to work. Silently. He knew well enough how to build up a wall, and he dug in. His mind wasn't on the task, because how could it be? All he saw was Carmen's gorgeous dark eyes and all he could taste was her kiss. He punished himself with thoughts of her, knowing he'd never been enough. Why she thought he was, he didn't know. But in no time at all, she would realize her mistake in believing in him. She'd move on. In fact, it appeared maybe she already had.

"Might, uh—"

Lander flinched as Asher grabbed the nail gun from his hands. The oldest of the Driscoll brothers looked back at him with severity in his wide hazel eyes. Lander knew the look well. It was one he'd used himself with countless new or temporary ranch hands. Except now, he needed correcting because he'd been so deep in wandering thoughts that he'd nearly let a loaded nail gun fall to the ground right in front of him.

Asher set the double safety and placed the tool carefully inside the building. "Might want to watch that," he finished, backing off. He brushed one hand through his golden-brown hair and went to work measuring siding, taking the next piece around the house to be cut.

With a sigh, Lander rubbed his face, hoping to wake himself from the stupor he was caught in. All he really wanted to do was hide away in bed covered with blankets. But he didn't have a bed, just a cabin floor. He'd set up a cot well before the storm, but when the wall had caved, it destroyed one side of the frame. So, he was left with no other option. Eventually, he'd make a lodgepole bed, but at the moment it really didn't bother him where he slept.

It took a lot of refocusing, but he managed to concentrate on his work for the next few hours. He forced thoughts of Carmen out of his head almost before they could start. When he thought he caught the scent of late fall blossoms in the wind, he pushed away the perfect image of her amber hair. How he loved the softness and smell of it. And when his horse whinnied, bringing back the memory of riding to Cedar Lodge in the saddle behind her, with her falling asleep leaning against his chest, he had to brush both gloved hands roughly across his face before he could break down.

Just one piece of frame at a time. Just one portion of insulation. Just one strip of siding. The effort to hold his attention to the task was excruciating, but he managed it. No one spoke to him, or hardly to each other. They just worked and communicated when they needed clarification on the project. Other than that, it was only the sounds of the forest blanketed in snow, which were few. He caught a wandering eye here and there as if they all knew what was hiding under the silence, but no one asked.

It wasn't until the job was done that they spoke. Lined up, each with their arms folded, the Driscoll brothers talked amongst themselves, agreeing that the wall was well-made.

Lander turned to them, and their conversation stopped. "I, uh..." He turned back to his cabin, nodding. "I appreciate the help, everyone. I know you have plenty to do at the lodge, so... thank you."

They took turns mumbling their approval and patting him on the back as they made their way around the cabin. There was a lot of equipment and supplies still to clean up, and they got right to it. But Lander stayed, studying the cabin wall as he slowly lost the battle with his thoughts, and images of Carmen filled his mind.

"Is..."

He turned to see Asher remained, even as the others were loading equipment. His hazel eyes were intelligent, and they peered into Lander's gaze. It had Lander fearing he was giving away every thought he'd ever had. But Asher's expression was kind.

"Is Carmen coming back out today?" The oldest brother shifted his weight, scanning the trees and turning back to the house.

Lander forced down the burst of pain in his chest, shaking his head. "No," he said as firmly as he could.

"Tomorrow?" Asher's gaze was soft as he turned back to Lander, even though he spoke casually.

It seemed there was a completely different conversation going on beneath the surface of their words, and it made Lander's heart ache with longing for Carmen. But again, he only shook his head. "No," he said, quieter this time. He prayed Asher would stop asking, because the firmness in his chest was cracking apart, and his vision was beginning to blur.

"Anything you want me to tell her?" This time, Asher reached out, placing his hand on Lander's shoulder.

Lander's emotions overwhelmed him. His firm expression crumbled, and he covered his face with one hand, breathing deeply. He rubbed his forehead and brushed his hair aside, struggling to overcome the moment. "No," he said again, with his voice breaking.

He cleared his throat and turned, walking away. It was no use. He wasn't strong enough to answer even one more question. What he needed to do was help with cleanup and shake each one of their hands. Load the gear and tie it down to the sleds so they could make their journey back. He needed to look each one of them in the eyes and thank them personally for taking the trip out and sacrificing the entire day to help him. Asher, William, and Chance. Each of the Driscoll brothers deserved that respect.

But Lander's hands were shaking, and his mind wasn't right. He was falling fast and all he could do was saddle his buckskin and turn toward the far valley where his cattle were grazing among a scenic layer of snow. All he could do was tap the strong sides of an animal that moved more willingly than usual as if it knew Lander's descending mood. He didn't know if the Driscoll brothers were watching him, talking about him, or cursing him. If they were, he couldn't help but agree with them. He was a curse on the wind.

It was a strange thing to ride away from those who had so selflessly come to his rescue. But the alternative would be falling apart in front of them. And that was something he simply refused to do.

Chapter Five

Carmen must have stared out the window for an hour before she noticed it. Her eyes were dry, finally, and she'd cooked a pot of spaghetti. The meal had been fresh and hot, giving her an energizing boost. It's when the tears finally subsided. But now, as she stood staring out the back windows that provided a view of the fields and Teton mountain range behind them, she realized something.

Past the fence line and south of the mountain view, where the forest crowded the fields, a slender stream of smoke trailed up from the treetops and into the frigid, blue sky. She knew exactly where it came from. It was the cabin that Lander and her Grandpa Tagen built together. The one he sold to help pay off the debts attached to Cedar Lodge after her grandfather had died. There had been enough left to fill up a good reserve of cash, too. Apparently, from the look of the smoke trailing from the chimney, the new owner had moved in. There was a separate dirt access road to the property, which would explain why she hadn't seen anyone or anything until now.

If you've got land, walk it.

Her grandfather's words surfaced from her memory. She recalled his advice to her on one of many horseback rides through the mountains. At the time, his words had seemed silly to her childish mind. She'd tried to imagine why her grandfather would have to walk all over his land as if it would simply lift up and float away without the pressure of his boots keeping it down.

Carmen smiled.

"Now that, I'm glad to see."

Her eyes flickered up to see Maddie's reflection in the window, standing behind her. She spun around, relieved to see her friend was dressed and ready, her short hair smooth and shiny and her face vibrant. "Looks like you're doing better." Carmen crossed the room to give her a hug.

"Mmm." Maddie sighed, always one to make a hug sound yummy. She stepped back from Carmen and her happy face turned critical, complete with an eyebrow raise. "Why isn't Lander with you?" Her at-first teasing tone quickly melted away as Carmen's sadness eagerly returned to pull at her lip and tighten her chest.

Maddie's eyes widened. "Does it have anything to do with you staring out the window for hours?" After a longer-than-usual silence, she gripped Carmen's arms. "No, Carmen," she whispered. "How could things go wrong? You two are so perfect together."

"No one's perfect," Carmen said, hurrying to get past the emotion. She shook her head, and her neglected hair danced around her face. Carmen pulled her jacket from the back of the couch and threaded her arms through. "I'm heading out to walk the perimeter—"

"I'm coming!" Maddie shouted, dashing down the hall.

Carmen sighed, wishing she could be alone. But she was relieved that Maddie was well, and telling her to stay would just make her feel worse inside. Especially when her friend returned in a rush, hopping on one foot as she wiggled her foot into an enormously fuzzy sock.

"See?" Maddie said, laughing as she zipped up her pink ski jacket. "You didn't even have to wait for me."

"There are some snow boots on the deck outside," Carmen said, working hard to force a lift into her voice. "Let's go." She was used to being the cheerful, expressive one, especially when compared to Maddie. But as they walked, Carmen found it hard to keep her gaze from falling to the ground. She listened to Maddie chattering away talking about the book she'd read while she was sick and realized the tables had turned a little in their personalities. But for now, it would have to do. Because sadness clung to her like a suffocating fog that would never leave.

"... I couldn't believe it when he turned out to be a were-wolf disguised as a regular guy! And actually, he was so amazing that I was even rooting for him by the end. But no, he ends up sacrificing himself so she can go live her dreams, or whatever—"

A rush of laughter bubbled up from inside Carmen. Maddie stopped in the middle of her explanation and Carmen smiled at her friend. "I'm really glad you're here."

"Oh, my goodness, Carmen." Maddie squeezed her in a sudden hug and then stepped away quickly. "I have no idea what you need me to do. And I know you don't want to talk about him—so I've just been going on and on and on, nonstop like a crazy person, and didn't know what else I could possibly say. You know I totally made that last book up, right? The whole werewolf thing and all that—never happened—"

"Maddie!" Carmen laughed again, and this time, it was almost genuine. Her friend's green eyes were studying her face, waiting. It was clear she wanted to know what had happened with Lander, but Carmen just wasn't ready. She started down the trail again. "I was just going to say it's only about a half mile farther, then it bends around the backside of the property."

"Oh, okay," Maddie said quietly, clearly disappointed that Carmen hadn't mentioned anything significant yet. They continued, trudging through the deep snow with their frozen breath surrounding them.

The mountains towered into the sky ahead, strong and majestic, especially with the white blanket that had fallen the night before. She thought about her race up the mountain to Lander, riding Dax dangerously fast through the storm. She'd worried that he was already dead, or that he'd gone into the forest and was struggling with hypothermia. There were so many fears. She'd felt blind with them. But now, she didn't know what to fear. Her dreams had come true and been ripped away all in one night. Everything was still spinning.

"So, Carmen," Maddie said, kicking at a drift of snow. "What have you done with the kids' camp you wanted to get started? I mean, I know you don't need to clear away the debt anymore, but you seemed really excited about it?" She ended with a question, with her head tilted back at Carmen. "If you still want to do it, you should get hold of Aries. I'm sure she's got the entire thing planned out by now." Maddie laughed, and Carmen joined her. Aries was definitely a force. The right person to put in charge of something like this, that was for sure.

"You're right, I really was excited about it," Carmen mused. "I still want to do it, I just haven't had a minute."

"Well, what about now?" Maddie asked. "Looks like everything is frozen out here, so what else is there to do? Let's get some names and donations and get this party started. What if—" Maddie stopped suddenly, turning to Carmen with wide, excited eyes. "What if I stay on until the camp and help you with everything? Then I can return to New York after. That would be a decent timeframe for me."

Carmen had a sudden thought. Something she hadn't even considered since Maddie had decided to stay instead of returning to New York. Now, as her friend planned someone else's life, it seemed clear she was only escaping her own. Carmen eyed Maddie, feeling suddenly guilty that she couldn't see past her own pain. "Is there something going on back in New York that you're trying to avoid?" she asked. "Is that why you stayed at Cedar Lodge?"

Maddie's excitement fell quickly, leaving behind an honest shame. She sighed with a shrug as if the charade were over. The real Maddie was returning, leaving behind a babbling, giggly farce. This was the Maddie that Carmen knew. She was keen and intelligent, thoughtful, and always aware. And now, as Carmen's eyes had finally dried, she saw a sheen of moisture gathering in Maddie's.

"I just couldn't stay," Maddie said, with a quick shake of her pixie cut. "And it's not that I'm running away, either." She turned to Carmen forcefully. "That's not what I'm doing. Cedar Lodge is where I'm meant to be right now, I could feel it the moment I stepped out of that car..." Her lip shook and she swallowed hard, squeezing her eyes closed.

Carmen clasped her hands together, holding in the concern. She knew that Maddie would need time to finish her thoughts. But her heart ached for a pain she'd never seen on her sweet, gentle friend.

"I know you think I always run away from guys," Maddie said. Her emotions were held at bay, and her voice was calm. She looked out toward the mountains as she spoke. They were gorgeous with the sun shining down so hard, leaving the deep green trees and craggy rocks to stand out brilliantly.

"You, Aries, Violet." Maddie sighed. "But I don't mind. I mean, really, you're right." She wrapped one arm around her back, holding on to her elbow in a flip-flopped sort of self-hug. It was one of the traits that Carmen hadn't yet told her she loved. "But I..." Maddie's gaze wandered back to Carmen. "I met someone. He, uh... I thought he was perfect at first. Ginger blond hair and the stormiest gray eyes I've ever seen. His smile made me catch my breath the first time we met."

Carmen studied her face, but there was no swelling of excitement in her eyes, no touch of color on her cheeks; nothing that would accompany the emotions of a new relationship.

Maddie shrugged. "His sister works with me. I hired her six months ago to handle marketing and public affairs. When I met him, I liked him right off the bat. But things weren't going in the right direction with his sister. She was pushing the bookstore into an almost all-digital, social media format, and it wasn't what I wanted." Her voice was gaining strength as she spoke about the bookstore. She'd always been confident in her vision for it. "It was really distressing, and I knew I needed to talk to her. The entire feel of the store was changing, and I could see it on the customer's faces the moment they'd walk in. They could tell."

She started walking again and Carmen kept pace with her as they rounded the back of the property. It was the closest they'd been to the trail that led to Lander's place. Although she tried not to, Carmen couldn't help looking up the mountain, following the line of the trail. Searching for him. But there was only snow.

"I went to talk to her, and Kevin was there. That's his name." She glanced at Carmen and then resumed the watch of her feet. "He just stood there when I brought it up. And you know me well enough to guess I just blurted it out before any conversation. No warming up, no prep. Just, hey, things have to change. I mean, I was nice, but it was clear neither one of them appreciated it. He actually put his arm around his sister and looked back at me as if he wanted an apology." Maddie's eyes narrowed. "I'm the one who hired her. If there's an opinion that needs to be heard above any other, it's mine. I spent my life being easily railroaded in the professional world and finally thought that would stop now that I have my own business. And I knew I couldn't date anyone who wasn't willing to at least support me that much. I mean, he didn't give me a chance. Then, when I came out here, I could feel such a difference."

She stopped. Cedar Lodge was a beautiful backdrop in the scenery from where they stood, and it seemed to take away her words for a moment. She snapped out of it and started down the trail again. "I've had my fill of NYC for a while. I needed a change."

Carmen thought back to when she'd learned Lander was

trying to buy the place out from under her. She'd run back to New York as fast as she could. Her friends had been there for her, and now it was her turn to be there for Maddie. Just the fact that she was speaking about a man and admitting how she felt about him meant that her feelings ran deep. Deep enough to be in considerable pain when it ended.

Carmen hooked her arm through Maddie's, saying nothing. She only walked and hoped Cedar Lodge would do the rest.

"Ho, there!"

The girls spun around together, with Carmen unable to hold back a gasp at the thought that it might be Lander. But a different cowboy was making his way towards them on a horse that quickly caught her attention. Its coat was a beautiful, blue-toned gray, dappled with lighter spots along its rump. Carmen had never seen a Gypsy Vanner in person before, but she'd seen enough horse calendars to know they were coveted. And it was no wonder. The horse's thick, black mane and tail swung gorgeously with each step. Its hooves were draped in the same dark, beautiful hair.

And then she noticed the cowboy.

He was nowhere as stunning as Lander had been the first time she'd met him, but he definitely had her heart skipping a beat. And beside her, Maddie had frozen like the ground under their snow boots. His hair was light brown, straight, and almost to his shoulders. She'd never seen a long-haired cowboy, but somehow it fit. Perhaps it was the way he mimicked his horse showing off its mane. There were leather strips like tethers around his neck and a tan cowboy hat hung from them, resting on his back. His eyes were a mixture of brown and green, Carmen couldn't quite tell which color was more dominant. But his smile was something she was sure got him out of a lot of trouble. It was a boyish grin on a man's face, and it had her smiling back without even realizing it.

"Hi," Carmen finally said when he was close enough that she didn't have to shout. He slid down from his horse and held the reins loosely as he stepped forward, offering a firm handshake to each of them.

"I'm Everett, nice to meet you," he said. "I just moved up that mountain a stretch." His head tipped back to where she'd seen the trail of smoke from before. Lander's cabin. To Carmen, it would never be anything else. "I..." He glanced between the girls. "I just saw you out here and thought I should introduce myself."

Carmen stalled a moment and then gestured suddenly to Cedar Lodge. "That's my home, there." She glanced at Maddie, who had yet to say anything. "And this is my friend Maddie from New York City. She's out here until summer."

"New York City?" He looked to be fighting back a grin. "Is that where you're from too?"

"It is." Carmen didn't bother with an explanation. If she went on too long, it would sound over-compensatory, and too short would sound like an excuse. For what, she didn't know. Either way, all he needed to know was she was Carmen, and she owned Cedar Lodge.

"Nice to meet you both," he said again, looking between them. His eyes paused on Maddie as if giving her a chance to move or speak at all.

She didn't.

"So..." Carmen glanced back at the trees to where she knew his cabin lay. To where she'd once found Lander fevered and ill and had taken care of him as much as she could. To where she'd borrowed his sweats that he ended up giving to her. She still had them in the top drawer of her dresser and wore them every night.

"Yes?" Everett asked.

Carmen pulled her gaze from the trees to focus on him again. From close-up, she could see that the flecks of green in his eyes were more prevalent than the brown. But just barely. "What is it you do, Everett?" She finally finished, wishing again that it had been Lander that had called out to them. She swallowed away the disappointment and focused on him. He hadn't answered yet, so she tried to urge him on. "Are you working a ranch or running cattle?"

He grinned and tucked one side of his hair behind his ear. The gesture made him appear shy, although she would wager, he was anything but.

"No, ma'am," he said, reminding her achingly of Lander. "I like to live on my own, away from the buzz of it all. But it's not what I rely on for my livelihood."

She waited for more, but instead of explaining himself, he only nodded and stepped into the saddle again. He lifted his hand and looked between them. "Good day to you, ladies. It was a pleasure meeting you." He turned his horse, and its huge hooves began their majestic marching through the deep snow.

"Nice to meet you as well," Carmen called.

"Bye."

Maddie's quiet farewell had him turning around. A smile tugged gently at one side of his mouth before he turned away again.

Carmen looked at Maddie to find her friend's cheeks were pink and her lips were parted ever so slightly as if she was unaware that her mouth had dropped open. She continued to watch Everett as he rode away.

"Something tells me..." Carmen said.

Maddie flinched, turning back to Carmen. Her expression was unchanged as if her mind were still with the cowboy riding into the trees.

Carmen couldn't help laughing just a little. She hooked her arm with Maddie's and began walking back to Cedar Lodge. "Something tells me Kevin will be forgotten in no time," she finished, ignoring it when Maddie guffawed at the remark. It was obvious, after all. Maddie would fall the way Carmen had. Maybe it would end in heartbreak and maybe it wouldn't. But there was something about a strong man on the back of a horse.

Something impossible to resist.

Chapter Six

Carmen watched the choir as they sang. For such an amateur group, their melody was perfect, ringing through the high-beamed ceiling and aged wood frame of the old church. All different ages and skin colors, and yet their voices rang together as one.

Oh, Thou who changest not, abide with me.

She hummed along, one leg crossed over the other and her foot swaying to the melody. Her dress hung at her knee with frills at the end that fluttered to her movements, making the small flower pattern dance atop its cream-colored material. The song was a familiar one; one of her favorites. But as they reached the end, she felt a rush of sadness that Lander wasn't sitting next to her.

Shine through the gloom and point me to the skies.

He'd only come to church once in his whole life, and he'd sat next to her. His voice had sent chills down her arms with a depth that was mesmerizing. She turned in her seat, scanning the rows behind her. But it was the same as before. He wasn't there. Had she so thoroughly chased him away? Or had she built up their relationship so much in her head that it wasn't aligning with reality anymore?

That couldn't be it. She'd seen his face. Heard his words. He loved her more than she ever could have hoped for. Maybe more than she loved him. Maybe. Her thoughts remained with him as Pastor Evans began speaking on hope. She imagined what he was doing and why he hadn't made the trip out for church. She'd assumed he would.

Her hands were clasped, and she twisted them together, glancing back again. It was painful each time she did it, but she couldn't stop herself. Why hadn't he come? Maddie sat next to her, and while she'd turned around the first few times Carmen had, she didn't turn anymore. As if she already knew what she would find. Well, she didn't know Lander. He wouldn't just abandon her like this. Would he?

Before she knew it, the sermon was over and the benediction was said. "Amen," she murmured, standing and making her way out the back of the chapel. She smiled and said "Hello" and "Fine, how are you?" without even thinking about it. They were just filler. Noise. Just the conversations had her able to keep Lander in her thoughts while she could appear to be socializing.

Someone grasped her wrist, and she turned to see the pastor's wife, Mariana looking back at her. The woman's long, red hair was braided, and her lips were shining with clear gloss instead of the usual bold red. "Carmen," she said. There was no smile on her lips, no false greetings. The look in her eyes showed that she knew of Carmen's pain under the surface. "Come with me."

Carmen couldn't answer. She only fought back the tears

that crowded in her eyes while allowing Mariana to tow her around the side of the building.

Not here. She couldn't stop the memories of when she'd found out Lander was trying to buy out Cedar Lodge from under her. But she managed to blink back the tears and take a steadying breath before they stopped, and Mariana faced her.

"I see you're suffering," she said.

Carmen waited for her to continue, but she didn't. She only waited, staring back at Carmen with eyes that were full of experience and wisdom. All Carmen had to do was ask. But how could she get the words out without sounding foolish? To anyone else, she knew how it would appear. They would say she and Lander were on different paths, and that he'd chosen a different life. He was focusing on other things. He wasn't committed to her. But she knew that couldn't be it. There was something deeper there. She just didn't know what it was.

Finally, she took a deep breath, ready to try. But letting her walls down meant that tears would come. And they did. One trailed down her cheek even before she'd spoken a word. "I just don't understand what happened, but something did. He..." She shook her head afraid she would say it all wrong. "He's pushing me away and I don't know why." She didn't need to say his name. Mariana knew.

Her friend's arms came around her As if she just couldn't manage a conversation without a hug. "He does care for you, Carmen," Mariana said. She held Carmen's shoulders and stood back with straightened arms, tilting her head so that her gaze bored into Carmen's. "I've seen it. I know it."

"Then why didn't he come today?" Carmen's lip shook. "It's like he completely cut me out of his life. Why?"

"I don't know, honey." Mariana squeezed her again. "I'm so sorry." She stepped back, releasing Carmen and crossing her arms around herself instead. "But let's give him time. He hasn't grown up the way the rest of us have. He might need awhile to adjust to the idea of having someone in his life."

"Adjust?" Carmen couldn't think of a less flattering way to talk about their relationship. Adjusting. That wasn't the way she saw him. She saw passion and beauty and desire and intense admiration... everything good. And she thought he saw that in her too. When she remembered the way he looked at her, she knew it.

She shook her head. "That can't be it."

"Well, regardless of what it is, you can't rush things like this. Maybe he's stewing it over, just waiting for the right time to come and beg for your forgiveness." Mariana winked. "I would bet he's very good at apologizing. Excellenté."

Carmen felt a smile pull at one side of her mouth. It had Mariana giggling. Maybe she was right, and Lander just needed some time before he was ready to commit to a relationship. By the sound of it, he'd never had one before. The idea that she just had to wait for him to be ready made it possible for her to dry her tears and join the chitchat on the front lawn.

Maddie was there, talking to the Driscoll brothers and laughing as the sun streamed across her face, illuminating the light brown highlights in her hair. She'd formed it into loose waves, and it was beautiful paired with her red-smocked dress. She was right; Wyoming was doing her good.

Carmen approached the group, ready to lose herself a little in light conversation about the weather and what to bring to the next church potluck.

"Don't see everyone here today."

A low voice stopped her in her tracks. The entire group, Driscoll brothers, Maddie, Carmen, and Mariana, all turned to the two cowboys approaching. Hal and Ernie. Carmen knew by firing them, she'd been the one to cause all the anger and discord between them and the workers at Cedar Lodge. But while they weren't looking at her, she suspected they were enjoying her surprise just the same.

Hal's intense blue eyes were focused on Asher, the eldest brother. Ernie, the taller of the two with a black mustache and slender build, walked next to him with his arms crossed. A gangly bodyguard. Asher didn't look the least bit cowed. In fact, he took a step toward them that ended their advance on the group. "Not everyone can make it every Sunday," Asher replied. "You know that."

"I guess," Hal said. He was the shortest one in the group, but what he lacked in height, he made up for in brawn. "I just sorta figured Lander had more commitment now. You know, that he'd changed." His eyes swung over to Carmen's and she frowned back at him. "It's always so easy for cowboys to change their ways. Right, Miss Carmen?"

She half expected him to call her Miss Times Square as he had before. She didn't want to respond, but she knew she had to. He was clearly hoping to cause her pain and staying silent was verification enough. "I asked him not to come today," she said. Lying in church. What was that going to do for her? Well, not in church, but ten feet from the front steps. It was close enough. She knew it could come back around and bite her in the foot, but it had just happened so quickly. And to see that moment of unease on Hal's face felt completely worth it. "After that snowstorm, it's just too treacherous a journey."

"Lander wouldn't be scared of a little snowstorm like

that," Ernie spoke up, kicking one boot at the snow and watching his feet instead of facing the group. "But you know what he would do?" His eyes lifted, staring pointedly at Carmen. "He'd turn his back on ya as soon as look at ya. He's not a hero, Miss Carmen, no matter how much he's led you to believe that."

"That's enough." Mariana walked through the group.

Hal and Ernie stepped back as she approached them, and their eyes lowered.

"Now, this is a beautiful day, and we are among friends. Those who aren't here only need our prayers, not our gossiping tongues. Is that clear?" With her hands on her hips, she seemed like a teacher scolding young children. Carmen nearly laughed but for Hal and Ernie's words still chiseling away at her heart.

"Yes, ma'am," Ernie finally answered. Hal kept his eyes on the ground.

"You boys have a wonderful Sabbath." Mariana reached for their shoulders, one after the other, and kissed their cheeks. Then she walked toward the church and met with her husband, Pastor Evans, at the edge of the steps. He was talking to patrons but turned his attention to her when she approached. He wrapped his arm around her shoulders with a smile on his face and they continued their conversations.

When Carmen turned back to Hal and Ernie, it seemed all their desire to fight had melted away. Ernie sank his hands in his pockets with a sigh. "I don't mean to challenge you, Carmen," he said. "It's just that I've known Lander a long time, and I don't believe he's gone and become a righteous man overnight. Maybe you should consider it a good thing he hasn't returned." His eyes lifted and settled on hers with something close to compassion.

Carmen could only stare back in shock. He'd never used her name or spoken as calmly to her as he was now. It seemed completely out of character, and she didn't trust it. Still, she couldn't help but soften with the change.

He turned and strode away, back to his old truck with Hal following behind. The faded blue Chevy rumbled and shook as it drove away.

"If you ask me, they're just making trouble." Maddie stood beside Carmen, and she crossed her slender arms in front of her red dress. She looked back at Carmen. "Guys like them only want to stir the pot. They're all the same."

"I agree," Jake said. He'd walked up from another group, joining their silent one as they all stared after Hal and Ernie. Now he stood next to Maddie and crossed his arms, looking back at her. "They're trouble." He turned to Carmen and hesitated, his firm gaze softening. "I mean, if you don't mind my saying."

It was kind of him to consider her feelings, but Carmen knew what was going on. She'd allowed him to see her when she was vulnerable and hurt, and now, he thought of her as tender. Delicate. Maybe even less capable than he'd considered her before.

And she wasn't going to let that happen.

"I have an event I need to plan out in a month," she said, making all heads turn toward her. She'd commandeered the entire conversation and could see it was throwing the group a bit off-balance. But that was fine. Jake, at least, had straightened and nodded crisply. She looked back at him. "There's going to be a benefit camp at Cedar Lodge in the summer, and if we want it to be successful, we need to start it off with a bang. A premiere banquet and ball with dancing and special guests the week before Thanksgiving."

Heads were turning as the group glanced at each other, and she could hear a few whispers. She was sure Maddie wanted more of an explanation, but for now, she was just addressing Jake. "Can you find me an event space?" She paused for half a second, but not long enough for him to answer. "It'll need to accommodate two hundred and have space for tables and dancing, hopefully an outdoor patio where we could have fire pits, and a view of water or the mountains. Is there anything like that here?"

"Yes, absolutely," Jake said. He'd been holding his hat in his hands, but he slipped it onto his head as if ready to start on the project right away. Good.

"Great, can you nail down some venue prices and see if the dates will work?"

"I'm sure I can find a spot," Jake promised. He gave Maddie a quick smile, which she didn't reciprocate, and then left, presumably to begin interrogating event spaces.

Carmen watched him walk away, hoping she'd done enough to replace a little of the strength she'd clearly lost in his eyes. There was silence around their group until she finally turned back to them.

"Okay." Maddie held one hand up. "We're doing what now?"

"That's a good question," William, the redheaded, middle brother, chimed in. He scrubbed one hand through his overgrown hair with a smile. "Sounds to me, we all just got *voluntold* here. Wanna let us in on the secret, Carmen?"

"I'll help with whatever you need," Asher said. The eldest brother with his hazel eyes, golden brown hair, and wide smile garnered a few exasperated glances, which he ignored. "Winter is downtime at Cedar Lodge. The perfect time for a big event, if you ask me. And if your purpose is to gather donations for this camp in the summer, you'll hit at the right time. Just before most of the other charities begin their campaigns and right about the time people start feeling charitable. Bravo."

Carmen sighed. "Thank you, Asher," She gazed at the rest of the faces, realizing she'd just made a very big decision in a very small amount of time. But it needed to be done. "I'm sorry I just sprang this on everyone." She watched their reactions to see how much support she really had. So far, it was looking good. In fact, Maddie was the only one who still appeared confused. Carmen couldn't hold back a small laugh. "Let me catch you all up on it," she said, gesturing with her hands as she spoke. "Think glamorous, black-tie event. Lights, flowers, catering, the works. We'll snag a few big names to promote the night and cut the guest list at 200. I imagine a short speech, a great band, dancing, and a live auction at the end of the night." She shrugged, scanning their faces again. "And now you know everything I do."

Maddie's hand settled on her arm. "It sounds amazing. I can't wait."

"I'm there," Chance said. He gave Carmen a nod, and his blond hair fell into his eyes. "Wouldn't miss it."

"Me too," William said, donning the crooked smile of his that would always look a bit wicked. "I was just givin' you a hard time earlier."

"Looks like you can start handing out assignments, then," Asher said, patting her on the back as he headed to the parking lot. "Have a good Sunday, Carmen."

She thanked them as they went their ways, feeling strangely settled. A premiere banquet was something she'd considered before, but the idea just came shooting from her lips. Now that it was out there, scheduled in only one month, she felt a surge of energy to get started.

Maddie's face was split into a full grin when she turned to her. Carmen couldn't help smiling back, and they broke into laughter.

"Girl," Maddie said, shaking her head. "You are the most spontaneous person I know!" She linked her arm with Carmen's, and they started toward her grandfather's old truck. She still hadn't gotten a newer car. She didn't have the heart. The truck belonged out there, rumbling along the roads as a reminder of Grandpa Tagen.

"I can't wait to set Aries loose with this project," Maddie said, smiling back at Carmen. "Can you imagine? Her and Violet will be ecstatic."

"They sure will," Carmen agreed, glad she had such amazing friends back in NYC. And hopefully, her parents would be willing to help with the planning as well. They knew all the caterers and event planners in the area. Their shop on Fifth Avenue had really taken off, which might make it hard for them to find the time for something else, but Carmen needed to try.

All the talk of planning a big event helped to clear her mind, crowding away the pain of not seeing Lander. But it still hung in the corners and edges, always present. Always aching. She tried not to let her thoughts return to him, but she wasn't strong enough to stop them. How she wished he'd come.

She pulled the gear shift into drive and started down the dirt road that was now hard-packed with snow. Tightness formed in her throat, and she swallowed hard, fighting the pain. It was something she'd just have to suffer through for now. After all, she couldn't sit around waiting on a cowboy who was determined to live his life alone. As much as she just wanted to hide away and let the world spin without her, she needed to live her life. Get things done. As much as it hurt—and it hurt bad—her accomplishments were hers to own.

And this banquet? It would be phenomenal.

Chapter Seven

The snow was frigid and the wind that blew across its surface even more so. Lander had already stripped off his jacket and T-shirt, working the only way he knew how. Hard. The wind stung the bare skin of his back, but he didn't feel it. He only continued to thrust in the blade of his shovel, digging.

The storm might've laid a good pile of snow, but the ground hadn't frozen yet. So, there was no reason he couldn't dig out a foundation. It was a foolish thing to do on his own. He knew that. But with the way his thoughts were poisoning him, he had no choice. He'd ridden out to the far side of his land and knew the spot the moment he laid eyes on it. It was going to be the site of his home. A generous, inviting, sprawling cabin. He wanted it to be impressive in every way, right down to the I. In the back of his mind, he saw Carmen there, designing the interior, straightening a vase on the polished wood coffee table made from the trunk of a gnarled tree. But he pushed away those thoughts like the invaders they were. Traitors to reality. There was only so much a person could do to redeem themselves.

He paused, breathing hard, and sagged against the handle of his shovel. His lungs were burning, and his back throbbed, but he knew he wasn't going to stop anytime soon. He'd been going for three hours and the pain in his heart was only just easing. It had taken him the entire first hour to choke back his tears.

Why hadn't he seen it sooner?

If he hadn't let himself believe so wholly that he could have a future with Carmen, it wouldn't hurt like this. Like his heart had been clawed from his chest. The pain was unbearable. She might believe she loved him, but it would only be a matter of time before she realized she'd made a huge mistake. Before she began to see the depth of his faults.

He thrust his spade into the dirt and pressed his boot down on the step, lifting a chunk of dark, rich earth and hurling it behind him. The pile of excavated dirt was growing atop the blanket of snow. Soon it would be a small mountain, and then he could rest. Only then. Still, his mind wandered back to her. The honey and roses taste of her kiss and the smell of her hair like wildflowers. For some reason, the wind carried the fragrance of her whenever it moved, each time it brushed past his face it brought the dizzying scent of Carmen.

He paused again, stabbing the shovel into the dirt. Climbing out of the hole, he stood at the edge and gauged the time it would take him to finish. He could feel the energy lost from his body and knew he had to take it easy. Making himself sick out there with no one to call on would be a risky move. So, he relented and reached for his shirt, stretching it over his sweat-tinged skin. His jacket he carried with him, waiting until his body had cooled a bit to put it on. For now, the sun was enough. His anguish was strangely warming as well, making him wonder if he might be straining his heart with all this worry. Why had Carmen ever chased after him? Was it really all just anger, and then he'd persuaded her into a relationship? He thought back to her face and the things she'd said.

It all seemed sincere, but who knew anymore? After all, if she'd run into Jake's arms the moment she returned to Cedar Lodge, maybe her feelings really hadn't been as deep as his.

But no, he wasn't being fair. He'd practically chased her off, and he could see clearly enough by the body language between them that Carmen hadn't asked for physical comfort. She'd nearly collapsed, and Jake was conveniently there for her at the right time. The time when Lander should have made it back. Should have been the one to catch her. Console her and tell her what an ungodly fool he'd been.

He brushed his hand through his sweaty hair, letting the breeze tousle the dark waves. It would dry soon enough, causing the proof of his struggling and straining to vanish. That was the way of things. Wind blew tracks from the trail, scattering them to dust. The river's current washed the edges off rocks, molding them until they were glossy and smooth. Things recovered. They changed. Somehow, the natural world knew how to repair and blanket the marks of those who trod the land. Maybe the heart worked that way as well. If he could just give it more time, perhaps the throbbing, gaping wounds in his chest would be only a memory.

Untying his horse from a nearby tree branch, he draped the lead rope over his shoulder and let the buckskin follow. The deep snow slowed him down, but he didn't mind.

Suddenly he had the patience of someone who knew their life was over.

"Where ya been?"

Lander froze. Having just come over the hill and only a few hundred feet away from the repaired cabin, Hal and Ernie watched. No additional conversation. They just waited as he drew closer. But instead of confronting them, Lander led his horse into the tack shed and unsaddled and brushed it. He slid a buck knife into the waist of his jeans and secured the gate, finally facing the two men.

"I've been starting up a herd," Lander said, glancing across the small valley at the few dozen cattle that stood well within view. "Thought everyone knew it."

"Nah, not everyone," Ernie said. Always the leader. He was short, but that just meant he had to be mean to make up for it. And he usually overcompensated. Now his gaze bored into Lander's. "Carmen seemed to be looking for you at church today." He tilted his head as if trying to pry into Lander's thoughts. "Then when I asked her about you, she said she told you not to make the trip. Now, what does that mean?"

"It's really none of your business what it means," Lander replied, conscious of the weight of the knife against his hip, the impression of the blade. He knew each man in front of him had at least one weapon, although none were in view.

"She gone and left ya?" Hal sneered and then turned to spit into the snow. "Maybe for that young fella, Jake. He's got his act together. You figure she wanted someone who wasn't so full of holes she'd be spending her lifetime patchin' him together?"

Lander flicked his wrist and suddenly held the hilt of a

hunting knife in his hand. The smiles left the two men's faces. Hal licked his lips.

"We're not your enemies, Lander," Ernie said, holding his hands up, showing his palms. He glanced back at Hal.

"Nah, we're just willing to say the hard truth," Hal grumbled.

"Look," Ernie said, speaking more cautiously now. "We know what it's like to lose your livelihood and be left living off scraps, is all. Figured you might need somethin' to supplement your income until your—eh—cattle ranch gets up and runnin'."

He eyed their surroundings and Lander knew just what he saw. Half-built fence lines and a scrawny herd just trying to make it through the winter. Lander's ribs were even showing more than they should be. He needed a hearty meal like the land needed a good thaw. But both were gonna take time. Sure, his cabin was patched up, but it was still a pathetic dwelling for any sort of man. But even if that were the case, he doubted Ernie and Hal were losing sleep worrying about him.

He faced the two men squarely. "My livelihood is my business, gentlemen." He tipped his hat back down the trail. "Now kindly leave and don't bother checking in on me again."

Hal and Ernie looked back at each other, and Hal left without a word, trudging back through the snow to where their horses were tied. Ernie reached into his pocket and stepped forward. He held a business card and shoved it at Lander. "Take it. I was gonna work for him, but I got a job in town at the slaughterhouse. But this here's a good gig for someone who's not tied to any particular place, and I figure..." His severe eyes glanced across Lander's face in an uncaring way. "You ain't."

With that, he turned and followed Hal, stepping up into the saddle of a tall grulla mare. They headed down the trail without another glance in Lander's direction. Opening his hand, Lander read over the card quickly. A cattle ranch operating in Montana. He recognized the name as one of the largest beef operators in the country. He didn't doubt they'd have a job ready and waiting for him. What he did doubt was why Hal and Ernie would offer him a lifeline like this.

They couldn't know how deeply he was suffering. How he woke in the middle of every night drenched in sweat and shaking from the nightmares that tortured his mind. Thankfully, it wasn't memories of his past. The guilt of his parents' death seemed to wait, allowing this new pain to torture him anew. But what haunted him most never changed. Always, it was images of a future with Carmen. A future where she looked back at him with disdain in her eyes. A future where she was his and yet she hated him more with each passing day. It was his deepest fear; one he'd never allowed himself to confront, and yet it blazed through his mind each night.

He forced away the memory of his last dream, sensing the cold sweat on his brow. Swiping his hat from his head, he brushed the back of his hand across his skin and replaced it. The business card he stuffed into his pocket, and after checking that the two men were long out of view, he turned back toward the construction site.

Work was the only thing keeping his fears at bay. At least, until the day would end. He glanced warily at the winter sun hanging low in the sky. Only early afternoon and yet, it rushed the night as if eager to torture him. The cold sunk through his sweat-tinged shirt, replacing the heat of exertion. He jumped into the dug-out foundation and gripped the handle of an axe in both hands. Swinging with all his might, he sunk the blade into the earth, loosening a large section of clay-like dirt. He lifted the tool and swung again. And again. Warmth returned to his body and numbness to his mind.

Relief.

But he wasn't keeping a careful hold on his thoughts, and they catapulted back to the moment he'd told Carmen to leave. His heart throbbed like it would burst as he swung the axe, sinking the blade into the earth again. But try as he may, he couldn't lift it. The guilt was too heavy, pressing down on top of him until he sank to his knees in the cold dirt. Still gripping the handle, he wanted to stand and swing it again, but it was no use. He was drowning in sorrow and regret and all he could do was hold on.

He pulled the business card from his pocket and read over the information again and again, quickly memorizing the phone number. If this anguish was all he could expect out of his life in Wyoming, then maybe it really was time for him to leave.

Tears sprang to his eyes, but he reached for his cell phone anyway, entering the number. He wanted to stop himself, but it was useless. He was in misery and all he could think of was escaping.

He pressed call.

Chapter Eight

❧

"I love it." Carmen nodded her confirmation back at Jake. The young cowboy beamed. "Go ahead and get it on the schedule, and we can send a deposit over immediately."

"Will do, ma'am." He gave her a quick smile and strode away with his boots hitting solidly on the old wood planks of the ballroom. He disappeared down a back hall that led to an office and reception room where a secretary awaited their answer.

Turning a circle, Carmen couldn't have imagined a more perfect space. Along one side, there were five sliding doors in all, creating a panoramic view of the thick, deep green pines beyond. A sprawling, multilevel patio was strung with café lighting, gas fire-pits, and heat lamps. And to one side stood the Tetons. They combined the ruggedness and western mountain feel with the gracious comforts of the chic log cabin.

She gazed across the room. There was more than enough space for all the tables they would need, plus a raised stage.

Perfect for a band and dance floor. There were touches of old mixed with new. Thick wood beams and black iron lighting sconces and chandeliers were strong and elegant.

Crossing the big, empty room, her footsteps echoed as she pictured what the night would look like. After speaking with Aries and Violet, she was sure the guest list would max out quickly. A lot of big-name designers and models had shown huge interest. It had only been one week since she'd sprung the idea on everyone, and here, they'd found the perfect venue and had more than half the invitations spoken for. Even her mother and father had quickly claimed their spots. She'd been surprised by that. Their business was growing so rapidly, it seemed they hardly had time to call her anymore. But she was grateful for all of it... even, surprisingly, the part that Lander played in the big scheme of things.

She took a quick breath, trying not to let pain surface. It was always there, boiling deep below her casual smile. But she refused to give in to it. Instead, she worked to feel gratitude for all he'd given her. But pain suddenly swelled in her heart, and she pressed a hand to her chest, fighting. The tears came anyway, filling her eyes. She blinked quickly, taking a breath.

"Here we are," Jake said, appearing in front of her with an envelope. Carmen could see her name scrawled beautifully on the front, although it was blurry from the tears in her eyes. She took it from his hands and tried to blink away the moisture, but the moment she looked up, two tears trailed down her cheeks.

Darn her emotions!

And in front of Jake... again. She didn't try to apologize this time, or even explain. She just turned away and left him to stare after her. It was better than accepting his comfort a second time. If he were to offer it, she wouldn't be strong enough to refuse.

"We'll be ready first thing Monday." Jake's voice followed her into the hall and more tears fell.

Why couldn't she get hold of herself?

But then, she knew the answer to that question. It had been surprising to fall in love, and it caught her entirely off guard. If she'd known it was coming, she would have protected herself. Set up boundaries. But, no. She'd fallen for Lander without hesitation, plunging so deep that she never would have believed it could end. Not after a million years. And now, to have him turn around in hardly a month's time...

She stopped, standing under a quiet cover of pines, having taken a shortcut off the main trail. Her breath made thick white puffs in the cold, crisp evening air. The parking area was a few yards away and the snow around her feet was untouched. No one would come that way, which gave her time to breathe and consider.

Leaning against the rough bark of an icy-cold pine, she hugged herself. It took some effort, but she tried to see things from Lander's perspective. The worst part of it all was not understanding how he could be so devoted one moment and then push her completely out of his life the next. She needed to understand, or it would drive her crazy. There was a lot she didn't know about his life, but she knew enough. She knew his upbringing was unbearably hard, with the entire town convinced he'd killed his parents. Set the fire that burned them to death in their sleep. He'd run off to the mountains, ready to end it all, at least until her grandfather had stepped in. It brought tenderness to her heart to imagine her rough, western Grandpa Tagen confronting a young, broken Lander. What a miracle it had been.

She swallowed, not enjoying where her thoughts were taking her. But if Lander, at such a young age, had been saved from ending his life, he would feel a keen sense of devotion and love. He would have set her Grandpa Tagen up on a pedestal, and when he heard stories of Carmen from such a mentor, perhaps it would have developed in him that same altered vision. What if he'd already fallen for her before they ever met? Then, when she'd come into his life, the pieces would appear to fit together so seamlessly. There would be no question. Until, of course, he got to know the real her.

Was that what happened?

She looked out at the darkening landscape around her, shaking her head. It wasn't an idea she welcomed, but what other options were there? He'd been in love. She knew that, but now... now he wasn't.

Her heart throbbed, and she pushed off the tree trunk, completing the distance to her truck. Her boots crunched loudly as they pressed through the snow. With the temperature dropping, it left an icy layer atop that quickly exhausted her legs. By the time she reached the truck, she was breathing hard. She didn't see any other answer to the question of Lander's behavior. And if that was the truth—if he never really loved her—then what was there to cry over?

Her eyes misted as she thought the words, but she blinked rapidly and pressed the gas pedal down. She rumbled back to Cedar Lodge. Everything needed to change from that time forward. She knew it. No sense in lamenting something that was never real, at least on his end. For her, it had been so devastatingly real, it threatened to tear her to pieces from the inside out.

She fought back another wave of tears. It was enough. She had a great future ahead if she could get the benefit camp up and running at Cedar Lodge. A beautiful night of formally dressed, high-class names with glittering necks and wrists would bring in the press she needed, shining a spotlight on Cedar Lodge. It had been awhile since she'd headed up a big-name event, and she was ready to dig in. There was no fear at the thought of such a high-stakes night. She excelled at it.

The pain in her chest she ignored. As far as she was concerned, it was simply a bruise that would take time to ease. She'd find a way to suffer through her sorrow and come out stronger for it. No more thoughts of him.

She pulled up to Cedar Lodge and slowed at the entrance. The drive circled a large tree with the front porch of the lodge on the other side, and the old, rustic barn tucked away at the end of the lane. A memory struck her of sitting on the porch steps in the snow. Her snowsuit was wet from playing outside, and her hair was damp around her face. Mittens hot on her hands with her palms sweating inside. She remembered the air had been icy on her tongue with each breath. Her grandfather came and sat down next to her, and she'd hardly waited for him to say hello.

"It's not fair, Grampa!" she'd grumped, crossing her arms as best she could in the puffy layers of snow clothing. "They all ganged up on me. I'm the only girl!"

Her grandfather had taken his time in answering, and she remembered the impatience quickly growing inside.

"Well, Carmen, you know why that is, don't you?" His wise gaze had settled on her as calmly as his words had, but she kept her arms *crossed and her eyes narrowed. She didn't want to feel better, she wanted revenge.*

"I dunno," she'd answered, only wanting to get to the punishment part. The boys had been invited as guests to the lodge. It was their job to help clear the pathways, not throw a hundred snowballs at her.

"Those boys know how strong you are."

Her grandfather's arm settled warm on her shoulders, and she'd refused to lean against him, as much as she wanted to. It was a comfortable place to be. But instead, she kept her spine rigid and held on to her anger.

"Did you see their faces when you shouted for them to stop?" Her grandfather chuckled, and Carmen glanced up. His eyes were especially glittery when he smiled, and she couldn't help but enjoy it.

"What did they do?" She asked, her arms finally untangling and resting on her knees.

"Well, they were afraid, that's for sure. One of 'em, I'm certain, ran back to his mom."

"He didn't, either!"

"He did." Her grandfather crossed his heart with one hand and nodded his head. "You are powerful, young lady." Leaning forward, his glittery eyes sank deep into hers. "Never forget how strong you are, Carmen. A queen." He kissed her cheek and her anger vanished. She'd jumped up from the steps and marched back to the boys, ready to show them how queens win snowball fights.

The front door to the lodge opened, and Carmen woke from her memories. Night had long since fallen, but she recognized the silhouette against the porch lighting. Revving the engine, she encouraged the tires as they slipped over the last hundred feet.

A genuine smile split across her face as she got out. Annette hurried down the steps and wrapped her arms around Carmen. "My beautiful friend," she said, swaying side to side the same way Carmen's mother would do. After their hug, she held Carmen at arm's length and took a deep breath. "How have things been at the lodge? You making it through winter? I can't believe this early storm. Everything is white! When I left, it was still practically summer."

Carmen knew Annette's habit of talking too much when she was anxious about something. She also saw Maddie peek out from one of the windows, which meant Annette likely already knew about Lander. "We're having a party soon," she said, quickly steering the conversation in the direction she wanted it to go. "A big one."

"So, I hear," Annette smiled, shaking her head. She laughed—a sweet, soft melody—and glanced back at the lodge. "Your friend Maddie told me all about it. She doesn't seem the type to glam up, but she's sure excited about your party." She released Carmen, but instead of turning to the house, she folded her arms and glanced at the snowy ground between them.

A classic transition to a sensitive topic.

Carmen rubbed her hands together. "You freezing out here?" She asked, taking a step toward the door.

"Yes, it's chilly," Annette agreed, but she didn't move. Instead, when she looked up, her face held the compassion Carmen was hoping to avoid. "Carmen." Her voice was so quiet. "I've been meaning to ask you." She shifted her weight, pausing. "How would you feel about me taking a job in Ridgeville?"

Carmen sighed with relief.

Annette's eyes lifted quickly. "I mean, just for the winter months when the boys do most of the work around here. It wouldn't have to be a permanent thing. I love Cedar Lodge with all my heart, but Ben Driscoll's wife Saundra offered me a management position at her wool shop. Turns out it's been growing so much she needs quite a bit of help—"

"Annette," Carmen finally cut in, recognizing the hint of apology in her friend's voice. Annette looked back silently. "I think that's a great idea."

"Oh, good," Annette breathed, resting one hand on her heart. "I was so worried you'd feel abandoned. But you don't need me keeping things up around the house the way Tagen did. I'm just getting in your way."

Carmen wrapped an arm around Annette as they made their way inside. "You're definitely not ever in my way. I promise," she said. "Maybe after winter thaws out, you could come once a week? It really is a big property, and I'd be happy to pay you for some extra help."

Annette squeezed her in a quick hug. "Sounds perfect." They walked in to see Maddie snuggled up on the chair by the fireplace. An open book rested across her lap, and she was fast asleep, her head fallen to one side. She woke at the sound of the door closing and fumbled with her bookmark before setting it aside and standing with a stretch.

"You're back," Maddie said, walking to the kitchen. She pulled out a barstool and propped herself on top. "What did you think of the event place?"

"It was so beautiful." Carmen pulled out mugs for each of them. "Herbal tea, anyone?"

"Mmm," Maddie said, nodding.

"Yes, please." Annette set her boots by the front door and returned to claim the stool next to Maddie. "So, what event place are we talking about?"

A knock sounded on the door, and Maddie jumped up. "I'll get it."

Carmen gave Annette a curious glance, and they both followed behind. It was strange to have one of the Driscoll boys, or even Jake, come out so late on a winter night. Carmen's heart was beating a bit faster at the thought that there might be something wrong.

Maddie swung the door open, and Carmen's heart nearly stopped. Lander stood square in the doorway, dripping wet as if he'd been out working in the snow all day. His face was more rugged than Carmen was used to, and he only looked at her briefly before turning his attention to his hands. He was wringing them together.

Annette glanced between them, and her gaze narrowed a little.

"I was on my way over and came across something in the field behind your arena," Lander said. His chest rose in a deep breath, and his unnerving eyes slowly lifted to Carmen's. For a moment, he only looked at her, unraveling every ounce of strength she'd struggled so hard to build. A surge of anger overtook her and suddenly she wanted to shove him. Hit him. Scream at him for leaving her so easily. But in the same breath, she could hardly keep herself from clinging to him. To have his arms around her would be everything she needed. She was torn so heavily in those two directions that she couldn't even respond.

"You're going to want to see this," he said. His voice had fallen to a whisper and chills broke out along Carmen's arms at the realization that there really was something wrong. Dread filled her chest, but as much as she wanted to ask him her questions, she knew she'd lose all hold on her emotions if she tried.

Instead, she hurried across the room, pulled her coat from the hook, and followed him onto the snowy porch.

Annette and Maddie were right behind, and the group started off with Carmen and Lander leading. Her heart was in her throat. There was so much she wanted to say. But for now, there was obviously something more important to attend to. She snuck a glance at his face as she walked beside him, and her heart throbbed painfully in her chest. As hard as she'd tried to convince herself that she could move on, it was suddenly very clear she couldn't.

As much as she didn't want to admit it, she was still desperately in love with Lander.

Chapter Nine

❧

"I, uh..." Lander was watching the trail ahead of them. He held a small flashlight in one hand, and the beam was just enough to make out a line of footprints. They must have come from Lander on his way to the cabin.

Carmen couldn't ignore the fact that he'd been on his way out to Cedar Lodge before finding whatever he was about to show her. So, what was it he'd come for in the first place? She wondered as she looked back at him, awaiting his next words. She wanted them to, but his eyes didn't meet hers. He only gazed down the trail.

"I found one of your calves in the snow. He's dead." Finally, his eyes lifted, but he looked away quickly. "Normally, I wouldn't think too much about finding a calf like this. It's not uncommon. Life is rough out here." He glanced at her again and then stopped, facing her. His gaze deepened, and Carmen had to work to keep her focus on the news he was bringing her. As shocking and devastating as it was, her mind was filled with memories of them together.

"Carmen, I'm positive this wasn't an animal attack or a natural death."

She flinched, glancing back at Annette and Maddie before turning back to Lander. "What do you mean by that? What else could it have been?"

"C'mon, I'll show you." He reached one hand out as if to rest it on her back as they continued. But then he stopped, and his hand lowered again. "This way," he said, shining the beam of light down the trail.

There was something in the snow ahead. A lump of darkness where it should have been only smooth, crystallized snow. She walked slower, dreading the sight of one of the yearlings. Lander glanced back at her and slowed as well, staying alongside her. That small act had her aching to talk to him. What was it about her that had ended things? What had gone wrong?

"I'm sorry, Carmen," he said.

She glanced down to where he was looking to see her smallest calf. Her heart dropped. They'd named him Howard. He was curled up as if asleep, but the snow around him was trampled and stained with blood. His head was turned to the side so that his face wasn't visible, and she was glad. Normally he was a goofy little thing that loved to run and kick, but more especially he wasn't afraid of people and other animals the way the other calves were. Carmen wondered if that endearing trait was what led to his death. After a steadying moment, she turned to Lander. "What makes you think this isn't an animal attack?" she asked. "What else could it be?"

"Poor thing," Maddie said, lowering in the snow and gazing over the calf.

"Well, for one, there were no animal tracks around him."

Lander glanced around as he spoke. "And there are wounds on his body. The cuts are very sharp and straight." He looked into Carmen's eyes warily. "Almost as if caused by a knife. And see here?" He knelt in the snow, and Carmen lowered next to him, turning to see streaks of blood where he shone his flashlight. "And right there." His voice was deep, lower as he leaned closer. "It appears he was dragged a pretty good distance and left here where he would be more visible." He looked back at Carmen with his eyes bright and piercing. "I believe someone wanted you to find this animal. They killed it and left it here so you'd be sure to spot it before the next snow."

Carmen gazed back into his eyes, measuring his face as she tried to imagine someone doing something so terrifying. And why? What would anyone have to gain by killing one of her calves? She placed her feelings for Lander aside and stood, gazing back at Cedar Lodge, wondering if it could possibly be someone close to her. "But why would anyone do that?"

"That's a good question," Annette said. She rested heavily on one hip with her arms crossed. "Who do we know that might want to threaten you? Or that might want you to leave?"

Wind brushed past them, icy cold, whipping Carmen's hair around her face. Lander's hand reached for her again, this time settling gently on her back. She brushed the strands of hair out of her face quickly.

"Why don't you all head inside?" he said quietly. She could feel every inch of his hand on her back, even with her winter coat on. It practically burned through her. But in front of Annette and Maddie, there was nothing she could say. And then his hand fell away. "I can dispose of the body."

He glanced behind them. "Is the wood pile in the barn stocked?"

Carmen couldn't look away from his face, wishing she could just talk to him. The solution had to be so simple. She needed to find the answer; change something. Anything. Everything.

He turned to her, and her breath caught. "Oh—yes. It's in the barn." She felt a familiar tightening in her chest and throat as she walked past him and joined Annette and Maddie who were already making their way back. She watched Lander as she left. He bent down and lifted the little calf in his arms. "Thank you," she called, feeling a rush of emotion as he nodded solemnly back at her.

Too soon, the darkness came between them, and he was only a silhouette. She forced herself to turn away, walking with the others. Their pace was quick as the wind began to howl, pressing against them with a mighty force that only the Tetons could provide. Leaning forward, Carmen was glad they at least had a little cover from the barn and oak tree. Soon they were huddled at the top of the steps, sheltered from the wind.

"You and Lander seem..." Annette looked back at her with creases showing between her brows. "Different."

Carmen was still spinning with emotions. Thrilled at being with Lander and drinking in every moment when his eyes met hers. The touch of his hand on her back, the kindness in his voice, and the way he'd looked at her. None of it said he hated her, and yet he'd forced her away.

Finally, she focused on Annette, only able to give her a small shrug. What was there to say? He didn't want me. He changed his mind. Maybe he never loved me at all. Tears formed in her eyes, but her anger was stronger, and she clung to it, blinking the moisture away. "I don't know," she finally managed, although it was just a whisper. The silence around them was heavy with concern; she could feel it. But it was also uncomfortable because whatever question they might ask next, she wouldn't have a better answer. Not until she could talk to Lander herself.

Maddie stepped forward and wrapped her arms around Carmen's neck, squeezing her. It was her way to communicate when there were no words. Carmen knew that about her friend, and she loved it. "Thanks, Maddie," she said, accepting a hug from Annette next.

"What d'ya say we go heat up that tea?" Annette suggested, rubbing Carmen's back. It was a comfort that felt much like a mother's, and Carmen couldn't help but appreciate their relationship.

They all hung up their snowy coats and left their boots on a mat next to the door. The cabin was warm and quiet, blocking out the cold of the snow and the noise of the wind. Carmen couldn't stop thinking about Lander as she sat at a barstool while her friends warmed the tea.

Maddie pushed a mug of reheated tea next to her hand, causing her to stir from her thoughts. "Sorry," Carmen said, glancing between the two friends. They both dismissed her apology with a shake of their heads. Maddie took a sip of tea and Annette abandoned her cup on the counter.

"So, what happened, Carmen?" Annette asked, glancing at the door. Her voice was gentle, but it didn't make the words any less jarring. Carmen felt slapped in the face with the question. What did happen? She had no idea.

A thump on the porch had them turning around together. Carmen recognized the sound as it continued, of Lander stomping his boots to shake off the snow. But when the sound stopped, he didn't enter. There was only silence outside. Suddenly, she feared he might head back to his cabin without coming in.

She jumped to her feet and abandoned the hot mug of tea, crossing the room. "I'm going to talk to him," she said. Without waiting for an answer, she stepped into her boots and pulled the door open. Wind hurled a flurry of snow through the opening, and she gasped. Rushing out onto the patio, she closed the door behind her.

In a light T-shirt, she wouldn't be able to stay out for long, but it didn't matter. Carmen waited impatiently for her eyes to adjust to the darkness as the frigid cold bit the skin on her arms and face. There was only a dim glow from the snow-crusted porch light. She took a careful step forward, holding one hand up in case she ran into something.

Suddenly her eyes adjusted, and her gaze flickered to where Lander stood, slightly off to one side. So close. Her hand was barely an inch from his arm, and she wanted so badly to complete the distance. Settle her hand gently on his arm and touch his face and plead with him to tell her what was going on. But what if he wasn't suffering like her? What if all he felt was pity? She wouldn't be able to stand it.

Her hand lowered to her side.

He looked back at her intensely. Unmoving. His vibrant gaze she would never get used to, as it seemed to communicate so many wonderful things. But clearly, she was reading him wrong. Still, she couldn't look away. Her heart ached to hear his voice, but she was terrified of what he might say. Everything burned away inside of her until she wanted to spin around and run back inside the cabin.

But no. She needed this. As much as it hurt standing so close to him, she refused to rush it. Whatever he had to say, she would listen and try to move on. Otherwise, the unknown would drive her crazy.

Wind pushed at her back, brushing her hair in front of her shoulders. She hugged her middle as she shivered, still watching his beautiful eyes as they moved from hers for the first time. He gazed across her body and pulled in a quick breath. "Carmen, where's your coat?"

His voice was incredible. Her coat? Who cared? Maybe they could just share his.

His hand touched her arm, and she had to step to one side to keep from falling over. His eyes were measuring her.

"I just worried that you were..." She stumbled toward the door, glancing back at him, and abandoned her explanation. "It's right here." She pulled her coat from the hanger and whisked it out the door. Her arms slid inside the thick, warm fabric, and she zipped it up, but it didn't stop her from shivering. She was trembling with the tension of the moment. Fear. Joy. Devastation. Everything together was torture. She couldn't stand it any longer. He might take all night to answer. As amazing as it sounded to be with him until morning, she was sure she'd die of anxiety. Looking into his face again, she prayed her voice would remain steady even though her body shook. "I just really need to know what happened between us."

He swayed back ever so slightly, and she cringed, rushing to continue before he stomped away. "Whatever it was, it's fine. I'm fine. It's just... confusing."

She was lying through her teeth. Everything was absolutely terrible. Her world was crumbling around her. But the last thing she needed to do was confess how utterly and devastatingly in love with him she still was. She swallowed hard and tried to look casual, but her eyes were already misting over.

His reaction was difficult to read. In fact, he hardly moved. Just stood there looking back at her with his incredible eyes and perfect mouth and...

"I'm sorry, Carmen."

Her heart instantly ached at his apology. It felt like he was saying goodbye all over again with only those three words.

He took a heavy breath and shifted his weight from one foot to the other. His gaze never left her face, although it occasionally strayed from her eyes. He seemed to wander over her features and then return to stare intensely into them. She loved and hated it, as it twisted her emotions around. In one instant she would feel certain he loved her, and the next she'd call herself a fool.

"To be honest." His eyes steadied, piercing into hers. "I had reservations at the beginning and really hoped they would fade away. But with only a few days in the high country, I could see how hard this would be for..." He paused, seeming to struggle as a muscle in his jaw twitched. "For both of us."

Hard? Wasn't everything worth doing hard? She was sure she'd seen a hundred posters quoting that simple fact. But at least he was explaining, she had to give him that much. Even if it didn't seem to justify breaking apart a love like theirs. Or... like hers. She took a quick breath, determined to keep her emotions at bay. But at the same time, he had to know how she felt. If he walked away because he thought she couldn't handle it, well, she wasn't going to leave it at that.

"I see what you're saying," she said, impressed with how

calm her voice sounded when her insides were a blizzard of chaos. "But I'd like to be able to explain myself too."

His head inclined a bit, and his lips pressed together. A quiet nod was all the approval she got. But somehow, it managed to have her shaking harder with the pressure of it all. Here was her one chance to tell him how she felt without coming apart. She had to look away from his eyes or the battle was already lost. Gazing across the snowy night, she took a step closer to him. "I understand you think it would be difficult, but honestly, I'm okay with difficult."

Her heart was pounding, and something dragged her eyes unwillingly back to his. It had her throat burning and her eyes stinging with tears. She took another step, bringing them close enough together that she had to fight not to lean against him. Still, she held it together. "If you think I'm not strong enough to live out in the high country, you're wrong. I'd be completely willing to leave all this behind."

Her voice cracked and she could hear the hint of pleading in it. She needed to reel it in a little, but everything was pushing her forward. Her heart was throbbing so badly it felt about to burst. "I promise I'd be strong enough, Lander." Saying his name was devastating, and her vision blurred. "Please, give me a chance."

Stop it! You're begging. What are you doing?

But it didn't matter how she tried to stop; she was already reaching for him. Her hands were on his arms and holding him while a single tear escaped. "Maybe I could stay with you for one week and you would see—"

His arms came around her, and she couldn't stop the tears any longer. She fought as a sob quietly escaped, and another. Holding on to him, she leaned heavily against his chest and cried with an anguish she couldn't hold back. But his reaction was frozen. He held on to her, unmoving. Maybe he regretted ever coming at all. How could it hurt so badly?

Choking back the emotions, she brushed at her cheeks and stepped back. His silence was answer enough. She couldn't bring herself to look into his eyes again and dropped her gaze to the ground. When she spoke, her voice broke. "You don't need to stay. I understand." She could only stare at his boots. They didn't move. He only stood there, probably humiliated, and staring back at her like one of the biggest mistakes of his life.

Suddenly his boots turned, and he strode down the steps and away from her. Past the oak tree and around the back of the barn.

Crushed, she hardly knew what she was doing when she flew down the steps if only to see him for one more minute. She trailed behind him, wishing he would turn around. Waiting for it. But he was practically running. She came around the back of the barn, and he was just entering the glow of the floodlight when he stopped suddenly.

Hope burst to life inside of her, but then she spotted another man approaching on horseback. By the silhouette of his long hair, it was Everett.

"Hey, Lander."

Everett's voice rang out. Strong and bold. Carmen didn't hear Lander respond, but Everett continued just as loudly. "I saw the blood out by the trees and worried something might be wrong. Followed it back here and saw the burn pile. Is everything all right?"

Lander's voice reached her, but just barely. She couldn't make out the words.

"I see," Everett said. Carmen could see him nodding back at Lander. "Well, thanks again for allowing me to buy your place. Not many were willing to give me a second chance, so I appreciate it. Let me know if you ever need anything. Anytime."

Lander responded quietly again, and Carmen watched as Everett turned his horse away and faded into the darkness. Lander had his buckskin tied to the hitching post. He untied his gelding, stepped into the saddle, and never looked back.

Chapter Ten

✦✦✦

W hy hadn't he told her? The question blazed in Lander's chest, and he had no answer. Plenty of excuses, sure. She'll be better off without me. The longer you stay, the more painful it will be. You can't listen to what you want right now. You're hurting her.

Lander hunched forward suddenly, and his buckskin slowed to a stop in the quiet darkness. Snow flurried around him, and he wrapped his arms around his middle with the stabbing pain he'd been fighting off all night. From the moment he'd first glimpsed Carmen, it had dug straight through his flesh and bones together. But it was nothing compared to the agony of hearing her cry. Of having her sobbing into his chest and holding her knowing he was comforting her from a pain he'd caused. But she had it all wrong. She thought that the high country was the difficult part when really it was him.

They'd both be better off if she'd just hate him like she should. If she would only scream at him and slap him across the face. He could handle that. It would be a relief compared to all the compassion he saw in her eyes; the desperation and struggle to understand. She was giving him so many chances. Too many. There was a lot he didn't deserve in this life, but most of all was her kindness. The moment she'd begged him to explain, he knew he never could.

His buckskin blew a strong breath and shook out his black mane, and slowly Lander eased back into the saddle. They resumed a slow walk again. It was the safest way to travel in the deep snow. He'd spent most of the ride alert and searching for any sign of an intruder on Carmen's property along Cedar Creek. It had kept his suffering at bay until now. The guilt and pain twisted at his insides relentlessly.

He was getting close to his shack, as he called it in his mind. *Cabin* was too gracious a word. But it had a newly repaired fireplace, so at least he could get it warm in an hour or two. The night was already half over, and he was glad. He'd spent too many replaying his mistakes in his head until he'd chased off any chance of sleep.

The wind had increased, blowing through his layers of protection and biting at his hands and feet. He finally reached his tack shed and stripped the gear off his horse. The animal had just enough cover to use as a windbreak, and it stood with its tail against the wind and its nose to the wood siding of the small shed row. Lander gave him a good pile of hay to eat, assuring he'd stay warm through the rest of the night.

When he was inside, he took a handful of kindling he kept in a bucket by the fireplace and stacked it atop the grate. Larger pieces of wood were layered against the wall as high as he could reach. He took a propane torch to the kindling, holding it there until the wood was eagerly crackling. Then he added larger pieces until it was a proper stack.

Stepping back, he watched the flames grow. Their warmth was a small comfort, but it wasn't enough to chase away the pain.

It wouldn't last much longer. As soon as she found out about his plans, she would hate him. He was sure about that. He didn't allow himself to wonder if he'd made the right decision; it was no use. What was done, was done.

He crossed his arms and turned around, letting the fire warm his back while he looked out at the empty rooms. There was a bedroll and sleeping bag in the back room that served as his bed for now. He'd cut down a few slender pines he planned to use for a lodgepole bed frame, but that could wait. Everything could wait. There was no rush now that he wasn't planning to stay for long. He just needed to endure the handful of remaining days. That was all. His heart throbbed, and he wondered if he could do it.

The glow of the fire lessened, and he took a few logs, adding them robotically. He leaned against the wall and slid down until he was sitting, watching the flames. They managed to distract his mind just enough, and eventually, his eyelids drooped, and sleep found him.

It was well into morning. Sunday. Usually, he would be about his chores before the sun began lightening the sky, but on Sundays, he would allow himself a hearty breakfast and a restful afternoon. But today, he was still in bed. Sometime during the night he'd lifted from his cramped position on the wood floor and crawled under the covers and atop a pad that was too thin. But at least he'd slept.

The memories of the night before were still raw in his chest, and there was something he needed to do. He could feel the importance of his next move balanced on the tattered timeline of his life. There were too many mistakes along the way, but this wouldn't be one of them. He saddled his horse and followed their tracks from the night before, heading back toward Cedar Lodge.

But he didn't stop there. He continued on, taking the old country road that led west toward Ridgeville. A clean white church was in view before too long. It had always seemed a perfect location, but now, nestled in a layer of snow and with the Tetons as a backdrop, it was picturesque.

Lander tied his horse at the hitching post. In the summer months, there would always be two or three horses tied, but today it was just his. He patted the buckskin's rump and turned toward the building to the sound of organ music. Voices joined in as the service began and the congregation sang. Lander's stomach twisted into an uncomfortable knot. He'd been to the church only once before, but it hadn't felt as difficult. Back then, he had Carmen. Just sitting next to her had eased the moment when all eyes had turned to him, and so many whispers filled the pews. Speculating.

What would they think now?

He shook his head. It didn't matter. He wasn't here for them.

Still, he climbed the steps and stopped short of opening the door. He stared down at the handle, instantly wishing he'd never come. When the music from inside ceased and the church became silent, he knew he couldn't open the door and make such a spectacle. He decided to wait just until the interlude hymn, and then he'd sneak in. If there were no seats, he was fine standing in the back of the building in the shadows. In fact, he'd prefer it.

There was a faint sound of Pastor Evans speaking. He leaned closer, listening, although it was hard to make out more than an occasional word. Faith. Almighty. Repentance.

The message was hopeful enough, but it did nothing to bring him hope. All he felt was devastation and loss. The loss of a life he let himself believe in.

The pain returned, and he closed his eyes, wincing. He leaned his forehead against the cold wood door. He hoped Carmen was one of the members of the congregation, although he didn't know why he wished it. The sight of her would only bring him more suffering, but he didn't care. If he was going to leave Wyoming, he wanted it to be with a fresh memory of her face. Her smile. The glow of sunlight in her hair and reflected in her eyes. She was beautiful.

A hymn rang out, and he opened his eyes. His heart began to pound, but he turned the handle and eased the door open before he could talk himself out of it. No one had noticed the door opening, and he eased through quietly. Shuffling to the side, he found relief in a shadowy corner. Only one young boy glanced back at him, but the child seemed more intent on tracing out the lines of the ceiling beams. His young brown eyes rolled back, and he tilted his head, following the largest beam to where it ended at the organ. He didn't turn around again.

Lander was scanning each row, searching until he spotted her soft, wavy auburn hair and delicate build. Carmen sat in the second row with her friend Maddie and Annette. But he could only focus on Carmen. Once he'd found her, he couldn't look away. His breath caught when she turned around, but she only glanced at the row behind her. He could see the couple seated there had their heads close together as if they were talking. They leaned away from each other when she turned around, and back together again when she faced the front.

Clearly, they were gossiping, but he didn't care. He only

watched as Carmen threaded one hand through her hair and tossed it behind her shoulder. He could practically smell her intoxicating fragrance from where he stood. A woman was speaking at the pulpit, but his eyes were distracted, tracing over every single strand of Carmen's hair and the curve of her shoulders.

Music started up and a few people in the back row stood, chatting as they turned to leave. The meeting was over, and his view of Carmen was blocked. He inched to the side, but more than one eye caught sight of him, and every time there was a look of surprise. One woman with silvery-blonde hair and a velvet red hat gasped when she saw him. And another man glared openly. It was obvious he remained a topic of conversation in the small town, and no doubt more especially after being found lurking in the back of the room. He ignored it, working his way up to Pastor Evans while staying to the edges of the building.

He searched over the top of gently curled hair, gel-spiked styles, conservative hats, and a few bald heads. Finally, he spotted Pastor Evans. He was smiling and shaking a gray-haired woman's hand when he glanced up. Catching sight of Lander, the pastor froze, and a look of concern filled his eyes.

Desperation swelled in Lander's heart, but he tried to keep it out of his gaze. He nodded at Pastor Evans, hoping he would understand and meet Lander privately. If he was going to continue mingling with the entire congregation, Lander would just give up. Still edging around the crowd, he ended up behind the stage for the choir and next to Pastor Evans's office. Finally, out of the way.

He watched the group of churchgoers warily but didn't

spot Carmen again. No doubt she was already outside and on her way back to the lodge.

"Hello, Lander."

The pastor's voice had Lander's emotions rising to the surface. He'd worked hard over the past weeks to keep them down, but now they rose like the tide; no holding them back. He could feel the sheen of moisture in his eyes as he turned and faced Pastor Evans.

"Come," the pastor said, "let's talk in here." He held a hand out, guiding Lander into his office.

Lander obeyed, grateful for the few seconds he was given to compose himself. Pastor Evans closed the door behind them and walked back to his desk, although instead of sitting down, he stood in front of it, waiting.

"I..." Lander took a deep breath. "I'm not sure where to start."

"And that's fine." Pastor Evans gave a comforting smile. "Let's start with today. Why did you want to talk to me?"

"I..." Lander's eyes clouded again, and he held one hand over his face, struggling. He took a slow, shaky breath. "Do you really believe I can be forgiven?" The pastor looked about to answer, but Lander held a hand up, stopping him. "And even if you do, what makes you believe I can change who I am?"

"What is it you need forgiveness for?" the pastor asked. "What is it you've done?"

Lander shook his head. "I fell in love with a woman who thinks she knows me. But I've realized that... I can't be that man. There's too much darkness inside of me. I feel it every day." He took a heavy breath, fighting back tears. "If it wasn't for my choices, my parents would be alive. Her grandfather took me in, or I would have ended my own life. But he's gone now, and I can't be certain it wasn't because of the stress I brought into his life. I can't be certain of anything." A tear trailed down his cheek. "I can only put distance between us so I stop hurting her." Pastor Evans's hand settled on Lander's arm, and he was silenced, breathing hard.

"Lander," the pastor said, his voice gentle. "You're finding conclusions where there are none. You're a work in progress. We all are. Except unlike most of us, you've had a decidedly traumatic upbringing. The most difficult of anyone I've known. Do you really believe change would come in an instant? And since it hasn't come, do you believe it won't come at all?"

Lander brushed the trail of tears from his face, looking into the pastor's eyes. They appeared so certain as if he still had faith in him.

"You can't experience something like you have, then hide away for most of your adult life, and suddenly expect to recover in a handful of days." He smiled, holding on to Lander's shoulders. "That kind of change takes a thousand small, purposeful commitments. But I promise you, day by day, action by action, you can become that man. A man strong enough for others to lean on. A man stronger than you, or she, could ever imagine."

Lander had finally calmed himself enough to see clearly and to breathe normally. He hung on every word out of the pastor's mouth, but in the end, he sighed with defeat. "I don't know if I believe that."

To his surprise, Pastor Evans smiled. He squeezed Lander's shoulders and released him. "Well, for now, let's just have me do the believing, shall we? What I want you to do is open a communication with your Father—"

"My father's dead."

"No." The pastor shook his head. "Your Father." He eyed Lander seriously, pointing upward. "Talk to him. He wants to hear from you because you're His child, and He loves you. Okay?"

It took a moment, but eventually, Lander nodded. He would try praying again. It had never produced a heavenly messenger or life-changing answer, but he supposed that was a little much to ask for.

"One other thing." The pastor walked around his desk and gazed out the window. Snow had gathered in the edges and corners of the glass, framing the winter wonderland outside. "I understand your concerns, Lander. I really do." He turned around and folded his arms across his chest. "But are you absolutely certain you're not doing this on purpose?"

Lander frowned. "Doing what?"

"Sometimes," the pastor said, "when people suffer the way you have and lose those they care so much about, they begin to push others away the moment they start to care deeply for them. The moment they love them. It's a sort of self-sabotage in the way of protecting oneself from similar pain."

"That sounds completely ridiculous," Lander said, struggling to hold back the anger from his voice. Because he was angry. Did Pastor Evans think he was insane? Ruining his life on purpose? It was infuriating. He took a steady breath.

"I know how it sounds, believe me." The pastor held his hands up as if trying to calm the moment. "But I want you to try something with me. Think back to when your thoughts changed about Carmen. When they changed about yourself. When did you begin to feel that this life together wouldn't work?"

Lander didn't want to answer. He avoided the pastor's

eyes as he recalled the sickening moment he'd wondered if he was enough. "I was alone, in the high country," he said, feeling sick when he remembered everything that had happened. "It was when I first worried things wouldn't work out."

"You worried," Pastor Evans repeated. "So, you could say you feared?"

Lander's eyes flickered up to the pastor's impatiently. "Yeah. I didn't know what to do, so of course, I was afraid. It was devastating. Why would I do that on purpose?"

"Lander, do you know where fear, doubt, and discouragement come from?" The pastor looked back at him peacefully, with a smile lingering on his lips. "They come from the father of lies. The enemy of your soul. He delights in misery and sorrow. It's no wonder he attacked you when you were so close to a turning point."

Pastor Evans walked back to Lander, placing his hand on his shoulder again. His blue eyes were deep and sincere. "Don't listen to him, Lander. Believe in yourself. Believe in your happiness. Let yourself live through the pain to experience the reward. The joy."

Lander's chest tightened until he could hardly breathe. Had he possibly ruined his relationship with Carmen for nothing? The question stung, and he shoved it away. A sudden burst of infuriation swelled inside, telling him this was all just mindless talk. "No," he said sharply, marching toward the door. He wrenched it open. "You're wrong, and I can't stay here anymore. I'm moving to Montana because it's the best decision for my life right now. Period."

He spun around and stopped short at the sight of Carmen. She stood inches away, her seething expression proof enough that she'd heard him plain and clear. Her eyes flashed with what he could only assume was bitter and unrelenting anger. Why did she insist on showing up at the most inopportune moments?

She rolled her slender shoulders slightly, and the heated color of her cheeks cooled. "I, uh..." She shifted her weight and her beige, tiered skirt brushed to one side. "I saw your horse." Her eyes wandered into the office behind Lander and then back into his eyes, making him flinch. "You're leaving?" She asked, her voice suspiciously calm.

Lander could hardly think straight. The last thing he wanted was to see her cry again and know it was his fault. But as he struggled to answer, a change came over her. The muscles in her jaw constricted, and her gaze narrowed. She looked back at him with an expression as close to uncaring as he'd ever seen on her. His heart pounded, and he ached inside, wishing he'd never come to the church in the first place.

"You know what?" she asked. The tone of her voice was like shards of glass that cut. "Leave." Her chin lifted and her eyes seared back at him. "You were right all along. We're no good for each other."

With that, she whipped around and strode out. Lander clutched the doorframe. It was the only thing keeping him from falling to his knees.

Chapter Eleven

✦❧✦

Her eyes were dry as she stormed from the church. She was glad most of the others had already left, making the trip to her vehicle a solo one. The road was slick, but she pushed the old truck harder than usual, letting the tires slide a little with each turn. At the turnoff to Cedar Lodge, she cranked the wheel, and the backend whipped around, spinning her in a full circle. But she wasn't panicked; instead, she felt relief at being out of control. No more choices; it was all fate from here. The truck continued spinning until she faced the old highway she'd turned off.

The sound of her breath was all she heard. There were no cars or people. No voices calling out. Just her sitting on an empty country road. Alone. Still, the tears didn't come. It was like her heart had vanished from her chest. She didn't even feel the pain anymore. All she felt was anger, but even that was muted as if committing to be angry was just too much effort. She was exhausted from the inside out. Deep down, she'd believed all along that she and Lander would be together. She believed it after he drove her from his cabin. She believed it when he came to Cedar Lodge and then left her. She believed it right up until hearing him shout that he was leaving.

She didn't believe it anymore. Let him leave.

With a quick breath, she cranked the wheel and jammed the gas down, spinning a cookie and then easing off the accelerator. The old truck took her abuse well, rumbling toward the lodge until she shifted into park and released it. She tore the keys from the ignition and shoved them in her purse. But her head was spinning; it was just too much.

Clasping her hands, she held them to her forehead, closing her eyes briefly. She couldn't talk about what happened. She didn't want to. But she needed help. "Forgive me," she whispered, letting the words ache in her chest. Lander was gone from her life forever now, but even worse was the thought that she'd hurt him. He clearly hadn't expected her to hear him like she did. A deeper communication touched her heart. An understanding and plea for softness, but she didn't want to feel it. The tears would never stop if she allowed them to come.

She pushed the door open and slammed it closed behind her, her boots crunching through the snow.

"Hello, Carmen!" Maddie waved from the door. She'd driven home with Annette when Carmen had mentioned she was going to stay and talk to Pastor Evans. Now she smiled, all ease and cheer, the way Carmen usually felt after a church meeting.

Carmen exhaled slowly, locking her vanished heart away. A smile pushed at her cheeks as if by magic. "Hey, Maddie," she called, "want to help me today?"

"Uh, sure." Maddie shrugged, stepping aside as Carmen walked in. "What do we need to do?"

Carmen hung her coat, using the moment to avoid looking into Maddie's eyes. Her friend could always tell when she was hurting with only a glance. She hurried into the library, waving at Maddie to follow. But when she entered the room, all she could think of was her grandfather's favorite chair and how Lander snuck it away and had it repaired for her. She turned from the corner where the chair sat and pulled open the desk drawer. "We need to place the orders this week. Tomorrow, if we could. So, with your artist's eye, we can sketch out the design."

She smoothed out two large sheets of paper and set a sharp pencil on top, turning to Maddie. "Want to get started?"

"Yes, absolutely," Maddie said, but then she turned toward the door. "It's just that Annette was busy getting lunch together. Should we eat first?"

"Oh." Carmen glanced at the clock. It was nearly 1 p.m. "I suppose we should."

"And, did you want to change?" Maddie shrugged.

Carmen hadn't noticed her friend was in sweats and a hoodie. It seemed like an annoying time waster. Changing clothes and eating. Who needed it? All Carmen wanted was to be busy. But it would be strange of her not to do those things, so she nodded back at Maddie. "You're right," she said, managing a small laugh. "I'm just really anxious to have this banquet go well." She stood, heading to her room. "I'll go change and help with lunch."

"The banquet will be amazing," Maddie said, her voice following Carmen as she disappeared down the hall. "Promise!"

Carmen wandered into her room. The shades were drawn, making it hard to see, but she didn't need the light. She stripped down and pulled on a pair of bootcut jeans and a button-up flannel shirt. The colors were a beautifully faded blue and purple that looked nice with her hair. She worked with the first button, taking awhile to get it buttoned, and then moved to the next. By the time she moved to the third, she realized her hands were shaking.

She dropped the fabric and took a deep breath, catching sight of her reflection in the mirror. Her face was pale; she could see that much. But other than that, she looked irritatingly normal. With how horrendous she felt on the inside, it was strange to look the same on the outside. But one thing was for sure, she was going to get over this. If Lander was going to leave, then fine. That was his choice. She just hadn't been expecting it. She forced her thoughts back to the banquet. Her summer camp depended on its success.

Her hands were a little better, and she returned to the buttons.

"Turkey and provolone?" Annette asked when Carmen came back to the kitchen. She held a plate with a nicely layered sandwich on one half and a pile of fresh sliced fruit on the other.

"Thank you." Carmen sat at a barstool, reaching for the plate. "Sorry, I meant to help. But it looks like you're done."

Annette and Maddie both had similarly decorated plates in front of them, but when Carmen glanced at her friends, there was an apprehensiveness passing between them, and then the look vanished as quickly as it had come.

"It's okay," Annette said, brushing aside Carmen's offer with a wave of her hand. She took a big bite of sourdough and roast beef. Maddie dug into her sandwich as well, and

Carmen felt a prickling of suspicion as she turned to her plate. Maybe they were wondering why she'd stayed and talked to Pastor Evans, but it seemed strange that they would give it much thought.

Lunch was mostly quiet, with a little talk about a winter storm in a few days and some comments on the messages of hope shared at church. There were no questions or suggestions; nothing that would explain the look Carmen had seen between her friends. She kept an eye on them over lunch and was eventually rewarded. Just as she stood to take her plate to the sink, she saw it again. Maddie glanced at Annette, and both their expressions were guarded. Maddie even looked a little afraid. It didn't fit with Carmen's guess that they might be curious about her time at church. There was something else going on. But Carmen didn't have room in her thoughts for anything more. She'd had enough. She needed to get out for a while.

"I'm going to check on Dax," she said, setting her plate in the sink. "I'll see you guys in a bit."

"Okay," Maddie said. Annette only smiled.

Carmen wrapped up in her thick winter coat and boots and stepped outside. Her eyes watered against the blinding afternoon sun reflected off the snow. But it provided little warmth against the bitter cold. Dax whinnied when she got close to the barn, but she didn't go in. She would check on him on her way back. For now, she just needed wide-open country.

The Tetons were beautiful and white, spotted with dark craggy layers of pine trees and granite cliffs. From far away, they only gave the mountain a beautiful, heathered appearance. But she knew what a formidable monster the mountain could be in the winter. Completely impassable. Still, its danger and strength only added to the beauty.

She came to the spot where Lander had shown her the calf. A new layer of snow covered any physical reminders, but she could still see the poor little animal in her mind. If someone really had meant the animal's death to be a warning, who could do something like that? Shivers touched her spine, and she continued on, looking ahead down the trail. It was the same perimeter path she'd walked with Maddie. Although hard to make out with so much snow piled on the landscape, she could see where the trail curved along next to the woods and then circled the back of the pasture.

Her eyes traced out the lines and wandered into the shadows of the trees. They were darker now that every branch was thickened and heavy with snow, leaving the forest a haunting, deep expanse. She searched the deepest sections of darkness as she walked, remembering the wolf pack that had terrorized her herd not long before. She'd shot one and managed to drive the pack away, but there was no doubt in her mind that they'd return. How could they not? Winter was long and harsh, and food was right there in her pasture, just waiting for them. Any day, she expected to see a glowing pair of eyes in the darkness, staring back at her. But not today.

She rounded the back of the pasture, where there was an open meadow and a breathtaking backdrop of the Tetons. They were practically on top of her. Stopping for a moment, she gazed at the scene, then closed her eyes, and took a deep, frigid breath. The thought came that anything could have happened to that calf. It could have become tangled in the fence and then dragged off by any number of creatures. Maybe an animal did kill it and was frightened away before it could finish it off. She'd heard of mother cows killing the calves of other heifers. Maybe that was it.

The idea that it had been an animal seemed a thousand times more likely than someone actually killing a baby animal to scare her. Besides, there had been that horrible storm. Who would possibly risk their lives just to send her a warning? It wasn't logical, and that had her feeling considerably better about things.

She turned to continue on and caught sight of a stream of smoke rising from the forest beyond. She figured she'd have to start calling it Everett's cabin, and maybe when she got to know him better, it would come more naturally. But for now, all she could remember was being there with Lander. Tending to him when he was sick, finding he'd kept her grandfather's harmonica, and then returning home wearing his sweats. When Chance had seen her that way, he'd jumped into quite a few assumptions, as well as a good lecture.

She smiled. Chance really was a good friend, however unwanted his good intentions had been at the time. But now, as she approached Cedar Lodge again, she wondered if she should have listened to him. Maybe Lander was someone to stay away from. After all, he was leaving her behind and hadn't even—

With a start, she wondered if that was what he'd come for the night before. Had he come to say goodbye? And then, after finding the calf and with everything going on, he never got the chance. She chewed her lip as she slid back one heavy barn door, squeezing through the space. She closed it behind her and sighed in the warmth of the barn and the smell of hay and horses. Such a comforting space. Winter light streamed in through the windows and the horses took turns nickering at her. Carmen sat on a bench next to the tack room, considering.

She didn't like where her thoughts were going. Being angry at Lander was easier than thinking she'd jumped the gun and possibly driven him away. After all, wasn't he speaking privately with Pastor Evans? Maybe he was really struggling, and here she'd gone and lashed out at him. She propped her elbows on her knees with a sigh. If she wanted to face the truth, she knew that whatever was going on with him, it likely had to do with more than just her. It hurt to think of him, and she didn't understand it. But maybe it was true that all he needed was time.

She got to her feet. Reaching for a brush, she opened Dax's stall and joined the black Appaloosa, brushing out his shiny coat. The spattering of white on his rump was gorgeous; bold and brilliant. He was bushy with his thick winter coat, and she brushed the bits of dust and dirt out, running her hand over the fuzzy hair like a plush blanket.

He turned his head, bending his neck around until he touched her cheek with his muzzle. She rubbed his head behind his ears. "I don't know, Dax," she said, looking into his huge dark eyes and enviously long lashes. "It might just be out of my control." She leaned against his warm side with a groan. "But I hate that."

The door to the barn squeaked, and she jerked upright, spinning around. But it wasn't Lander easing into the barn and out of the storm. It was Maddie, then Annette. The looks on their faces were solemn, and Carmen gave Dax one last pat before leaving his stall. "Hey, you two," she said, glancing between them. "What's up?"

Maddie glanced away, scanning the barn. But Carmen knew she was just buying more time as if unsure how to start. Annette stood boldly and clasped her hands in front of her. "We heard a rumor at church today," she said, glancing at Maddie. "Now, normally I'm not one to pay any attention to rumors, but when everyone in the room is whispering the same thing, you need to at least know about it."

"Yes, you do," Carmen said. She fidgeted with the zipper of her coat, feeling anxious. "What was the rumor? I'm guessing it has to do with me."

"Well, yes and no," Annette said, hesitating. "They say Lander tried to steal the lodge out from under you and that you drove him away, up into the high country."

Carmen frowned, turning this information over. "They've got it all wrong," she said. "Maybe his intentions weren't always the greatest, but Lander practically saved the lodge. I would have had to sell if it wasn't for him."

"We know that," Maddie assured. "But somehow, everyone has this idea. After you left to talk to Pastor Evans, I heard it from four different people. I guess they believe he's tormenting you. One person even said he's been spotted multiple times circling the Cedar Creek property on his horse. But Carmen..."

Maddie crossed her arms, increasingly agitated. "They talk like he still lives in his old cabin. So, when they say Lander is the one circling your property, they're mistaken. Because Lander doesn't live there anymore. I got to thinking about it and realized that if someone is coming from his old cabin on horseback, it has to be..." She hesitated, finally looking into Carmen's eyes.

"Everett," Carmen said, her voice feeling heavy. "It would have to be Everett."

Chapter Twelve

"Who's Everett?" Annette asked, clearly taken aback. Her gaze shifted from Carmen to Maddie, looking a bit irritated. "And how do I not know him?"

Carmen sighed. "He bought Lander's old cabin." She glanced at Maddie. "He was out here riding when we were on a walk, and we met him. Seemed like a really nice guy, although he made it clear he was out here to get away from it all."

"Hmm." Annette frowned. "I don't like the sound of that. I mean, everyone is out here to get away from it all, obviously. But when he brings it up to you like that, it's as if he's intentionally creating distance." She paused, combing her fingers through her hair as she thought. "Did he seem rude at all?"

"No," Maddie said. Then she turned to Carmen with half a smile. "He was really nice, actually."

Carmen nodded. "He was." She thought back to when Everett had confronted Lander about the calf. "But then, I did overhear him talking to Lander." Both Maddie and Annette leaned in, waiting. "Eh... he said he was grateful for Lander giving him a second chance. Like they knew each other before."

"When was that?" Annette asked.

Her eyes were sharp and thinking. It made Carmen nervous, and she wanted to know what thoughts were brewing behind those eyes. "It was just last night," she answered. "He said he'd seen the blood in the snow and was worried."

"The blood in the snow that was just right out here by the pasture?" Annette tipped her head out toward the Tetons. "So, he was riding around just behind the lodge?"

Carmen felt a pinch of discomfort in her middle. That didn't sit right with her, having a stranger riding up to her house at night. But she hadn't thought of it like that until just now. "I guess he was." She looked at Maddie, seeing resistance in her friend's eyes. It was clear Maddie had a crush on Everett, but even she looked unsure of what that would mean.

"So, he was there before or after the calf was killed?" Annette asked. Her voice had lowered and Carmen's heart beat faster.

"What are you saying?" Carmen knew and respected Annette's logical thinking, but she was questioning it. She'd met Everett, and he seemed like a perfectly good guy.

"I'm just saying, there are strange events happening that have never happened before," Annette said. "And there is a new person who has never been here before. That's a strong coincidence."

"Maybe it is," Maddie chimed in, "but I'm sure we could just talk to him. Get a better idea of who he is."

"We should," Annette said firmly, glancing back at them through the silence. "All three of us. Let's ride out there and talk to him."

"When?" Maddie asked, her voice small.

Annette glanced out the window, and Maddie followed. To one side, above a gorgeous section of forest, a stream of smoke spiraled lazily into the sky. Annette turned around abruptly. "Now."

"YOU KNOCK," MADDIE WHISPERED, BACKING AWAY FROM the door. She'd frozen the moment her hand was an inch from the stained wood. Now, she glanced unsurely around them. Their three horses were tied to the hitching post at the front of the house, swishing their tails.

Carmen stepped forward and rapped on the door. It echoed around them in the quiet treetops, and a few birds chirped their disapproval, lifting from their perches to flutter away.

"Maybe he's out," Maddie whispered.

"Out where?" Annette's voice was strong, and she crossed her arms and turned around to gaze out toward Cedar Creek land.

"Can I help you?"

The three women whipped around at the new voice, surprised to find Everett striding toward them from the forest. He wore canvas work pants with suspenders that hung down at his sides and a T-shirt that clung to his chest. Sweat marks lined the cream material, proving he'd been hard at work when they rode up. His long hair was tied back, but a single strand had escaped and hung aside his face. He stopped just short of the deck. "You ladies need something?" he repeated, a little softer this time as if he wagered he'd surprised them.

"We wanted to talk to you," Carmen chimed in, hoping they were doing the right thing in coming to interrogate their new neighbor. Hopefully, they could make it into more of a friendly, get-to-know-you conversation. "I feel bad we never welcomed you into the area." Carmen wished they'd brought a loaf of home-baked bread or some cookies. "Uh... and we wanted to invite you out to the lodge for dinner tonight. Would you be free?" She could feel her friend's eyes on her, but she kept a watch on Everett.

He shifted his position, and she spotted a long, sleek knife in his left hand. It looked closer to a tactical knife than the more traditional hunting blades she was used to seeing in Wyoming. It seemed decidedly out of place. But then, he wasn't from around there.

In one quick, smooth movement he slid the knife into a sheath strapped to his waist. "I'd like that very much," he said, with a gentle nod. "Want to come in a moment?"

"If you're not too busy," Annette said. She glanced at Carmen.

"Right this way." Everett stepped between them and took a key from his pocket, unlocking the front entrance. He pushed the door open and stepped aside. "After you."

The cabin was the same as before, while also being completely different. With Lander, it was kept in order and showed off his sleek taste in everything from dishes to furniture and rugs, and now, Carmen had to work hard to keep from cringing. Garbage was crumpled about the floor as well as T-shirts and jeans. A few dirty socks were tossed on the couch. There were dishes scattered across the kitchen on every surface and dirty boots in the center of the room.

"I haven't been one for cleaning since I got out here." Everett glanced about the place and then back at Carmen while she tried her hardest not to look appalled. He reached down and picked up a crumpled burger wrapper, tossing it into the sink. "It's not like me, usually. Something about this move just has me breaking out. Doing what I want for once and not giving a—"

He stopped, glancing across their faces with his mouth half full of a word he seemed to suddenly deem inappropriate. "I mean, uh..." He adjusted the leather belt around his waist, situating the knife. "It's given me a bit of freedom, and I'm ashamed to say, I've regressed in age by about fifteen years." He chuckled.

"Well." Annette smiled and shook her head. "I'm not one to disagree with making some changes in your life when you need it, that's for sure."

Maddie nodded in agreement while she watched Everett carefully. Carmen watched him too, and as she did, she noticed his amusement fade away. Shadows appeared on his face as he gazed out the window to the snowy view beyond.

"We approached from the east when I came to take a look at this place, Lander and me." He tipped his head toward the window. "That way. I felt lost in the wild and agreed to buy it immediately. The solitude was a savior for me. My life's been a little... rough lately." His gaze wandered back to Carmen and then to Maddie. She blushed. "I didn't even know Cedar Lodge existed until I went for a ride the morning that I ran into you both. It was a surprise, but a pleasant one." He turned back to Carmen, smiling a bit, although there were still edges of darkness along his features. "If it was anyone else, I'd have to run them clean out of the area."

The air felt heavy around her, and Carmen took a breath. "You said you've had it rough lately. Is there anything we can do to help?" She looked over at Maddie and Annette, thinking back to when she'd inherited Cedar Lodge and then learned of the massive debt on the property. So many friends and neighbors had jumped in to help. Maybe they could do the same for Everett.

But when she looked back at him, he was eyeing her with something close to suspicion. She hardly knew what to say.

"Where's your horse?" Maddie asked. She'd walked to the window and stood gazing out. Everyone turned to her, and Everett crossed the room to look out the window as well. "He's right inside there." He pointed far to the side, and Maddie leaned closer to the window peering over.

"Oh, I see," she said, smiling.

"You want to take a look?" he asked, turning back to Annette and Carmen.

Carmen wasn't sure if she was imagining it or not, but she could swear his gaze hardened when he looked at her. She nodded anyway, anxious to see his incredible horse again.

Everett walked to the back door and waved them along, pushing the door open. "Let's go, then."

Carmen and Annette followed behind. When they passed a hallway, Annette gasped, pulling on Carmen's arm. She gestured down the hall to where a bedroom door stood open, revealing a long table with a rifle on top. It was mounted onto a small tripod and stood facing directly out the window. Carmen gave her a small nod, and they hurried to the door just as Everett turned away from the trees and back to them.

"So, Everett," Annette said when they were halfway to the barn. "Do you enjoy hunting?" He turned back to her, and she watched the ground as she walked. "There are plenty of mule deer and antelope in the area. Wolves and bears as well, although I don't encourage hunting them unless they're posing a danger."

Everett didn't answer right away. Carmen looked up from the rocky ground and stumbled on the next step. The same look he'd given her before was back, except now it was more intense. She could swear he didn't trust her, although unless he could read minds, she hadn't given him any reason not to.

"I don't hunt," he answered, disappearing into the small barn.

Maddie followed after him. She appeared oblivious to any strangeness in his responses. Annette gave Carmen a quick glance before following, and Carmen ducked inside last to find Maddie rubbing the silky black nose of Everett's Gypsy Vanner gelding. It was so tall that its front shoulders were visible above the stall door. Everett stood on one side of the big horse, and Maddie stood on the other. She looked even more willowy and petite than usual when compared to him and his huge steed.

Everett glanced over at her. "I always wanted a horse like Blaze, but never thought it would actually happen."

"He's beautiful," Maddie said, rubbing its neck.

"Where did you move from, Everett?" Annette asked. She held her hand out to Blaze, and he extended his neck, sniffing her.

"You know what?" Everett's voice boomed through the barn. "I'm finished with this interrogation. You can leave—

all of you." He backed away from them and crossed his arms. His neck was reddened, and his jaw was firmly set.

"Everett," Carmen ventured, feeling a bit panicked. He was an intimidating man when he wanted to be. The boyishness in his face she'd admired when they first met had vanished. "We don't mean to pry. We're just trying to get to know you a little."

"Hmph," he grunted. "Right." His gaze narrowed, the hazel-green color glowing in the shadows of the barn. "Oh, and I just remembered." He began walking away. "I've got something I need to work on tonight. I won't be able to make it for dinner."

"Everett—" Carmen argued.

"Goodbye," he said, stepping inside the tack room.

"C'mon, Carmen," Maddie said, tugging on her arm. "We'd better go." Annette was already out the door. Reluctantly, Carmen followed them, glancing back into the barn once more. Whatever Everett was so keen on keeping from her, suddenly she had to know.

The ride back to Cedar Lodge was a quiet one. The sound of the horses' hooves pressing through the snow echoed around them. Strong afternoon sun had the snow melting off the pine needle branches. It fell regularly, dripping off branches and treetops into the untouched snow and digging a pattern of holes through the top layers as it went. To Carmen, it was a ticking clock. She couldn't stop imagining the rifle Everett had propped up in the back room, pointing out the window. Had it been directed toward Cedar Lodge? Toward the pasture, maybe? The angles of his house were a little hard to be sure of. She swallowed hard. It couldn't be. Besides, that calf didn't have bullet wounds.

"I think we need to stay away from Everett for a while,"

Annette said. They'd reached the barn, and she slid down from the saddle, taking the reins in her hand. "I don't think he means us any harm, but he clearly needs some time to himself."

Carmen nodded as she dismounted, swinging her leg over Dax's rump. But she couldn't answer. She worried that Everett's intentions were darker than Annette or Maddie suspected. But to be sure, she'd have to find out about his past. And the only person she knew who could let her in on that little secret was Lander. Monday would come early with lots of chores to start on, but as soon as things were in order, and if he hadn't left for Montana yet, she was going to talk to him.

Chapter Thirteen

✦✦✦

Carmen swore she'd never go running after him again. Let him stay away if he wanted; she couldn't spend her life chasing him. And yet, here she was on a Monday afternoon, riding Dax up the same mountain trail she'd used before to stop him from leaving. It was the worst feeling of déjà vu she could imagine.

They came to the edge of the hill that looked down on Lander's small, renovated cabin. There was no smoke coming from the chimney or lights glowing in the windows, and in this frigid weather, that meant he was likely out working. She led Dax up to the cabin and stayed in the saddle, gazing over the pasture beyond. Lander's herd was young and still small, but there were easily thirty in all, calves included. It would be a rough winter for them, as some of the young ones looked like they were born too late in the season. Their scrawny little legs and bellies hardly seemed ready to take on four months of snow.

She scanned the area, searching for Lander. He would be easy to spot against the white landscape, especially atop a horse. But he wasn't there. Stepping down, she led Dax to the shed where Lander's buckskin usually sheltered to find it empty. She tied Dax and headed for the cabin, just in case. A quiet knock at first, and then after a few moments of silence, she made a proper fist and knocked firmly.

Nothing.

Returning to Dax, she patted him and studied the ground. It looked like it was well used, that was for sure. But the fresh layer of snow helped a little. There were tracks from a horse that seemed recent. It was a slow walk headed to the pasture as if going to inspect a fence or check on the animals. Maybe search for predators. She stepped into the stirrup and swung her leg over Dax again, following. Of course, she could be wrong, and the tracks were older than she thought. Maybe Lander never came back to his cabin after attending church at Ridgeville. But it was the best clue she had, so she followed it.

Dax seemed to like the high country. He lifted his head more when they were up in the mountains, always gazing across the forest and trees and mountains. When a cool breeze blew, he would stand still and turn his nose to it. Carmen usually enjoyed being high in the mountains, but this time, she was only filled with nerves. It would be easier if she could just pick an emotion, but everything inside of her was battling.

She was angry at Lander for leaving; for changing every-thing. She was lost and so confused. Why wouldn't he just tell her what was going on? If they could just talk it over, maybe things would be fine. But above all, she was so in love with him that it ached with a pain that seemed to be swal-lowing her whole from the inside out. She wanted to hunch over and wrap both arms around her middle just to fight it off, but she didn't. Lander was out there somewhere, and the last thing she wanted to do was fall apart the moment she saw him. Shouting at him would be a better alternative, so she spent the time reminding herself of all the reasons she should be angry.

The herd of cattle was bedded down in the snow, and they called to her in their low, solemn baritones as she passed. She counted out the calves nestled next to their mothers, finding eleven. It was a great number for building a herd if they could last through the winter.

She came to the back of the pasture. It was the farthest she'd ever been, and she could feel the land rounding again as if it was preparing to offer a glimpse of something amazing ahead. Some grand vista or lookout point.

She leaned forward as if to peer over the land, and that was when she spotted him. Lander rode his buckskin toward her, far down the other side of the hill. He pushed his horse forward so hard that it slipped a few times on its way to meet up with her. A mule followed behind him, hopping a little as it trotted to keep up. It was strange to see him practically racing to meet her, and her pulse beat faster at the idea that maybe he'd changed his mind. Maybe everything was okay, and he did want her with all his heart, the way she did him. A wave of emotion cut off her next breath.

But when he came within the last hundred feet, she could see him well enough to know she'd been wrong. He wasn't coming to take her back; it was something else that drove him to her. She could see the caution in his eyes and the low-set line of his mouth. He wore a dark blue Henley shirt with a heavy canvas jacket over it, unzipped. His jeans were always a little loose, and now they hung over his dark boots, lifted a little as if he'd been riding a long time. His cowboy hat hovered perfectly above his gaze, and she wondered if he were oblivious to the striking combination of the two. There were only a few minutes left until they were together, but it was just enough for her to be able to steady her breathing and ease the pressure building in her chest.

Calm. Be calm.

"Hello, Carmen," he said, breathing a little harder than usual after his race up the mountain.

Hello, Carmen? That's it? He wasn't at all curious as to why she'd ridden two hours up into the high mountains to talk to him? Carmen steadied herself in the saddle, taking a minute to adjust the reins and angle her boots in the stirrups. "Hello," she said, tying a loose strap on her saddle. Finally, she looked into his eyes, forcing her expression to remain unfazed. "I came out here to ask you about Everett."

Lander visibly flinched, and his gaze sank. Darkness settled in his eyes, and he wrapped the reins around his hand. "Everett," he repeated.

Carmen tried to move things along, fearing he would ride away and leave her behind without an answer. He was all too good at that. "Yes." She lifted off her toes, settling in the saddle again. "Honestly, I need to know that we're safe with him around."

This time, Lander really changed. His mouth dropped open with an overtly perplexed expression. "Of course, you are," he blurted out. "There's no one safer."

"You're sure about that?" Carmen asked, tapping Dax's sides. She let him move in closer to Lander until her heart throbbed in her chest. His face was mesmerizing from up close, she almost couldn't concentrate. She shook off the feeling as much as she could. "Because he has a rifle set in his back bedroom, mounted with a tripod and facing out the window. But he claims he doesn't hunt." She couldn't look away from his eyes. They were incredible. She forced herself to continue, but she couldn't stop her voice from softening. "He's good with a knife too, but it's not a knife like I've seen anyone else in this area use."

"Well, he's not from—"

"Around here," Carmen interrupted. "Yeah, I know. He's from somewhere else, which leads me to ask..." She leaned in, wishing they were standing so she could be even closer. The horses were keeping them far too separated. "How do you know him?"

Lander was silent. His head tilted ever so slightly as he gazed over her face. "I'll tell you how I know Everett," he finally said, glancing around them. "But the sun will be going down soon, and you have a lot of ground to cover on your way back, so it'll have to be quick."

For the first time, Carmen noticed Lander's mule was loaded with gear. It carried packs and blankets and supplies as if Lander were going to be gone for a very long time. Her heart raced in her chest. "Are you leaving?" She asked, hating the panic in her voice. But it was too late to cover it up. She studied his face as he fidgeted in the saddle, glancing back at the mule and then into her eyes.

He sighed. "I am."

"For Montana?" Carmen could hardly get the words out. They squeezed through her tight throat painfully. She hoped it didn't show.

"Yes, that's right."

She didn't know what else to say. There it was, plain and simple. He was leaving her for good. His cattle still grazed in the field, meaning he likely had plans to return for them, or at least to hire out some workers for the winter. But either way, it didn't matter. He was leaving. The truth of that statement boiled inside of her, destroying the hope she'd harbored for them.

"Everett worked with my father in security, back in Cheyenne. He was at the beginning of his career, and my father was at the end." Lander watched the trees as he spoke. "They were both detailed to Senator Jackie Thomas. There were rumors she'd gotten herself involved in a smuggling operation and things had gone very public, which made everyday life for Senator Thomas pretty dangerous. Threats started to trickle into my father's private life before things calmed down. At least, from what I heard. After that, he decided to retire early and move out here."

Carmen was waiting for his eyes to return to hers. He continued watching the trees, and eventually, they began to wander back. But instead of looking directly into her gaze, he became distracted with the length of his reins, evening them out in the silence. It had always been so easy to look into his eyes and see that he was holding back; that he really loved her. But now, she wondered. Maybe she'd seen only what she wanted to see, and he'd been indifferent to her all along. It was devastating. She wanted to kick Dax's sides and race away, but she needed to use this moment as much as she could before he was gone forever.

"So, what about Everett?" she asked, still not catching his glance.

He turned back to check on his mule. "Well, he, uh—it's a rough life." His eyes flickered to hers, then returned to the mule that was standing still as the Tetons behind them. "I'm sure he just wanted to change things up."

She wasn't going to let him get away with that. "I feel like there's something he's hiding," she said, lifting her eyebrows when he turned to her, hoping to hold his gaze. It seemed to work as he didn't turn away. "So, there's no other reason? He was just a bodyguard who wanted the quiet life? Because he was pretty upset when we asked him where he came from."

"We?"

For the first time, Carmen faltered. She tried to think of a reason it was a bad idea to visit Everett with all three of them, but it seemed the smartest thing to do considering they didn't know him. He could be anyone—and clearly, he had a past that should be at least respected if not feared. She shrugged a little. "Yeah. Maddie, Annette, and I."

"I see," he said. His green eyes didn't leave hers, and as much as she tried not to react, she could feel the warmth growing in her face. "Well, he might have felt a little attacked in that case. He's worked hard to get himself off the beaten path." He seemed to notice her confusion, and he sighed, sweeping his hat off. Rotating it in his hands, he looked down at it, causing a few strands of dark, wavy hair to tumble forward. Apparently, he was still growing it out. Carmen remembered running her hands through his hair. She turned away, trying to forget.

"Something happened two months back," Lander said, "and he contacted me. During the time after my parents died, he didn't come around at all. He practically vanished. And he apologized for that. But he also asked for help. Said he was getting heat for a call he'd made to stop a hold-up situation. Usually, he worked across the country, but this was right in Cheyenne." He paused. "He had a clear shot, and he took it. Dropped the guy where he stood and freed twenty-one people from the oil refinery plant where he'd held them, demanding a cut of the company's profit."

"And people were upset about that?" Carmen asked. She

waited for him to look up, but he never did. Just rotated his hat in his hands.

"Well, he didn't recognize the man with the bandana he'd pulled up over his nose and chin. Turns out it was the son of a well-respected family." He sighed and turned to Carmen, his gaze a bit unsteady. "He'd stopped taking his medications and got a little out of control. Although he'd shot two security guards, they both survived." He shook his head. "But snipers shoot to kill, and the situation was desperate. They were completely barricaded in, and he'd lined the hostages up."

"That doesn't sound right," Carmen said. She couldn't imagine Everett being seen as anything but a hero.

"Sometimes people believe what they want, no matter what actually happened. The grief of losing that young man just exploded within the community and mobs of people would gather around Everett's car. His house. He lived twenty miles outside of Cheyenne, but they tracked his place down. His reputation and his career were over."

Carmen couldn't help seeing a few similarities between Lander's experience and Everett's. Neither had done nothing wrong, and yet, they were practically driven away. It had seemed Lander was able to beat it and change people's minds, but now the rumors were starting up again and he was leaving. She couldn't exactly call the two things unrelated. "I see," she said. "Well, we'd heard he was seen riding around Cedar Lodge and..." She stopped when his gaze swung back to her. "And, uh, we just wanted to get a feel for who he was. He didn't give us much, though. Even with your story, I can't say I trust him completely. There's something dark behind his eyes. Something he's holding back."

Lander didn't answer—he didn't argue. He only looked

back at her quietly as if he was considering her words. But in the end, he lifted in the saddle and took a deep breath. "Look, the one thing I know is, he's safe. You don't need to worry about him." He settled his hat on his head and a smile tugged at his mouth.

She hadn't seen him smile completely in months, and this one she could tell took a little work as if he only attempted a smile because the situation required it. Sadness washed over her. "Are you sure you have to go?" The question came out before she could stop it. Before she truly thought it over. She just couldn't understand why he was doing it. Was it all her fault? Had she single-handedly driven him away?

His gaze settled on her softly and everything stilled. His horse, his hands, even the wind ceased. "I've committed to a job already," he answered quietly. "I'm..." The words froze in his mouth as if whisked away by dark magic. He only looked back at her with his lips parted and the words poised on his tongue. He didn't seem able to continue.

Everything rose from the chamber where she'd locked it away. She wanted to climb off her horse and into his arms and shake him until he changed his mind. If only she could break him out of this spell he was under. He was running away—anyone could see that. But the reason was important. Was it because his feelings weren't what she thought, or because they were?

Her heart was breaking all over again. Only this time, she was able to keep it under the surface of a calm expression. She could feel that her face was flushed, but beyond that, the torture stayed inside. Twisting and aching.

She pulled Dax back, creating space between them. He didn't need to finish his answer. They both knew he wasn't staying. After a tense breath, she managed a smile. "Have a safe trip, Lander." His name was devastating as it came from her mouth, stinging on her lips. But she wanted to say it one last time to his face. She watched his reaction—she'd always been able to find it before. The draw of his eyes and the laxness in his jaw. But now there was nothing.

"Thank you," he said, his voice sterile as if he'd washed away the emotions that had been there before. The feeling and heart and longing. The love.

She turned Dax away and encouraged him into a trot, creating a space between them as quickly as she could. There should have been tears streaming down her face, her heart breaking, sobs racking her body. But there was only a cold, empty realization that for him... it was over.

Chapter Fourteen

❦

Lander clung to the reins, watching her go. He wanted to call out for her to come back, but he couldn't. What was the point of putting her through more when she was clearly moving on? It hurt like nothing he'd ever felt before, but at least she hadn't come farther. At least she hadn't seen the cabin.

He swung the horse and mule around, continuing down the hill and onto a small vista. From where he stood, the view was picturesque. She'd come so close to it. The frame of the cabin was perfect, towering between the pines and backed by the mountains. It was incredible. But if she'd seen it, she wouldn't have understood. She would have asked him questions that he wouldn't be able to answer. Questions like, why was he building it? Was he ever going to finish it? Did he have plans to return?

Of course, he had plans to return, but he didn't want anyone to know it. Especially not Carmen. Pastor Evans's words came to him frequently, but he didn't believe them. There was something broken inside of him that he feared would never be whole. Carmen didn't need to struggle through life with someone like that. She deserved more.

He hoped it was the right decision to tell her about Everett. There was nothing he'd left out, but in the end, how much did he really know? He hadn't ever gotten to know the man very well personally, but his father had never spoken more highly of anyone. Everett had been key in saving his father's life more than once, and maybe even his own. If only his father was around to ask questions, he was sure he could have an easier time with the decisions he'd made, especially concerning Everett. Having him move into the cabin was either completely inspired or unintentionally risky. Everything hinged on Carmen and her safety.

Oh, how his heart ached!

He closed his eyes, intending to ask his Father like he'd been counseled. But no words would come. He only felt the pain and directed it away, reaching out for help. There was no answer. No communication. Only the ability to take the next breath, and the one after that. Maybe that was all he needed to do for now.

But the daylight was waning. He turned his buckskin's nose to the trail. There was a small town up north where a truck and trailer waited for him. From there, he'd load up his horse, mule, and gear, and head out to work the ranch. Every step felt harder than the last, but he didn't pull back on the reins. He only focused on the work ahead and hoped the burning in his chest would subside in time. It was all he could do.

THE AFTERNOON WAS GETTING LATE. CHORES HAD TAKEN more time than usual since the heater she used for the cow's trough had shorted out, causing the water to freeze solid. It took a little help from the Driscoll brothers to get it patched up and thawing. But at least she'd made it out to Lander, as difficult as it had been. Learning about Everett's past should have had her feeling better about him, but it didn't. It only added to her suspicions.

First off, Lander only knew what he'd heard from his parents. And his father was a bodyguard. An agent. Which would possibly make him an unreliable source as he likely had hoards of classified information he'd never divulge. And Everett? She'd bet anything the rifle he had in his window was a sniper. But why was it positioned pointing out the window? The thought was chilling. And no matter how she turned his past around, she couldn't deny her intuition that there were shadows in his eyes. Some darkness he was holding back. Something he didn't want her to know. That fact alone meant she couldn't trust him, at least not completely.

She tightened her hand around the reins, and Dax pulled to a stop, turning his head to glance at her. His ear flicked back and front again, and he chewed at the bit, swishing his tail. He attempted to graze, but Carmen's grip didn't budge, and he lifted his head again, turning his ears back in irritation.

Twisting in the saddle, Carmen looked back the way she'd come. There was something she'd brushed aside that perhaps she shouldn't have. If her suspicions about Everett had been right, then perhaps she wanted to pay attention to what she noticed when she'd first seen Lander coming up over the hill. It was like he was stopping her from going farther, and he looked panicked about it too. Like there was something she would see if she continued on. If she'd rounded the hill and followed it down the backside.

She tugged at the reins, turning Dax around, although he didn't seem in a hurry to go back the way they'd come. He stood stiff-legged as she leaned forward in the saddle, nudging his sides. After a click of her tongue, he relented and began a slow walk forward. Carmen smiled and patted his neck. It would only take ten minutes to go back and peek over the hill, then she could return to Cedar Lodge before nightfall. She prodded Dax on, who swished his tail every time her heels tapped his sides. It was his way of disagreeing with her direction changes, but at least he kept walking.

She pushed against the stirrups with the balls of her feet, lifting in the saddle. The leather creaked as she gazed across the view in every direction. A breathtaking winter day. The air was cold, but not unbearable. Not brittle, like it had been the night of the storm or the few days after. Late afternoon had calmed even the mild breezes of the day, and now she could find enjoyment in the frozen wilderness surrounding her. But even in midwinter, life was buzzing in the forest. Tracks of wild hares and foxes were plentiful under the deepest cover of pine branches, and tiny star-like tracks from mountain chickadees left trails of wavy, looping lines as they scoured the snowy landscape for pine nuts and seeds.

Their old tracks were still fresh in the snow, and she followed them until they came to the point where she'd stopped. Lander's tracks were mere feet in front of her, coming and then leaving. With a sigh, she urged Dax on and adjusted her grip on the reins, panning every inch of the horizon as it came into view, anxious to see just what Lander might've been hiding. The drop-off along the back of the hill was a steeper decline than she'd expected. She sat back in the saddle, letting Dax move slow and steady with each step, shifting his weight right to left as he worked his way down. They followed in Lander's tracks, and she kept her attention on the ground ahead of them until it finally evened out. And there, across a small valley of snow and nestled into a beautiful grove of tall, slender pines, had to be what she'd been searching for.

He was building a cabin. And not just any cabin, either. This one was a work of art, with two chimneys clearly framed out, and a complex footprint designed much differently from someone who might just want four walls and a roof over their head.

Carmen stepped down from the saddle and scanned the area carefully. All was quiet. She tied Dax to the closest tree and explored the framework, stepping up onto the concrete pad and walking through the strips of two-by-fours. There was a base work of stairs leading to a second level, although no railing or walls. It had her feet tingling, but she went up anyway, taking caution when she was at the top. Sheets of plywood were laid down at her feet and huge spaces between the framing showed where a host of windows would eventually be placed. Their angles were perfect, taking in the views of the Teton mountain range spectacularly.

Just what was Lander up to? He was moving to Montana, so why would he spend so much time and money on a cabin only to leave it behind? The answers she could come up with were unconvincing at best. Maybe he wanted to sell the whole ranch and figured a buyer would be more interested in a new cabin. Or perhaps he was going to live out here after all and just planned on avoiding her forever... or... what else could it be? She tossed her arms up, exasperated.

Dax's shrill whinny had her spinning around. She raced down the steps, fearing wolves. Why hadn't she thought of that before? Why did she leave him alone out there, tied up and hindered? He called again, and she dashed through the framework, jumping off the foundation and sinking into the snow. Scanning the area, she saw nothing, but she ran until she reached Dax, breathing hard. The panic that had coursed through her remained. She searched between the trees and along the snowbanks, looking for tracks or glowing eyes. Wolves were the stealthiest animal she'd come in contact with yet. Bears were less afraid and much bolder, and mountain lions were practically ghosts. But maybe that was it. Maybe Dax had smelled a big cat, even if he hadn't seen it.

She rubbed the Appaloosa's velvety coat, but his agitation didn't calm. He continued snorting and digging at the snow with his front feet. Pulling his lead rope free, she wrapped it around the saddle horn and climbed into the saddle again. This time, he needed no urging from her. He spun on all four legs and charged up the hill.

"Whoa, Dax!" Carmen shouted, squeezing her thighs, and catching the saddle horn in one hand before she could roll off his back. He didn't listen, and only dug his front feet in again and again, launching them up the hill with his strong hind legs.

When they reached the top, he didn't slow. But he began watching the trees. In a flicker of movement, he would turn right and left, weaving a little in each direction as he did. Carmen could feel his body tremble beneath her as if he could explode at any moment. The fear he exuded sunk under her skin. Something crashed in the trees, and he skirted to the side. She held on tight, peering into the branches in search of the culprit.

"Whoa, Dax," she said again, quieter this time. It seemed to help as the frenzy underneath her began to slow. He was breathing hard, and she could feel the power surging through him. Another wave of panic could hit him at any time, but she pulled back until he was stopped. His belly expanded and contracted. She rubbed his neck and shoulders, telling him he was a good boy while she searched the trees again. But there was nothing.

After a few minutes, she sat up again, ready to click her tongue and ask him to walk. But before she had the chance, a gunshot echoed through the air followed by the sound of a bullet ricocheting off a tree. Carmen threw her arms up, shielding her head. Dax shied and her heart raced. Who's shooting? Why? She kicked her legs hard, and Dax bolted forward again. She stayed ducked down against his neck, gasping for air and waiting for the next shot. The one that would hit Dax and have him fall to the ground. Or the one that would hit her, making life fade away. She could hardly see with the panic flowing through her, blood whooshing in her ears. Clinging to Dax as he raced to save both their lives.

They passed the lookout point, but she didn't turn her head to see the view of Cedar Lodge. She only held on. Soon they began the downhill, and finally, Dax slowed. He walked, but quickly. Still searching. Still afraid.

Carmen couldn't speak. She couldn't tell him that it would be okay. The only thing she could do was get home as quickly as possible and call the police. It was all she could think of. When they reached the barn, Dax turned toward it. But she pulled on the reins and took him around to the lodge, right up the steps, and onto the porch. He looked a little unsure but stood there just the same.

She swung out of the saddle, and her legs gave out. Her knees hit the wood, and she dropped her hands down too, shaking hard. Breathing through the pain in her knees, she forced herself up again. Whoever was shooting at her could be miles away if they'd gone in the other direction. But something told her they didn't. She imagined they'd followed right behind her, and she would see them any moment.

Stumbling in through the door, she saw Jake first. He held a plastic cup in one hand half full of a dark cola, probably Coke as he mentioned it was his favorite. Maddie was on the couch, smiling back at him and Annette, who stood in the kitchen holding a stack of small paper plates, the kind that would be used for dessert.

"Carmen!" Annette shouted, looking angry. But that couldn't be right.

Jake stepped forward and grabbed her hard around her middle. His fingers dug into her ribs and his drink sloshed out, splashing on the floor.

"We tried calling, but you left your phone here." Maddie's voice was muted and fuzzy.

It took a moment to realize she'd almost passed out. The world was tilted and suddenly she was sitting on the floor. Everything was taking too long! She needed to call the police. She could hear questions from all three of them, but one answer would satisfy them all.

"I was out at Lander's ranch, and someone shot at me," she blurted out, catching the sound of Maddie's gasp, but in too much of a hurry to turn to her. "We need to call the police. I don't know if they followed me and Dax." Carmen turned to the door with her eyes wide. "Dax."

"I'll get him," Jake said, holding her arm. He waited until she looked back at him. "Okay?" he asked, still waiting.

"Yes, okay," Carmen rushed, appreciating his intentions but angry at him too. *Just hurry up. Everyone.*

It felt like she waited forever. And then, suddenly, everyone had crowded inside. Everyone was rushing her. Question after question, one asked before she had time to answer the last.

Why did you go out there? Did you see Lander? Are you sure he left? Did you feel the concussion of air from the bullet? Are you sure it was fired at you, or did you only hear it? Where was Lander? Did you see where he went? Why would he leave if he was in the middle of building a cabin? Was he lying? Could he have circled back and fired the shot to drive you away?

Carmen stared unblinking at the deputy standing in front of her. His voice had come as if echoing in a tunnel. A deep, angry tunnel. She shook her head, confused. "What?" She asked. Their questions were going in the wrong direction. They made no sense. She took a deep breath, wanting to rise to her feet and shout at them. Get them to understand. But her entire body was shaking. She could hardly speak loud enough for them to hear. "Lander left. He wasn't lying. Now please, go out and search for this person who was shooting at me."

"Ma'am." The deputy was a little younger than Carmen, she guessed. His hair was dark, and his skin was a creamy tan. He had deep brown eyes and a rounded nose. His slender lips were pursed as if he was already disagreeing with her, even though he'd only said *ma'am*. She waited for more, but he only stared at her.

A taller, older man with thinning yellow-blond hair and

freckled skin came forward. He was the police chief, but she couldn't help noticing his boots were obnoxiously loud on the wood floor. "We've gotten enough information for now, Ms. Rivera," he said. "I'm sorry for what you've been through this afternoon. Try to relax and we'll call you in the morning at the latest—"

"Are you going to search for him?" Carmen asked, although it was practically a whisper. Even so, the effort had caused her voice to crack.

"We've conducted a thorough search of your property," he said, nodding as if this were enough. But it wasn't. None of it was enough. "You're safe now, ma'am. I assure you." His cheeks squished into a smile, but it was brief. "You've been through enough. Now, your friends have agreed to stay with you tonight. So, you won't be alone."

Alone.

Thoughts of Lander flooded her mind. How dare they imply that he would do such a thing. He was the most incredible man she'd ever met. Maybe she'd go on for the rest of her life with a memory of him like a ghost. It would follow her in the shadows, to remind her every day of the depth of love she was capable of. At the same time, torturing her like a demon. Like an empty glass of water in the Mojave. Like a life raft in the Bermuda Triangle, always out of reach. She would be known as the "Woman of the Lodge." Curious and odd and always alone.

"Ma'am?" The police chief had knelt in front of her, and for the first time that night, he looked genuinely concerned.

Carmen forced herself out of her daydreams, coiling her lips into a smile. "I'm sorry, I guess I am pretty tired," she said, finally able to muster more than a whisper. She continued, working to raise her voice enough to wipe the concern from his eyes. "Thank you so much for coming out." The last thing she wanted was to be whisked away to a hospital where she'd be forced to tell them the truth about her sadness. The reason for her distractions. How humiliating if Lander ever found out she couldn't handle being without him. How humiliating if he knew how her heart was breaking.

Chapter Fifteen

Three weeks later...

THE DAY HAD THREATENED TO RUIN HER EVENING WITH its howling wind threading through the trees. All day long it had torn through the mountains. They weren't even able to drape the pale silk fabrics across the trellises until three hours prior to showtime. But it had also done something magical. The clouds and winter haze that had settled along the horizon were whisked away to reveal a clear evening. Now that the sun was beginning to set, the entire sky glowed with light and serenity. The wind ceased and lanterns were lit. Catering was being brought out and arranged, and guests were even beginning to show up.

Carmen stood at the mirror in an upstairs dressing room. She was glad she'd decided to come up a little early, leaving her friends to help the caterers with their finishing touches.

It was just the time she needed to settle her mind and calm the twisting in her stomach. She'd formed her hair into silky smooth waves, which added another few inches of length. Now it came fully down her back, nearly brushing her hips. Her dress clung to her torso with straps intertwining around the back of her neck. The shimmering material split open just above her knees and trailed to the sides, becoming longer in the back so that it brushed the floor. It reminded her of flower petals with the way its rosy-peach color gradually darkened to a deep wine-red from her neck to her toes.

"Carmen?" A soft tap on the door had her turning around, and the cool silk of the dress brushed softly against her legs. Violet's blue eyes peeked in through the doorway. Her left hand clutching the door showed off an impressive ring and her blonde hair was swept back in a messy bun. "Can I come in?" she asked. The smile fell from her face when she took in Carmen. "Oh, my goodness," she said, a soft gasp escaping her lips. She stepped inside, closing the door behind her. "You look incredible."

Carmen looked down at the dress again. "It's a very pretty dress. You guys did good."

"Here, turn around." Violet took Carmen's wrist and spun her slowly. "Wow, this mountain life has really toned you up. I mean, you've always been slender, but now look at this definition in your back. And the dress hugs you perfectly." She dropped Carmen's hand and shook her head. "Wow." Her eyes searched Carmen's face a moment before she continued, and Carmen wished she would have had more time with her friends before the event. They'd hardly arrived two hours earlier, which meant Carmen was deep in the hustle and work of setting up and putting out all the fires that came with a big event like this one.

"I've been meaning to ask you." Violet folded her arms. She hadn't gotten dressed yet and wore gray sweats and a purple sweater, but even in those she was beautiful. She was just that kind of girl. But now, as she looked back at Carmen, her eyes were somber, and her lips drooped at the edges. "Is Lander not coming tonight? I mean, is he still living out there in the high country? Because I was so sure we'd find him back at Cedar Lodge by now."

Carmen had a few regrets that night, but this had to be the biggest one. Why hadn't she told them what had happened between her and Lander? Why, oh, why? Because now, no matter what she said or how she phrased it, they would know the pain she was in. They would see right through her to the devastation and suffering. Why else would she have kept it from them? It was too obvious.

Even so, Carmen tried to think of an excuse that might satisfy her friend. She reached for the sides of her dress, letting it trail through her hands and fall from her fingertips. "He had to take a job in Montana, actually," she finally said, trying so hard to keep from getting emotional that her voice came out as more monotone than anything else. She cleared her throat. "I was hoping he'd make it back for tonight, but I guess he'll miss it by a day or two."

Stop, Carmen! What are you thinking? You're lying to one of your best friends.

But her thoughts didn't change her mind. Nothing right then seemed worse than admitting that Lander didn't love her—that he'd left her behind.

"Oh." Violet's relief was obvious. She exhaled in one gust as if she'd been holding her breath. "Well, I'm sorry to hear he won't make it tonight, but so glad he's coming back. How long has he been out there?"

"Uh... a few weeks." Carmen turned to the mirror and pulled at her hair, distracting herself before she could take everything back and crumble to the floor in a big, crying mess. "Things here have been really busy, so the time hasn't been as hard as I thought it would be."

Stop. Tell her the truth!

"Well, I'd better hurry and get ready if I want to turn any heads standing next to you." Violet winked on her way to the door. "I might be engaged, but I still like to make an entrance every now and then."

"Always," Carmen said, smiling as her friend left the room. But her smile was whisked away the moment the door closed, and she looked herself in the eyes, disappointed. For tonight, she would just have to fill every conversation with talk of the summer camp. One lie didn't have to turn into a hundred more. She just had to keep the topic far away from Lander, and then, once the party was over, she could pull Violet aside and tell her the truth. Beg her forgiveness. Try not to turn into a pathetic, sappy puddle.

She swallowed, turning from the mirror. It was too late to take back what she'd said. Guests were downstairs and so should she be. Memories of countless fashion shows and galas had her assuming a role she'd played many times. A persona of perfection, from the taut smile on her lips to the purposeful swing of her hips when she walked. It was a routine she'd memorized. A display of confidence that no one had ever seen through. Tonight, she used every piece of that New York City education as the doors to the elevator slid open and she strode out into the banquet hall. The lie she'd told Violet would have to keep because she'd just stepped on stage.

A scan of the room and a swift walk meant she had somewhere to be. Those who didn't know her understood it wasn't the time to interrupt. Those who did might assume there was something that needed to be done. Perhaps they were sweating the moment, racking their brain for what they might have overlooked. She'd seen it so many times before; it wasn't something she felt bad about anymore. It was just part of the show. Act I. Let them scramble a bit; it was good for business.

"We'd like to welcome all who are in attendance this evening." Ben Driscoll stood at the microphone in front of a string band. He was calm and a natural at commanding attention. The entire room hushed, and most of the guests found their seats quickly. His voice was deep and resonated effortlessly through the room. "Please help yourself to the buffet tables, and we will begin with introductions in about forty-five minutes. Thank you."

It had been Carmen's idea to start with food and mingling, and she was glad she'd done it. There was much less pressure that way. Plus, those who came late wouldn't miss their chance to donate. By the time the microphone was handed over to her, most of her nervousness would ease, or so she hoped. For now, it was gnawing away at her insides. She couldn't even look at the buffet tables, as the very thought of food made her sick.

She wandered out onto the patios. They were beautifully lit, and the sky had darkened just enough to allow the lanterns and string lighting to glow. Carmen clasped her hands together and rested her forearms atop the black iron railing, staring into the sunset sky. Its orange and pink colors blazed against the dark silhouettes of pine trees, and she took a moment to breathe. Behind her, she could hear the string band begin to play. Their melody was elegant and peaceful. She turned around just as guests began to make their way outside, holding plates piled with a variety of foods. Everything looked incredible, but Carmen only smiled at the faces she passed as she returned to the banquet room. Eyes followed her full of interest and questions, but she didn't engage in conversation. It was just as well. Her head was spinning with anxiety. But she could tell it didn't show. The looks of admiration and awe attested that the role she played, she played well. No one suspected thoughts of Lander, plus the guilt of lying were taking turns tormenting her.

Inside the banquet area, she spotted two groups right away. Seated at a table close to the band were Violet, Aries, and Maddie, with Maddie looking the most casual. Violet and Aries gazed around the room with stars in their eyes, clearly not used to the lodgepole pine frame and mountain backdrop. Violet had kept the messy bun but paired it with a sparkling silver dress that was moderately low cut in front and form-fitting as far down as Carmen could see. Aries had chosen a bright fuchsia ball gown with large pleats and an energy to match the wearer. Her hair was bigger than usual, tendrils of dark brown curls tumbled atop her head. Maddie was dressed in a delicate silk maxi of pale lavender. She was smiling, but not awed like the others. She was more accustomed to the scene, although her eyes did trail over the room often. Carmen's eyes wandered to find Jake at the other end of the room, looking back at her.

She smiled, keeping up her act as she went to meet him. The other table, where Annette sat with Ben Driscoll and his wife and family, was next to him with an empty seat not far from where he stood. They gave Carmen varying looks of surprise, with the Driscoll brothers being the most noticeable. All three of them appeared shocked at seeing her in something other than denim and leather. One other seat was left vacant at their table.

"Mind if I join you all tonight?" She asked, happy to be at the back of the room where she could assess the feel of the party and the guests. It was a good vantage point.

"It would be our pleasure, I'm sure." Jake nodded, having removed his hat. "Can I get you a drink?"

"You're not old enough to bring me my drink," she said, noting the turn of his countenance. It had her feeling immediately guilty for the jest. There were light chuckles coming from the table beside them, but Jake's face was somber. "I meant cider, of course," he retorted, although his tone was a little rough.

"In that case, thank you," Carmen said, watching as he strode past her to the drink table.

"Strong words tonight," Annette said. She wore a strappy red dress with sequins that hugged her all the way down to the floor. Ben and his wife Saundra gave her looks of sympathy while each of their sons looked a little intimidated.

"I suppose I have to act the part," Carmen said, pulling out a chair. She sat down, keeping her back straight and throwing a smile at a stranger who had caught her eye.

"I suppose you do." Annette lifted the champagne glass in front of her and took a sip. "Just remember we're all friends here. At the end of the day, everyone else goes home."

Carmen turned back to Annette, sinking in her gaze. It had taken only a matter of minutes for her to shake at least one cherished friendship without hardly trying. Mixing the world of her past with the world of her future was taking its toll, and it was taking it quickly. But she needed to be seen as almost untouchable in this world of glamor. These people held her to different standards.

She trailed one hand through her hair, closing her eyes. When she opened them again, Jake set a glass of amber liquid down in front of her. Bubbles trickled up from the bottom.

"Sparkling cider, Ms. Rivera," he said, taking a seat beside her.

She lifted her glass and turned to him only to see his gaze wasn't what she expected. He wasn't cowed or embarrassed. His gaze was firm and dominant, challenging her. She may have just tried to shun him, but clearly, he wasn't going without a fight. "Thank you, Jake," she said quietly, as the other members of the table spoke amongst themselves.

"My pleasure," he said, never looking away.

The band started up a new tune, lively and vibrant. It was getting close to the time she'd planned on speaking, and she knew she should leave the table. Go up to the stage and wait for her moment. But her gaze stayed locked on Jake's.

He pushed his chair away from the table and stood, reaching a hand out. "Dance with me," he said. Carmen glanced around to see two other couples using the center space the way it had been intended, although it was a little early in the night. She stood and took his hand, holding it unmoving when he tried to walk away. "Can we dance later?" she asked. She took a deep breath, keeping everything locked down deep inside.

He seemed to see more in her eyes than he had before. Slowly, his grip on her hand softened. "Yes, ma'am," he whispered back, squeezing her hand just before releasing her. He took his seat at the table again, and Carmen began her walk to the front.

She trailed along the side of the room, watching the guests as they enjoyed their meals. There were a few faces she recognized, but only a few. Aries no doubt had done a job getting everyone there. The fashion industry was on great display as she counted the number of Lauren's and glittering Tiffany's. At the front of the room, near the band, a small group was gathering. Aries, along with a woman she knew to be her aunt, although they'd never met. A taller, dark-haired man was with them, showing a possible family resemblance. But Carmen wasn't sure about that. She only smiled and joined them as the song came to an end. Aries approached the microphone and small makeshift podium. Carmen listened as her name was announced.

Everything was happening so fast. She stepped up to the microphone and gazed across the faces smiling back at her. Thoughts of her summer camp came to the forefront of her mind. Memories of the two schoolchildren who had inspired the idea blazed in her memories. They needed this; all the children did. Coming to Cedar Creek would change their lives; she knew it.

She lifted her head, about to speak as a man walked in. He was dressed in a sleek tuxedo, perfectly tailored to fit his firm shoulders and slim hips. Her breath froze, looking back at Lander paused in the doorway just as his gaze found hers. Freshly shaven, his deep wavy hair was brushed back from his face. The cut of his jawline had never stood out to her as much as it did now. It complemented the lines of his face beautifully. And his eyes. She could see their glimmering aqua-green from across the room.

Her heart dropped to her feet, and she looked down at

her manicured hands on the podium. Every thought in her head vanished, and the act she'd stepped into melted away in that one second. Each breath gusted in her ears, filling her head with dizziness as her heart pounded. If she didn't fall to the ground, it would be a miracle. Nothing in the world could have prepared her for seeing him. Not now, of all times. Of all places. How could he be here?

God, please help me.

Chapter Sixteen

❦

Carmen tried to gather herself, but when she looked up from her hands, she could feel the devastation rising. All her confidence, and even her smile, was wiped away. People began to notice, many of them glancing to the back of the room where her eyes continually strayed. But she couldn't let them put the pieces together.

With a deep breath, she started in on her speech, although she couldn't find her smile again. It was lost, vanished in the crushing emotion that had drowned her at the sight of him.

But she needed this event. If she was going to make staying at Cedar Lodge a lifelong thing, the benefit camp needed to be at the forefront of her plans. So, she spoke about the schools and the kids she'd talked to. She spoke about her own time at Cedar Lodge growing up and what values it instilled in her at a young age.

People's eyes glittered. Their faces were entranced. They stared back at her adoringly. It's how she knew she was saying just the right thing, even if her thoughts were miles away. All she saw in her mind was Lander. She couldn't pull her mind from the fact that he was there in the very same room, looking back at her. Perhaps he'd moved from where he stood in the back. Maybe he'd sat down. Maybe he wasn't even watching anymore. But in her head, she saw him standing there just as he had the moment he'd entered the room. His look. His eyes. Everything stayed exactly the same, blazing in her mind.

Before she knew it, she was tearing up as she ended her speech. People were standing. Clapping and cheering. She smiled and waved and backed away from the podium, not daring to look again at Lander. Maybe he'd never even been there at all.

"Amazing job, Carmen!" Aries squeezed her tightly. "You are so good at this, woman." She stepped back and hesitated. "Are you okay?"

Carmen nodded emphatically, taking a huge breath, and forcing a smile onto her face. "I'm great, thank you, Aries." She gave her friend a quick squeeze. "Thanks so much for doing this for me. All the planning and arranging, I know how much work it is." Her eyes inadvertently lifted, and there he was. Lander remained at the back of the room, but he'd moved to the side, more in the background. He still stood out, though. Nothing could stop that.

"It was really..." Aries started to speak, but then she stepped back, studying Carmen's face. Carmen tried to look more engaged in the conversation, but it was too late. Aries had noticed her distraction. She twisted around and caught her breath. "Oh, he's here!" She gushed, grinning from ear to ear. "Violet told me you were worried that he wasn't going to make it, but here he comes and surprises you. No wonder you were flustered. Oh, how sweet. This is so exciting." She directed her grin toward Lander, and Carmen noticed him straighten a bit. But there was something else that needed her attention. Like the fact that Violet had talked to Aries, and now she needed to apologize to both of them and set things straight as soon as possible... especially with Lander here.

"Aries," she said, but the band behind them started up again. This time they got to their feet and swayed as their arms and hands flew across the instruments. The room bounced to the new beat and whole tables emptied as people filled the dance floor.

"I've gotta check on the desserts," Aries shouted above the music. "Did you want to come?"

Carmen nodded, taking Aries's hand, and towing her away from the spotlight. The sooner they had even a few seconds to talk, the better. She wanted to wait until Violet and Aries were together, but she had a feeling that would take too long. One of them was bound to talk to Lander before she had the chance. She had to tell Aries now.

But as they rounded the lively crowd, Violet came into view. She was charging straight for them, but there was a big problem. Mainly it had to do with the fact that Lander's arm was hooked with hers. Carmen could see the confusion in his eyes even if he was wearing a smile. Her chest pounded with dread. How was she going to fix this now?

She jumped into conversation, shouting above the noise. "I had no idea you were coming back for this," she said. Lander looked about to speak, but he didn't get the chance.

"Can you believe it?" Violet shouted, much too loud. A few people close by glanced back at them. "Here you were saying he wouldn't be back until next week." She nudged Lander and released his arm. In his eyes was a question

Carmen hoped desperately he wouldn't ask. "But clearly, he's the type that won't let you down," Violet continued, bubbling over. "And he's good at surprises. I mean, look at this. He comes all this way to support you. That is adorable. You two..." She winked at Carmen. "I love it."

Lander's gaze never wavered from her as if he were piecing her lies together with every word Violet spoke. At the end of it all, he only pressed his lips together briefly.

Carmen wanted to die. The only thing she had going for her was the lighting. It was low enough that she hoped they couldn't see the heat of her embarrassment radiating through her face, hot on her skin. She wanted to look at the ground, but that would surely give away her discomfort. So, she only stared back at Lander while she waited for a brilliant answer to pop into her mind. But nothing came. Eventually Violet and Aries began glancing between them. Carmen could feel their confusion growing. It was clear they didn't understand the frozenness between her and Lander.

Lander's face settled into a gentle smile. "I really hadn't planned on it. This event was something I should have kept better track of. I'm glad I got word of it in time to come out." He stepped forward, although Carmen could see the stiffness of his movements. She hoped her friends couldn't. He hugged her briefly, but all she felt was pathetic. What must be going through his mind? What would her friends say now when she tried to explain the truth? It was all a big mess.

The music behind them phased into a new melody, slow and wandering. Lander glanced across the room and then back at Carmen. She could see what he was about to do.

"Want to dance, Carmen?" She spun around at the voice behind her and the touch of a hand on her arm, finding Jake.

His eyes lifted to the group, and he faltered. "Oh, Lander." He took a small step back as if unsure what he should do next.

"No, it's fine," Lander said. Carmen turned back to see him turning from the group. He gave her a small nod. "Go ahead and enjoy the song—keep the dance floor warm. I'm going to get something to drink first."

First? Did that mean he was going to dance with her next? She had no idea what she would say to him if he should ask why she'd told all her friends they were still together. But for now, she was being led to the center of the room by Jake. There was another conversation she'd be happy to avoid.

"I'm sorry, I didn't realize Lander was here," Jake said, as they started swaying together. "Or, that he was coming back." His eyes were steady on hers, and his hand felt heavier on her back than she remembered. "Ever."

"I know," Carmen said, hoping to dial back the warmth in their conversation, although after having collapsed into his arms and sobbed on his shoulder, she knew he expected more. Avoiding it was the best she could do. "It was a bit of a surprise for me as well. I'm sure he'll be leaving again soon. I might have to hire someone else if any of the Driscoll boys end up heading to new adventures in their lives."

She'd been scanning the room but brought her gaze back to Jake. He was watching her intently. "Or you," she said quietly. "I'm sorry I acted like a jerk earlier. I was just nervous and impulsive and I got carried away. I hope you'll forgive me."

A rather mischievous grin showed on his face, something she was more used to seeing on William, the youngest Driscoll brother. Now, it was clear he hadn't been the least bit damaged. "You used to live a different life out in New York, didn't you?"

Carmen shook her head, "I wasn't like that, even in New York. It's just..." She took a steady breath, lowering her voice. "Ever since that night, I've been worried that you see me as weak, and it's the last thing I need. It'll damage our working relationship and my reputation at the ranch. It's not easy commanding a team of men as a woman—"

"Carmen," he cut in, chuckling quietly. "Sorry, I don't mean to interrupt, but you couldn't be further from the truth." His smile steadied and his dancing slowed until he was looking back at her with a somber expression. "I could never see you as weak. You're one of the strongest women I've ever known, and I admire you greatly." A shy smile crept across his face. "It's an honor working for you."

The tension in Carmen's shoulders eased, and she relaxed in his arms for the first time. There was a lot she didn't know about Jake, and it occurred to her that maybe she should start there. Forget worrying about his opinion of her and genuinely try to understand who he was. She looked back at him anew, a smile easily lifting her lips. "Do you have plans to go to college?" He'd been glancing about the room, but his gaze flickered back to her eyes. "I know you've spoken about it before."

"I don't know about that," he said, seeming reluctant at the subject. Silence lingered between them, and for the first time, he looked a little discouraged.

"Why not?" Carmen pressed, hoping to draw out this bit of their conversation. Besides the benefit of keeping the topic off Lander, she was curious about Jake and his future. College would be a great fit for an ambitious kid like him.

"I don't know," he said. "I've always wanted to, but I

guess it's just…" He glanced to the back of the room briefly, and then his eyes returned. "Hard to leave."

Carmen's gaze flickered to where her friends were watching. She'd suspected he was interested in Maddie for some time now, but putting off college in order to pursue her? That was a little more serious interest than she'd thought, if indeed that was what he meant. She couldn't be sure, but when his eyes strayed to the back table again, she would be willing to place a large wager on it.

Suddenly, he pulled Carmen close and leaned in. She stiffened as he spoke in her ear. "Do you think you could put in a good word for me with Maddie?" he asked, leaning away again with a nervous smile.

What was he doing? Didn't he know how it would look to everyone in the room?

Carmen worried his chances with Maddie had just crumbled. He might not have meant it to look so intimate, but with how long they'd been dancing, and then to have him lean in so close to her, she wasn't sure what to expect. With one swift glance back at their table, she could see a few slightly alarmed expressions looking back at her.

Thankfully, the song ended. She dropped her arms and clapped with the rest of the room. "I'll be sure to do that, Jake," she promised. "But you should talk to her yourself. Maddie would be happy to have more friends out here, at the very least."

He ran one hand along the back of his neck, looking a little reluctant. "Yeah, I've talked to her a little bit." When he straightened, he sunk his hands into his pockets. "Okay, thanks, Carmen." He patted her arm. "Enjoy the rest of the party. You've really done an amazing job."

Carmen took a small step to the side. He might not have

meant to bump her arms so strongly, but it nearly took her off-balance. She smiled back at him, but there were a few concerned-looking friends she needed to speak to. She turned to their table, heading back. Violet and Aries watched her, both with very slight smiles. No doubt they were becoming more confused with each passing minute. She needed to explain things to them. But before she had the chance, Lander crossed in front of her view.

She stopped in her tracks, her breath locked away as she looked up at him.

He held his hand out. "May I?" he asked.

Carmen's hand shook as she lifted it, placing it in Lander's. Her gaze only lifted to his chest. She couldn't bear to look him in the eyes. Instead, she walked silently beside him as he led her to a spot at the edge of the dance floor. No tables were nearby, and it was quieter there. It seemed not as many people were watching, which she appreciated. But she still couldn't meet his gaze.

His arm came around her back, barely touching her. The hand that held hers lifted, and he began to move with the music. Everything she'd been aching for was now so close. The scent of his cologne hung in the air, fresh and woodsy. It matched the backdrop of elegant pines in the windows, draped in white lights. They glittered against a sky that had long since gone dark.

She wanted to adjust her hand in his, but everything was frozen. She was terrified, balanced on this one moment and seeing it for what it was. Her last chance with the man she loved. Had he been watching her and Jake? Because there was no doubt how it would've appeared. She took a breath as the song came to an end, meaning to tell him her feelings.

But her entire body trembled, and her voice caught in her throat.

The music ceased, but they kept swaying and turning. He was smooth on his feet and a confident leader. She'd never expect anything less from him. A new melody started, and she cleared her throat, meaning to start again before this song finished. She doubted they would stay like this for much longer.

"Carmen."

His voice was deep and rich, and so softly spoken. It felt as if the pain swelling inside of her just might exist in him too. With a breath that felt as heavy as the world itself, she finally looked into his eyes. And when she did, she wanted to cry. Everything she'd never said collected inside, suddenly piled on top of her. So much weight that there was no way to talk about it. Any of it. She fought hard to keep her expression untouched, even after a smile graced his lips, and she could see she was wrong. He knew nothing of her pain.

"I knew that my time away would cause things to change around here." He glanced back to the table where Jake had joined her friends. "I see that things have changed, and I just want you to know, I'm happy for you."

So that's what this was? Three weeks later and he's wishing her well? She dropped her arms away from him, finally finding strength enough to speak. But now, it was hardly her love she wanted to profess. "Lander Casey," she said, her voice strong but shaking. There was no avoiding that. She was so close to breaking down, her entire frame shook. Anger swelled through her. "Just how many times will you do this?"

His face had fallen, but he still seemed unsure of what she meant. "Do what, Carmen?"

Maybe he actually believed she was in love with Jake. And if that was the case, she needed to set him straight. She crossed her arms, holding herself together for at least a minute longer. "How many times will you lie to yourself instead of asking me how I feel? How many times will you break my heart?" Her throat caught, and she pressed her lips firmly together.

He glanced around. She already knew more than a few eyes were peering back at them. Their conversation wasn't exactly lowered, after all, and people were taking notice. But Carmen didn't care about that. He stepped in close to her, bringing his arm around her shoulders. He turned her toward the patio. "Let's talk outside," he said.

She didn't argue, but she didn't need his assistance either. His arm across her shoulder was suddenly infuriating. She walked ahead of him, shaking with anticipation and devastation, love, and anger. If she could just hold on to the anger, she might be okay. The words would come, and he would hear them. But if she couldn't keep her emotions together, everything was already lost.

Chapter Seventeen

Lander could hardly stand the thought that he'd hurt Carmen. It clambered in his mind, shaking him up inside. But the night had taken an uneasy twist, and there was more than just the pain of hurting her. There was the thought that someone else might be a danger to her. Someone he'd trusted all along, all these years. He turned to the back of the room where Everett had been standing, but he was gone now. To see him at the banquet at all was startling. Sure, he'd moved into Lander's home, but he didn't expect Everett to join in with the community and Cedar Creek Lodge so quickly. For starters, it seemed out of character for the ex-sniper. But as Lander had walked up to him at the drink table, he'd paused. A memory he'd forgotten for all these years suddenly rushed into his mind.

Perhaps it was the crowds and low lighting, mixed with the circulating strobes of light from the stage. It was eerily similar to the moment he'd walked up to his home and learned his parents had died in a house fire. The night before, while he'd been glowering over their argument, he'd left them alone and worried, and the unthinkable had happened.

He always remembered speaking to the police. He remembered the looks in their eyes. It had been clear, even in his frightened teen mind, that they suspected him first and foremost. But it was moments before those conversations that Everett had found him. Outside of the lights and crowds of the crime scene, he'd approached Lander and asked him a question in a low voice.

"Did you see anything, kid?"

It all came rushing back to his mind so clearly. The tone of his voice, the look in his eyes. He even remembered Everett's black tactical uniform. It had been difficult to see him in the dark, even as morning was slowly coming on. Lander only shook his head, still holding out hope that his parents were alive. Still searching for their faces.

"These guys won't stop until they find answers," Everett said, and then he walked past Lander and away. Where he went, Lander never turned around to see. He only stared ahead at the pile of rubble still smoldering. He hadn't thought it was strange that Everett wasn't seen again during the entire investigation. His father's assurance that Everett was a good man and reliable partner at work was validation enough for him. But now, his mind was churning.

He'd said hello and snagged a drink from the table, taking a sip while he worked to clear his head. Everett stood there, not exactly smiling back, but seeming content. But the more Lander's head worked, the more it spun. Everett had been there that night. Why? And then he disappeared that night until recently when he'd asked to buy his place. So if by some insane chance, there was a connection between

Everett and the death of his parents, why would he come back now?

And... what about the calf? No one had ever searched for a gunshot wound. And if he'd used the right gun and the right ammunition, on a black calf at night it would be invisible. Could Everett have done something like that? He couldn't imagine it. But from Lander's old cabin, there was a perfect view of the cattle. Not many could make a shot like that, but for Everett, it would be easy.

Lander's face had gone cold and his hands clammy as he tried to counter the conclusions he was coming to. But Everett only finished his drink, tossed it in the trash, and said it was good to see him again. Then left without another word. The suspicion Lander was overcome with while watching him walk away was so intense it made him sick. It was impossible, and yet, it seemed so obvious at the same time. And now, before anything else happened, he was going to tell Carmen about it. Maybe she was in love with someone else now—he hoped she was. But she still deeply controlled the rhythm of his heart.

And now, she stormed ahead of him, walking swiftly in the long, vibrantly colored dress. It was mesmerizing the way her legs sent flicks of the shimmery red material swirling about her feet. Lander always knew she came from a classy upbringing, but the transformation she'd made for the evening was breathtaking. He admired everything about her from her long, wavy auburn hair as it brushed against her arms, to the perfect wet shine of color on her lips. She likely had no idea the force she was in that dress. But it ended all too soon.

The moment he'd stepped outside, she spun around and faced him. Her silky hair, layered in soft curls, swung over her shoulder. "So, are you going to answer my question?" She demanded, crossing her arms; her breath coming hard. Her dark, Spanish eyes cut deeper with each passing second.

But her question had been more than that. It was a knife, and it remained lodged in his center. How could he possibly find an answer for the declaration that he'd broken her heart? After only a few seconds of looking back at her, he could hardly feel his body anymore. "I'm—" He glanced away and then met her gaze again. Its severity deepened, and he focused on the stone at their feet. "I'm sorry, but I can't answer that right now. There's something happening here tonight that I wanted to warn you of."

He saw her weight shift in the small moment of silence that followed. Her toes were painted a bright red and the glittering straps of her sandals made her feet look delicate and beautiful. Everything about her was delicate and beautiful. And strong. And smart. And perfect. He felt suddenly sick as a rush of love surged in his chest. He adored everything about her.

"And that's why you came back here tonight? To warn me?"

He looked up to see her position had softened some, but her cheeks were still flushed with anger. Determined to stop cowering before her, he forced a bit more strength into his voice. He needed to think about Everett. The man was here for a reason, and with a jolt of fear, he wondered if this night had been planned for a long time—whatever Everett was about to do. What if it was only playing into his hands by allowing him to stay at Cedar Creek?

Lander took a quick breath, waking from his thoughts. He could see on her face that she was noticing his tension. A shadow of confusion crossed her features, and she waited silently for him to continue. His posture relaxed a bit. "Why I came isn't important right now. I believe there are plans that have been set, but I don't know what they are." He glanced back at the dance hall, catching Everett watching them from the window. His breath caught.

"Let's walk a moment," he said, taking Carmen's arm and leading her down the pathway. The fact that she was still waiting for an answer to her terrible question stung his mind, but her immediate safety was more important. With luck, she would understand later. For now, she seemed confused enough that she wasn't contradicting him. "I might've made a mistake in trusting Everett," he whispered, pulling candidly on her arm when she tried to look back over her shoulder. "Don't look at him."

She gripped his arm and jerked him to a stop. "You're acting like a crazy person," she shot back. "Don't order me around and expect blind obedience, because it's not happening. So, you'd better tell me what's worrying you." She pointed at the cabin. "Or I go back inside, and you leave my event for good."

It seemed his chance to explain himself had vanished. He took a heavy breath, although nothing could shake the apprehension tingling off his skin that something was terribly wrong. He could feel the perspiration on his face even in the frigid night, and he looked desperately into her eyes. "He was there that night we found the calf. You didn't see him, but when I made my way around the barn that night, he was riding up to the lodge—"

"I did see," she answered, lifting her chin. "I followed behind you and listened enough to know that you two have a history. So, why is he your enemy now?"

She'd followed him that night?

"I see," he answered, studying her expression for a moment. But she wasn't giving anything away, and he doubted they would be alone on the patio much longer. Someone would come out, maybe even Everett, and then he might lose the chance to talk to her at all. "Well, good," he said, rushing. "I'm glad you heard that, actually. The thing is, I've been trusting my father's opinion of him from nearly twenty years ago. Anything could have changed since then, and tonight, I..."

I what? Formed a suspicion? Remembered a question he asked?

"So..." She shook her head. "You saw something? Or, he told you something?"

"No, that's not it." Lander shook his head, but he didn't have an argument. He knew that. The reason Everett came to Cedar Creek was probably just to get away. So, why did he feel so horrible? "Something's going on," he insisted. "I just don't know what."

She took a heavy breath and looked out at the wilderness around them. Deep, fragrant pine boughs swayed in the icy breeze. "So, if he came out here after all this time..." Her voice was contemplative and completely mesmerizing. Lander followed her as she walked to the railing, staring out at the night. She turned to him suddenly. Her eyes jumped up to meet his, and he flinched, hardly aware of how hard he'd been concentrating on her. The beauty in her face was radiating. "Did they ever find an answer to what started the house fire?"

Lander's answer was quiet, and he felt suddenly overcome with exhaustion from the weight of his memories. "They told me an old outlet shorted and started the fire from down in the basement."

"Hmm," she murmured. He was frozen as she stared

deeply back at him. It was unnerving. He was anxious for her to look away, but she didn't. Instead, she moved in closer. So close, all he wanted to do was take her in his arms. It was suddenly so simple. He loved her. Why had he been such an idiot as to convince himself he couldn't have her? She was incredible, and for some reason, she wanted to be with him. Who was he to say what was best for her? If she wanted to waste her life on someone like him, why couldn't he just let her do it?

His hands moved toward her so slightly, she didn't seem to notice. And then the memories came rushing back, drowning him in nightmares of her trapped in a life with him. A life where she resented him more with every passing day.

His arms fell to his sides.

"What if there's some new clue to the case, and he came back here, but he needed a believable cover of some kind? So, he told you the story of needing to get away and change up his life." She clasped her hands together, clearly lost in her theory. But when her eyes wandered back to him, the sadness returned. Color filled her cheeks, and she stepped back suddenly. "I need to get back in there. Look, I understand why you'd be concerned about this, but there's no need to worry—"

"Is this about the gunshots?"

They both spun around to find Maddie walking up to them. Clearly, she'd caught the last bit of the conversation.

Tremors shook through Lander, and he waited for Carmen to turn back to him, but she didn't. He felt nearly faint with shock and hoped beyond anything that his assumptions were wrong. And if they were right?

Heaven help the man who pulled the trigger.

Chapter Eighteen

❧

"Gunshots?"

Lander's voice behind her was deep and strong. Since meeting him, Carmen had heard him call out from far away; she'd heard him when he was unsure and surprised. She'd heard him whisper soft and passionate. And now, she could almost imagine his hand brushing her hair aside and his lips at her ear as he spoke. He had a way of adding tenderness to his words that sunk through her skin.

"Carmen."

His hands touched her arms on either side, and Carmen leaned back instinctively, resting against him. She didn't want to look into his eyes. There was no point in turning around. The moment she did, it would all be over. But for this one small piece of time, his warmth was cradled around her like an embrace. She hadn't noticed the chill of the air on her skin, but now her hands ached with it. Her toes were numb, and she realized she was shivering.

"Oh." His hands left her sides, and his warmth vanished

only to return as he draped his coat around her shoulders. "I wasn't even thinking. Here." His hand was on her back, and she went inside with Lander and Maddie right behind her. Lander's coat on her shoulders smelled so strongly of him, she could hardly stand it. The moment they were inside, she handed it back. She wanted so badly to ask him again if he could stay. If he would stay for her. But Maddie was looking unsurely back at her, and Lander's thoughts were clear enough on his face. His expression hadn't changed from the moment Maddie had asked the question.

Suddenly, Carmen didn't want to explain about the gunshots. The police officers had ruled it out as nothing malicious. They said there was likely someone out hunting nearby and that the bullets weren't even sent in her direction. Disorienting echoes were common on that side of the mountain. But even as she wished he would ask about anything else in the world, the words came from his mouth in the same passionate tones.

"Tell me what happened."

She waited only a moment before giving in. Her explanation was brief, and she made sure to explain that the police had come, and an investigation was started. Everything was found to be okay. But there was a severity in Lander's turquoise eyes that deepened as she spoke, and all her assurances didn't wipe it away.

"Gunshots," he murmured. He held his coat in his hands as he scanned the room. The band continued to play and nearly everyone in attendance had flooded the dance floor. "I must not have been very far from you when it happened, but I didn't hear anything." He turned back to her, pausing as if waiting for her to interject.

But she didn't want to.

"Do you remember where exactly you were?" he persisted.

Carmen hesitated. She'd been near his new cabin. The cabin he was keeping from her. So, why was he expecting her to be so forthcoming when he couldn't even share something like that?

An anger like she'd never felt bubbled up inside of her, boiling over. Tears stung at her eyes, but she held them back. "I told you everything that happened," she said quietly, "Everything I know, which is more than I can say for you."

The surprise on his face was strangely satisfying. She'd been so desperate for anything from him. A word, a look. Any validation that his feelings were still there. Suddenly, all she wanted was to slap him across his perfect face and scream at him to go back to Montana and never return. Her hands were shaking now, but not from the cold. She was losing her grip on her emotions more with each second, and if she didn't get away from him, the tears were bound to come.

He was waiting for her to continue, obviously unsure of what she meant. She took a quick, heavy breath and returned her gaze to his. "You haven't explained anything to me, Lander. Or spoken to me since you forced me away." Her hands clenched into fists, and she rested them on her hips. "You know that night I risked my life to save yours? Remember?"

Her tone was rude, but she didn't care. All the words that had been bottled up were rushing out, and she couldn't stop them if she wanted to. And she didn't want to. "When I found you delirious and half frozen, I stayed with you all night. Made sure you were warm—held you." Her gaze faltered, and she bit down hard on her tongue to keep from crying.

Lander hadn't moved. He only stared back at her, tall and strong and handsome, holding the suit coat he'd draped across her shoulders. Even with their little standoff, she sensed women's eyes lingering in his direction as they passed by on the dance floor. He was something to look at, that was for sure. But he wasn't hers; hadn't been for a time now.

"Would you have even told me about going to Montana if I hadn't overheard it?" Her legs began to feel weak. He didn't answer, but she no longer expected him to. "And what about our relationship? It's just over without a word? Without..." The words faltered on her lips, and she tried to fight back the tears. His face blurred, and she cursed her emotions to the heavens. "I'm not in danger, Lander. You don't need to worry about anyone hurting me." She wanted to stop herself, but the emotions were too strong. Tears broke free and trailed down her face. "The only person who has ever hurt me is you."

Her voice broke, and she shoved past him, racing through the room. If only he would call out. Chase after her. Anything. But she knew it was pointless to even wish for it. He would go back to Montana, and she'd never see him again. She thought saying those words would be a way to get back at him. That somehow, they would give her strength. But they stung in her heart so painfully she could hardly bear it.

"Carmen!"

She heard Maddie calling to her, but she didn't stop. Not until she was safely through the back door and out of view of him. Finally, she turned around, brushing away the tears, although more trailed down behind them.

Maddie raced through the door and skidded to a stop, breathing hard. Her pixie-cut brown hair was sleek and full of movement, sliding like a silky curtain around her pale, delicate face. The green of her eyes was flecked with hazel as if mimicking the wild around them. Carmen hadn't told her how beautiful she looked, or that the pale gold-lavender of her dress was entirely flattering on her. She wanted to say something now, but pain still radiated through her so fiercely, she doubted she could get the words out even if she tried.

"I came to tell you..." Maddie paused, setting one hand on her chest as she took a few breaths. "Everett said there's a patrol car back at your place. I guess someone found another animal? One of your cows. It's... well, it's dead." She crossed her bare arms in front of her slender frame, shivering. "I thought you should know."

Jake stepped out of the door behind them, pausing at the sight of Carmen. She wished he wouldn't have seen her just then. Standing there crying, as always. It was becoming a humiliatingly common thing. She was glad she still had her purse on her shoulder and no real need to go back inside the banquet. It had promised to be such an incredible night, but instead, it was one of the most miserable she'd ever known.

"Can you drive Maddie back, Jake?" Carmen asked, taking a few steps toward the parking lot. "Something's going on at Cedar Creek and I need to drive out. I'll be back before cleanup."

Jake took a step forward with one hand lifting as if he were going to object, and Maddie frowned. But neither one of them replied. They seemed to be fighting with their desire to stop her and support her, and it was just as well. Because for the moment, she just wanted some time alone.

Even if it was only for the drive back. It would have to be enough.

"Thank you," she said, looking into both of their eyes as sincerely as she could before she made for the truck. The door squeaked as loudly as ever, and she had to twist the skirt of her dress in one hand and hold it up as she climbed in. But at least she was alone. She shifted the truck into reverse. At least she didn't have to look into the deep, luscious green eyes of—

The passenger side door flew open.

She gasped. But when she saw Lander, the breath froze on her lips. He jumped in and slammed the door without even acknowledging her. Pulling at his seatbelt, he buckled it and faced the front.

No. This was not going to work. The tears hadn't even dried on her cheeks. "Get out," she said. The cool, fierce sound of her voice surprised even her, and Lander finally glanced in her direction. Sweat shone on his forehead and his eyes were widened, perhaps a little afraid. It had her feeling just the least bit pacified.

His jaw muscle contracted. "All your farm hands are here at the party, Carmen. I'm going with you."

"What, for my protection?" Her voice had risen, and her hands shook on the steering wheel. Her temper was flaring. She gripped it tighter. "In case I didn't make it clear in there, I'm fine on my own." She shifted into park and leaned back in her seat. "If you insist on coming to Cedar Creek, come with Maddie and Jake." She glanced back to see both her friends staring back at her. Maddie had her hands clasped together and held in front of her chest as if pleading with Carmen.

She squeezed her eyes closed and pressed her hand to her

forehead, fighting the softening of her heart. She didn't want it. With that softness came pain like torture, and she wouldn't allow it. "Please," she whispered, desperate. All the strength in her voice had shattered, and she turned slowly back to him. Everything hurt. The beating of her heart, each breath in her lungs, and even the sight of him were painful. "Just... please go."

His jaw worked and his eyes studied her face. She watched his chest rise, and then he reached for the door, pushing it open. "I'll just change and meet you over there if you need me."

She stared down at the old dash, faded from years of sitting in the sun and weather. The door closed, and there was the sound of Lander's shoes crunching through the snow. She didn't look up as she pulled away. The tires slipped when she pressed down the pedal too quickly. She eased up on the gas and allowed the truck to amble along, keeping her eyes focused down the dark winter road and far away from any of them. If there was an animal suffering at her house, that was where her attention needed to be anyway. Saying goodbye to Lander yet again was not something she was particularly interested in. She managed to keep her thoughts on what she might find ahead, even if her heart was still hurting. It was strange that Maddie had been the one to tell her. Why didn't Everett speak with her directly? She'd been too preoccupied by other things to even ask.

As she turned off the main road and drove carefully down the drive, the lodge came into view. There was a patrol car with its lights on, and standing there talking to the officers was Everett. He hadn't spoken with her at the party because he wasn't there. He must've called Maddie on the phone. They must've gotten each other's numbers at some point.

She parked behind the small group and studied their faces in the beam of her headlights. Their conversation had ceased and the officers both looked back at her sternly. Everett's expression was softer, but not by much. The worry of what they were about to tell her swelled in her middle, making her feel ill. Something in their eyes had her tensing for the worst.

The air was frigid as she went to meet them. With her headlights turned off, there was only the glow of the porch light and the circling flash of red and blue across their faces. It was eerie, sending chills tingling along the back of her neck.

One of the officers greeted her, although his dark eyes trailed down her dress as he did so. "Hello, I'm Officer Shirley and this is Officer Tanner." He gestured to the woman officer next to him. "We'll give you a few minutes to change, Ms. Rivera."

"Yes," she said. Her heels slipped a little on the snow as she turned to the porch. "Thank you." She didn't look at Everett, mostly because she feared falling completely on the icy ground. She changed quickly, laying her dress over the back of her desk chair, and hurried out again. Her jeans, jacket, and boots combo dealt much better with the cold. Still, she braced herself when the same dark-eyed officer regarded her.

"A slaughtered cow was found on your property tonight," he began. "Follow us." The officer next to him had her blonde hair tied into a knot at the base of her neck. She touched the brim of her hat in greeting and then followed alongside Officer Shirley.

Carmen walked behind them, and Everett fell into step beside her. She could see him glancing over at her, but she was too focused on what might be ahead. Her heart had dropped at the thought of another deceased animal. But it was part of the business; maybe this one was from natural causes or a predator. Just because an animal died, it didn't mean someone was sneaking onto her property and killing the poor things.

They walked around the barn, where Dax whinnied from inside his stall. Carmen glanced inside, reminding herself that she needed to get him on a better training schedule. Even in the snow, she wanted to keep working him.

"Now, Ms. Rivera."

Carmen stopped suddenly, looking up to see they were poised at the edge of the shed where they stored the ATVs. Officer Shirley had stopped with his hand on the edge of the building as Officer Tanner peered around the other side. Carmen swallowed.

"I want to let you know before we see it," Officer Shirley continued. He turned and faced her. "This is something I haven't dealt with before, and I've been an officer around here for twelve years. It's not anything common, not something anyone here would do as a joke or..." He shrugged. "I don't know what to think of it. The cow has been mutilated very purposefully and displayed in a way that was likely meant to bring about shock or fear." He sighed and glanced at his partner, crossing his arms. "Actually, there's really no reason why you have to see it right now. Maybe we could just photograph the evidence and show you—"

"No, it's fine," Carmen said. "I'd like to see what happened." They both looked back at her quietly for a moment, and then Officer Shirley sighed again. "Well, then," he said. "Let's go."

Carmen's knees were jello as they rounded the corner of the building and found the scene. Her breath caught in her throat. The animal had been sectioned apart and strung up like some strange artwork. Its head was severed and lifted up on a post, while the legs were hung separately with twine along the edge of the building. The rest of the body had been split open and left rib-side up. It was sickening. Carmen brought her hand to her mouth, breathing as evenly as she could. "Who would do something like this?" she asked, although she was sure they wouldn't have mentioned a name if they had one. "Why?" She looked at each face, stopping at the one most familiar to her of the three. Everett. "When did you find it? I thought you were at the party."

Everett nodded. "I was. But I managed to ask the most unsteady woman in the room to dance and she spilled her red wine all down my shirt." He patted his coat, where Carmen assumed there was a soiled suit shirt underneath. "I came through this way because it's a shorter route." He swept his hand across the scene. "I called the cops right away. I mean, it's clear someone is trying to scare you, or..." He grew silent, seeming as unsure as Carmen was.

And she was unsure. About a lot of things. She glanced at the officers, who were both looking at Everett. Her eyes strayed back to him as well. At first, she'd thought there must have been an accomplice to the slaughtered cow. After all, it was a big job. But then, Everett was a big man, capable of dragging the cow where he wanted to.

Shivers tingled down her spine.

If he'd come back from the banquet alone, it would have

given him the chance to complete the crime and then call the police.

"You say there was wine spilled on your shirt?" Officer Shirley took a step closer to Everett. He nodded his head, gesturing to Everett with the brim of his hat. "Want to show us?"

Everett's expression froze. He smiled, but his eyes had hardened. "Of course, officer," he said. Unzipping his coat, he pulled it open, revealing a dark stain down the front of his suit coat and the white button-up shirt beneath. On the white shirt, the color of the wine was easily distinguishable.

But Carmen couldn't help noticing the way his voice had risen with each answer as if a hint of anxiety was creeping in. He seemed nervous, his eyes jumping from one officer to the other. Even if Everett's story were true, it was clear he wasn't telling the whole story.

Chapter Nineteen

❦

By the time Carmen got back to the banquet, the last of the guests were leaving. She must've missed Lander, Maddie, and Jake on the back-and-forth roads to the lodge. With any luck, they wouldn't come back to the banquet. She wasn't sure she could handle even one more encounter with Lander. She started up the walk, still dressed in her jeans and work coat. It had seemed a little silly to change back into her dress after the night she'd had, especially when the party was over anyway. With any luck, it would generate the interest she was hoping for.

Eager to help with the cleanup and hoping that her friends weren't taking it all on themselves, she went inside. The string lighting had been turned off and was being taken down. It left the room in more shadows than before. Suddenly, her mother and father appeared in front of her. She felt bad they hadn't been able to spend hardly any time together at the banquet. But from the smiles on their faces, they weren't upset.

"Oh, Carmen!" Her mother gushed, wrapping her tightly

in a hug. "This was such a wonderful idea. It turned out beautifully." She stepped back, and Carmen's father held her quickly in his customary brief, but warm, hugs. "I'm glad we caught you before we left," he said, smiling quietly as he stepped back, returning his arm around her mother. "I heard you had to step out, but Aries gave a polite and equally pressing speech." He winked. "I'm sure you'll have donors step up."

Carmen was just happy they were there. She shook her head, and a broad smile stretched across her face. "That you made it at all is incredible." She hugged them together. "Thank you so much." She stepped back and her eyes settled on her father. It filled her heart to see him back in Wyoming. To her knowledge, he hadn't returned even once since meeting her mother all those years ago. It was clear there had been a rift between her grandfather and him, but she'd never gotten much information about the subject from any of them.

He glanced into her eyes somberly as if knowing where her thoughts were. "I hope you can forgive my actions in the past, Carmen," he said quietly. "I wish I could change the way things were. But honestly, I wasn't welcome here."

"It's true, Carmen," her mother said. "Grandpa Tagen refused to invite us out. Only you. You changed him."

"Changed him," Carmen repeated, feeling the sudden burn of bitterness in the pit of her stomach. Did men really change? She wanted to argue but knew how bizarre that would be if she did. To them, the conversation was a pleasant one. So, she bit her tongue and smiled back. "Thank you."

They spent the evening fielding phone calls and calculating donations. It was like a special kind of therapy to be with her parents. Everything they said and did was familiar and comforting. The kind looks they gave and the hugs that were never-ending. She began to miss New York for the first time since she'd left. Although she never felt completely happy in the city the way she was at Cedar Creek. At least, until recently.

"That's it," her mother said, scribbling down an impressive five-digit number. "The last one. Oh my, you really had a successful night." She lifted the paper she'd tallied. "Nearly a million dollars, Carmen!" With a squeal, she threw her arms around Carmen. "You're so amazing. Just look how they believe in you." She leaned back and gazed deeply into Carmen's eyes. "Just look at the opportunity you've been given."

For the second time that night, Carmen didn't know what to say. A million dollars? She lifted the paper, reading it from top to bottom. "Is this for real?" Back in New York City when she'd wanted so badly to run a benefit for the kids at inner-city schools, she'd been crushed when it all fell apart. Now, she wanted to go back and find every one of those kids. Every single one.

"That's right." Her father's hand settled on her shoulder. "You did it."

Her eyes drifted up to meet with her parents and a smile pulled at her lips. "I did it."

TWO WEEKS LATER, LIFE BEGAN TO SETTLE INTO A STRANGE new rhythm. At least, it felt strange for Carmen. It had been wonderful to see Violet and Aries, and her parents too. But they'd returned to New York and life had gone on one day at a time. Her favorite thing had become driving into Ridgeville with Maddie nearly every day for lunch. They enjoyed the surprisingly good salads at the old western café and especially wandering through Saundra Driscoll's wool shop. It seemed there was always some new creation. Maddie held up a multicolored poncho, giving Carmen a glittery-eyed grin. "I need this," she whispered.

Her personality had opened up completely since moving to Wyoming. Carmen could hardly believe she was the same girl who used to be closed down to any social attention of any kind. Staring into books and never really showing her smile. Now she smiled all the time. Carmen had even caught Maddie walking around the lodge, completely alone, with a smile on her face. At peace.

Carmen winked back at Maddie, who still held the poncho. "You have my approval." Maddie draped the handmade treasure over her arm and continued browsing. For Carmen, home decor was her favorite section. She always wandered over to it and quickly fell in love with the natural textures and colors in each rug, pillow, and afghan. It snuck up on her softly at first, and then the pain would hit. The realization that what she was searching for was a way to dress up a new cabin. Not her grandfather's lodge, but the big, beautifully angled, and masterfully built cabin in the high country. The one Lander meant for them. Or maybe he hadn't. Maybe he only wanted solitude. Maybe he really did scare her by firing a rifle into the trees.

Maybe.

It was a horrible word because it meant nothing... and everything. A hundred conclusions could spring up from those two syllables. And yet, it seemed to go nowhere.

"Find something you like this time, Carmen?"

Carmen woke from her thoughts to see Saundra smiling down at the afghan in her hands. Her full, gray hair was pulled into a loose bun at the base of her neck, and her brown eyes were vibrant, framed by bright red glasses. "Uh, yes," Carmen said. "Always, actually." She shrugged, wanting to tuck the beautiful blanket back onto the shelf, but feeling bad at the same time. It was probably rude to come to browse the shop day after day and never buy anything. Still, it hurt to think of buying something she was only imagining in a future that would never come. But those were thoughts she was just going to have to get over.

She smiled at Saundra and handed her the afghan. "I'll take it."

"Wonderful," Saundra said. She turned to the register and then stopped, swinging around again. "You don't need to buy anything, you know. I don't want you to feel obligated. Most of my sales are online anyway." Her eyes swept the store. "This place is just for the love of it."

"No, I really want it," Carmen insisted, as they made their way back to the register.

"I'm coming too," Maddie called, hurrying down the aisles with at least two more items in her arms. "Hurry before I buy the whole place." She laughed.

"You're getting to be my number one customer, Maddie," Saundra teased.

Carmen and Maddie left the store each with a bag in hand. Maddie with two, and she swung them cheerfully as they walked.

"You know, Maddie," Carmen said. "You seem very happy here. Does that mean you've gotten over a certain person?"

"Definitely," Maddie replied, without hesitation. "Kevin is long forgotten." She smiled in a relaxed, comfortable way.

"I've never been so completely happy on my own before. You know how I love reading, but I haven't even been reading as much as I used to. There's always so much to do. But then, sometimes I just look out the window and can't believe I'm here. It's the most incredible place."

Carmen smiled, stepping into her old truck. "I agree." She set her bag aside and started the engine, but just like always, the sadness rose up as if waiting for a chance to challenge her. To remind her of the pain she held inside still. It never went away, it only spread like mold, darkening any light it touched until all her hope seemed to vanish.

"How about you?" Maddie asked. Her voice had softened, and Carmen glanced over to see her turned in the seat, her green eyes full of sadness. She knew. Of course, she did.

"I, uh…" Carmen checked the rearview mirror and pulled into a U-turn, pointing them back toward Cedar Creek Lodge. She already determined she couldn't bring up Lander. The only way she'd gotten through the past two weeks was by keeping him out of any and every conversation. She would notice the looks she got from the Driscoll boys or from Maddie every now and then… and especially from Jake. But she still couldn't handle it. "I'm so happy here," she said, trying to get some volume out of her voice, but the words came softly. "The camp next summer is going to be amazing." She shook her head. "I still can't believe we were able to get all those donations. It's unbelievable."

"I had no doubts," Maddie said, giving a wink. But then she paused, and her face fell a little as if awaiting more. Likely she wanted the truth for once. But that wasn't going to happen. Not today.

Carmen turned off the main highway and onto a snowy side road. The tires began to skate over the slick surface, and she slowed. "Aries and Violet are already making up promotional flyers and images. They've sent me about a dozen different ideas for schedules." She smiled. "They've set aside the time from work and even started contacting caterers and party planners from New York until I told them not to." She glanced over at Maddie. "I want everything to be provided locally."

"Smart move," Maddie said, nodding. She leaned back in her seat, looking a little less interested, and leaned her head back.

Carmen glanced over again to see her eyes had closed. Feeling a bit of relief, she settled into her seat as well and looked ahead to where the road curved into the trees. Cedar Creek Lodge was just beyond that.

"I'm glad there haven't been any more dead cows," Maddie mumbled, keeping her eyes closed. "That was so sad."

"I know," Carmen agreed. "So am I."

The rest of their drive was quiet, with Maddie seeming asleep. Carmen's mind strayed to the calf and cow they'd found. Both had been shocking, but the calf most of all. It showed just how devoid of compassion the attacker was, to kill such a young, affectionate creature. She'd tried to convince herself it was animals, but she knew the truth. Chills shivered through her, and she twisted her hands on the steering wheel anxiously. Even if it hadn't happened in recent days. that didn't stop her from looking deep into the trees as they pulled up to the lodge.

She glanced over at Maddie still asleep with her head reclined. It had been a nice lazy Saturday so far and wouldn't hurt to let her friend sleep a little. Keeping the engine running and the heat blasting, Carmen leaned her chair back and closed her eyes. But like a thief of opportunity, her thoughts turned to Lander. His face and gentle voice. The way he'd held her. Kissed her. She would have sworn to the heavens that he loved her fiercely. She would have sworn that she knew it clear to her bones. Nothing would have ever caused her to doubt his devotion.

Until he'd walked away.

She hadn't let a tear fall in two weeks but felt helpless to stop it now, and they quickly gathered under her lids. Wishing for sleep, they slid down her cheeks one at a time. A slow, solemn procession, each one a painful reminder of the truth she kept locked inside.

LANDER TRIED TO LOSE TRACK OF TIME, BUT IT WAS IN vain. He'd felt every minute of the past fifteen days like needles under his skin. After the banquet, when Carmen had ordered him out of her truck, he'd meant to go to the lodge. He wanted to. But something held him back. He watched Maddie and Jake drive off, declining a ride with them. And then he'd pulled the business card from Montana out of his pocket. The decision had been quick and freeing.

He left.

And now, here he was, looking out on miles of grazing land. The snowfall had begun later than usual, giving them just enough time to complete the fencing. It wasn't typical to raise fences at the start of winter, but the late fall had produced unseasonably warm temperatures. And the foreman had gotten a wild hair about fence lines. Lander helped set up nearly fifteen miles of fence line since he'd arrived, and today was the first time he could see the endpoint. It stood over another hill and across the pasture beyond. They were almost done. But realizing that brought him no relief. He didn't want to finish anything; he only wanted to work. Hard. For the rest of his life.

He took a short break and removed his gloves, tucking them in the back of his jeans. His hands felt the sting of winter air, the breeze born from miles of open, snowy land. But he didn't mind it. There wasn't much that brought him discomfort anymore, aside from memories of Carmen. But those, he kept buried deep down inside. From what the other workers knew of him, he was a quiet, ornery worker just looking to be left alone. And he didn't necessarily mind that image. Let them gossip about him. All he needed was the next job. He wiped his forehead and made a mental note to ask the foreman about it as soon as the fence was completed.

Before he had the chance to don his gloves, his phone rang. Strangely enough, it had sat silent in his front shirt pocket for nearly two weeks. He unzipped his coat and loosed the button from his flannel shirt, retrieving his phone. The number on the front was unknown to him, but he answered anyway.

"Is this Lander Casey?" A strong male voice inquired.

Lander glanced at the screen again, seeing the call came from Cheyenne, Wyoming. "Yes," he said. "This is him."

"Lander." The voice sounded relieved. "This is Detective Peter Hollingsworth, head of the Cheyenne Investigation Bureau. How are you today?"

Lander hesitated, reviewing any possible reasons why a detective from his father's previous workplace might be contacting him. He couldn't think of a single one. "What's this about, detective?"

"Yes, sorry for the abrupt nature of my call." He cleared his throat. "I worked closely with your father's security team. I'm not sure if you're aware of this, but the actual cause of the fire at your home those years ago was never determined. The case was considered cold." Again, he paused. "It's been on my mind almost constantly, and with my retirement in six weeks, I knew I wouldn't be able to rest. So..." He sighed. "A few months ago, I reopened the case."

"Sir." The world shook under his feet, and Lander slipped on his gloves before returning the phone to his ear. "I'm in the middle of my workday. Perhaps we could talk about this later."

"Oh, I see—" Detective Hollingsworth stumbled about a bit on his words, sounding taken aback by Lander's reply. But he couldn't help it. Something inside of him was crumbling.

"Can I call you this evening?" The detective asked. "Or better yet, give me a call when you're available. It's never too late."

Lander knew he was talking about the time of day, but his words were a dagger. Never too late? Of course, it was too late! Years too late. Painful, torturous, abusive years that'd turned him into a shadow of a man. Years he feared he would never be free of. All this time he'd assumed he was the one and only suspect, but that wasn't what Detective Hollingsworth was saying. He was talking like they were searching for someone else. Like his parents had been murdered.

"You still with me?"

Lander took a breath of cold mountain air, glancing around to assure none of the other workers were around. "I'll give you a call tonight. Goodbye." He ended the call, suddenly breathing hard. Everything spun, and he grit his teeth, fighting hard to keep his vision. But it narrowed into a darkening tunnel. And then the world vanished.

"HEY, KID. KID!"

Something smacked his boot, hard. Lander jerked upright, to find himself lying in the snow. "What're you callin' me kid for?" he grumbled. His gear was scattered about, and the fence was still unfinished, even as nightfall was coming on. He looked up to see the foreman, gray-white hair, and pale skin. His eyes were a twinkly light blue that gave him the appearance of always smiling.

But he wasn't smiling. "Cuz you are," he shot back, lifting Lander from under his arms. "Here, get up before you freeze to the ground. I ain't strong enough to carry ya back. You think you can walk?"

Lander shuffled to the side a little and then straightened. "Yeah, I can walk," he said, trying not to sound angry, even though he was. Furious. But not at the foreman.

"You sick or something?" The foreman's blue eyes peered into his, and then he dropped the question with a grunt. "C'mon, let's get you back. Probably didn't eat anything all day, did you?" Lander kept his eyes on the ground as he walked, but he caught the head movement as the foreman looked over at him. "Yeah, that was probably it. Young guys think they can survive on nothin' out here, but that sure ain't the case. You need a meal that can carry you through a blizzard."

The old man talked all the way back, even after they

loaded their gear onto an ATV and began driving. He talked about food and sleep and staying warm. And after that, he kept talking. But Lander had quit listening. His mind retreated to that horrible night. The one he'd blamed himself for almost the entirety of his life. If there was even the slightest chance someone had caused that fire on purpose...

His hands balled into fists, and his insides felt torched by fire. If they did, then he'd find them. And he'd kill them.

Chapter Twenty

C armen stepped onto the concrete and walked through the framework, aching. Why? Why had he stopped loving her? It hurt too much to not know the answer, and she clung to the pine-fragrant redwood lumber. She knew she shouldn't come back to the cabin. She'd done it once already and promised herself she'd never return again. And yet, here she was one week later.

Her heart felt like it was crumbling inside of her, and she wrapped her arms tighter around the wood post. Tucking her head, she lost all hold of her pain and broke into sobs. If only she'd never come. If only she'd never set eyes on Lander.

The sound of heavy boots on the concrete slab silenced her. She caught her breath and listened as the steps grew closer. Was it possible he'd returned? And here she was falling apart in front of him.

"You shouldn't be out here, Miss Carmen," Hal rubbed one hand over his mustache. He stood beside Ernie, both with scowls on their faces.

Carmen spun around, brushing at her cheeks quickly. Anger chased away the pain and gave her a strong voice. "And why's that?"

Ernie looked up at Hal, who stood a good foot over him. But Hal's eyes narrowed, glued to Carmen. "Wolf pack moved in over the mountain. I even caught them roaming around the cabin a few days ago."

"And why were you out here?" Carmen's anger sizzled inside of her. "This is Lander's property."

"Yes, it is," Hal said, his jaw as firm as ever. "He asked me to look out for it while he was away. We just came out to check on the place. Saw you ladies riding out here and had to let you know."

"He told us to clear anyone off his land," Ernie said, his voice as mean as ever. "And that includes you. So, I suggest you get."

"Carmen, maybe we should just go."

Carmen gasped, spinning around to see Maddie at the edge of the cabin. She stepped down from the foundation and onto the snow. "It's fine. We saw what we came to see."

It was nice of her to pretend they'd come together, but Carmen didn't answer. She turned back to the two men who had given her the most trouble since she came to Cedar Creek. "Lander wouldn't kick me off his property, and neither will you." She could practically feel the fear radiating from Aries and Violet next to her, but they didn't speak.

Hal took a slow step forward, then another. His dark eyes were unnerving. "I'm not runnin' you off. Just letting you know you could have some unwelcome company." He took another step closer, looking down at her. "Stay if you want. I'd prefer you did."

A thrill of fear tingled through Carmen. Something about

the severe calm in his eyes was terrifying. But before she could answer, Ernie stomped forward.

"Well, I am," he shouted. "Get outta here!"

Carmen couldn't help taking a step back. But she didn't want to leave. She wanted to stay right here, where she could feel Lander's presence. Where she could see the work of his hands. She belonged right beside him. It took every ounce of strength to turn back and join Maddie. She could hear Hal and Ernie behind her, commenting to each other. Chuckling.

She spun around to see they'd followed her. Hal was balanced on the edge as if ready to jump off. "You have any more problems with your cows?" he said, looking far too pleased. "Funny how the moment he left"—his head jerked back at the house—"your problems went away. Coincidence, you think?"

"Let's go, Carmen." Maddie pulled on her arm, and she finally turned back to the horses.

"The case is reopened, you know," Hal continued. "They want to figure out who killed his parents once and for all. Strange that he skipped town at this exact time. Nothing says suspicious like a runaway."

Carmen spun around. "That's enough, Hal. I doubt Lander ever asked either of you for a favor. You better believe I'll be checking in with him."

"See that you do," Ernie said. "Now, get along."

Carmen studied his face, watching the way his eyes flickered to Hal. Deep in his gaze, she thought she saw a shadow of fear. It sent her thoughts spinning, and her perspective shifted, leaving her off-balance. Maybe Ernie was just trying to get them out of there and away from Hal.

She gave him a nasty glare and turned on her heels. "Let's go," she said, walking fast. Maddie didn't need any encouragement; she practically jogged up the hill. As soon as they were in view of the shed, Carmen heard Dax whinny. She glanced behind her, relieved that they were out of view of the two hardened ranch hands. Whatever happened back there, she was glad to be away from them. The idea that Lander had asked them to watch over his property was laughable. There was no way.

"Are you okay, Carmen?" Maddie asked, glancing around them.

"Yeah." Carmen untied Dax, but instead of climbing into the saddle, she turned to Maddie. "Did you follow me last time too?"

Maddie sighed. She took a moment to look into Carmen's eyes, and when she did, the pity there made Carmen feel sick. She hated feeling so pathetic, but somehow, she just couldn't stay away.

They set off together, although quietly. When they eventually reached the peak of the hill, Carmen turned in the saddle to spot two horses in the distance. Hal and Ernie were coming. "They're following us," Maddie said. "Do you think they just wanted to get us out here in the middle of nowhere?"

"Why would they do that?" Carmen whispered back. But no one answered. She kept Dax moving, right past the lookout and into the downhill.

In the trees ahead of them, a horse snorted. Carmen pulled up on the reins, holding her hand up and signaling for the others to stop. Their horses' hooves shuffled, and tails swished as they stopped reluctantly. Clearly, they'd been excited to get back to the barn. But someone was in the trees.

"Do you think they circled around us?" Maddie's voice

was afraid.

"No," Carmen said. "They couldn't have." But she wasn't sure. Maybe they did.

A big, shaggy horse emerged from the trees, and Carmen exhaled, laying one hand on her chest. "It's Everett," she said. But as he got closer, she tensed. Her mind battled it out. Which was worse? Should they be more worried about Hal and Ernie or Everett? She didn't know anymore.

"You all okay?" Everett's voice was strong and kind, and Carmen tried to trust it.

"I texted him after Hal and Ernie showed up," Maddie said. She shrugged when Carmen looked back at her. "I didn't know what to expect with those two. But I trust Everett."

There was no time to answer as Everett approached. He pulled his horse to a stop and looked across their faces. "Everyone all right?"

"Yeah," Carmen said, pushing Dax on. "But we'd like to get back as soon as possible."

"Hal and Ernie causing problems?" Everett's voice was stronger than before, and he glanced up the hill. "There they are," he said.

They all turned to see the two cowboys standing at the lookout, watching them. Perhaps they'd never intended to come any farther, or perhaps it was Everett who stopped their pursuit. Either way, they turned their horses around and disappeared from view.

"They won't give you any more trouble," Everett said. "I'll talk to them."

"Thank you," Maddie said, smiling. "Sorry to sound so panicked on the phone, but I didn't know what was going on. They were acting crazy."

Everett nodded. "Wish I could've gotten here sooner," he said. "You want me to go with you to the lodge?"

"No, we'll be fine," Carmen said, although she caught sight of Maddie's disappointment. "Thank you for coming out."

"Anytime." Everett gave them a nod and turned his horse, heading back into the trees and up toward Lander's old cabin.

Carmen rubbed her hand across her face, exhausted. "Let's just get back and let the horses relax for a bit," she said. Behind her, the girls agreed quietly, and they finished the trip in silence. But in her head, Carmen was a blizzard of thought. She knew Lander would never ask those two for a favor, and she wouldn't trust a word out of their mouths. But if the case really was reopened and Lander left for Montana so suddenly, it wouldn't look good. It didn't look good, even to Carmen. Dread built up steadily in her chest until she felt half-drowned by it. Was that the real reason he couldn't move on with his life? Did he get word of the case and knew their future was over because he would finally be convicted of murder?

No.

He didn't do it. She reminded herself of when he'd spoken about losing his parents, every detail. The sheen in his eyes, and the tenderness in his voice. The anguish was so near the surface, it had pained her to watch. She'd known in her very soul that he was innocent. The victim of a terrible tragedy.

She pulled up suddenly on Dax and kicked her heels, spinning him around. He snorted, digging in his front foot as he reacted to her energy. Her breath was puffing in front of her face, one after the other. If the case was reopened, and

Everett had worked with Lander's father, he had to be the whole reason he'd come. All this time, it had to be what he was hiding. Maybe no one else knew, not even the local police. They wanted to catch the guilty person unaware, and who else would they suspect but Lander?

"How'd it go?" Jake called from the barn. Carmen urged Dax on suddenly, sending him charging past Maddie, Violet, and Aries. Their eyes were each wide with fear. "I'll be right back!" She shouted, turning back to them. "Jake can help with the horses."

Dax was in his element while running, even in the snow. He had a way of settling into the movement, not rushing it. His steps were purposeful and light, giving her a smooth ride. She wanted to urge him on faster, but she resisted. They were making good time and would be there soon. No sense in making their trip unnecessarily dangerous.

When she turned into the trees, she pulled him back to a walk. The cabin came into view, and she saw Everett's horse tied out front. He must've planned on taking him out again. She patted his horse and tied Dax on the opposite side of the hitching post, just in case they decided they weren't friends. But for the moment, they seemed unconcerned with each other.

She hurried up the walk, slipping in the snow a few times on her way. When she got to the door, she knocked, trying not to pound her fist on it.

Footsteps came from inside, and the door opened. Everett's expression filled with surprise, and he leaned out the doorway, glancing around. "Carmen," he said, stepping back. "Please, come in. Is everything all right?"

"No, actually." Carmen hurried in, pacing through the clutter. Boxes and random things. Just the way someone would treat a house if they didn't plan on staying for very long. Her heart raced, and she just wanted to get the words out so he could confirm all the pieces she'd just put together.

Everett's hand settled on her arm, and she skidded to a stop, looking up at him. "Carmen," he said, holding a hand up as if trying to calm her. "What's going on?"

"Did you know the case was reopened?" She blurted out, watching his face with a laser focus. But he'd frozen so successfully, nothing was given away. Just the same look of surprise he'd greeted her with. "It's why you came here in the first place, isn't it?" She pressed. "You knew. But..." Her eyes glanced across his face, pleading for answers. "Lander didn't, did he?"

"Hold on, Carmen." Everett released her, and he began pacing. But she was still, watching him and hoping for honesty. "There are things I can't talk about with anyone. Literally, word for word on my contract. With anyone."

"But you didn't talk to me about it," she urged. "I talked to you. I figured it out on my own." She thought about telling him she'd heard it from Hal and Ernie but stopped. There was still enough that she didn't trust about him. And admitting where she'd heard it would give him an easy out.

He stopped directly in front of her, his eyes widened and jaw hard-set. "Just what have you figured out besides that the case is open? Do you know who did it? Do you have evidence?"

"I know it wasn't Lander," she said firmly. But to her utter and disgusted surprise, he laughed. Not just a little chuckle, but a burst of laughter that gusted in her face. Her eyes narrowed.

"I'd like to stand up for him too, believe me." He nodded and appeared to have a difficult time reining in his amusement. He held his hand up again. "I'm sorry. I don't mean to make light of this, but I've been under an enormous amount of pressure. And I really shouldn't talk about it."

"Tell me what you know," Carmen demanded, knowing how obstinate she sounded. It didn't matter. She wasn't trying to be Everett's friend, especially when he refused to stand up for Lander. "Who do you suspect? Because there can't be that many who were there that night."

"Practically the whole town was there," he returned, grumbling. He walked to the couch and sank into it. "And I can't talk about it."

Carmen sat down next to him, feeling desperate. "Please, Everett." His eyes lifted to hers. "Please let me help. What can I do?"

He sighed, leaning forward, and resting on his knees. His eyes watched the floor a moment before lifting to hers, but his expression was nearly devastated. "You can accept the fact that the man you are clearly still very much in love with could be a murderer."

Carmen shot to her feet, holding back the words that flew to her tongue. She wrestled to keep her emotions under control. "How can you possibly defend someone when you don't even believe in them?"

"I'm not here to defend Lander." He stood, looking back at her gently. But the turn of his mouth was all-business. His emotions were set aside. "I'm here to solve a case, and believe me, I've seen plenty of good, beloved men and women do terrible things. Things no one would ever believe them capable of. Things they would swear on their life the person didn't do. And yet, they did. And Lander was seventeen, Carmen. You didn't even know him then."

"No, but I know him now." Carmen's voice broke, and

she cleared her throat. Maybe she couldn't set her emotions aside like Everett could, but she didn't have to. "I know him now. And I know what he's told me and what he's shared with me. Besides, if he were guilty, he wouldn't have held on to the lie this long."

"It gets easier with time," Everett said. Easily. Casually. "Tell me why he moved to Montana so suddenly, then."

Carmen's emotions swelled, but she didn't want them to show. She bit back the pain as best she could. "He didn't do it."

"If he didn't do it, why did he run outta here like he was being chased? Why did the threats to your cattle vanish the same time he did?"

"What?" Carmen shook her head, taking a step closer. She wanted to punch him. "Why would he be the one to do anything with my cattle? It makes no sense—"

"To scare you away," Everett was nearly shouting now. "You got too close, and he knew it. He wanted you out of here, but when you wouldn't leave and he learned about the case, he skipped town."

Carmen's mouth dropped open. Everything he'd said was ridiculous and untrue, but every word hurt like he'd stabbed her. Is that what people thought of him? Is that what they were saying? He didn't stand a chance with an argument like that. Lander would be overcome with guilt over dragging her into it and he'd never be able to defend the argument. But she could.

Clenching her fists, she pointed her finger at him. "You're wrong, Everett," she said, her voice rising. "He didn't do any of that. I know it!"

He grabbed her wrist, but she jerked her hand away,

pushing against him. But he wouldn't budge. Tears came to her eyes. "You're wrong!" she shouted.

"Carmen." His voice was soft, and his hands rested gently on her shoulders. "I understand that I could be wrong, but..." He shook his head. "There's very little chance of it."

"Stop saying that!" She was losing her grip now, and the words were rough from her lips. Covering her face with her hands, she gave up. What else could she say? What could she do? There was nothing to prove him innocent, and she knew it.

His big arms came around her lightly. "I'm sorry Carmen. I wish you hadn't found out about this. But maybe it's for the best that you know now, before..."

"Before what?" She stepped out of his arms, wiping her cheeks for the second time that day. "Before you drag him to jail? You need to stop, Everett. You need to believe in him like I do. Because he isn't like all those other dishonest fools you've dug out of hiding. He's someone who worked his way out of an experience no one should ever go through. He blamed himself for most of his life, but not because it was his fault. Only because he hadn't been there to help them, and that's not the same as guilt."

She crossed the room and opened the door. Pausing, she turned back to Everett once more. He was watching her silently, her tear stains still visible on his dark shirt. "If you turn around and accuse him of the one thing he's worked so hard all his life to overcome, I don't know what it will do to him." Her vision blurred, and she swallowed, biting her lip when it shook. "At least think about that. Consider it. Be open to what might have really happened that night if it wasn't Lander." She shook her head, shrugging. "Because it wasn't."

Chapter Twenty-One

❦

It had been so many years, but Lander knew his mother's voice the second she spoke. It seemed to jolt through his body like electricity, and he dug through the darkness, frantic to find her. Then suddenly she stood next to him, as did his father.

He didn't try to speak, somehow he knew he couldn't. That it wasn't the purpose of their visit. They were here to tell him something. But he didn't know what, and at the moment he didn't even care. He only looked from one face to the other and back again. Drinking in the sight of them. Just like that, all the pain he'd endured since their death was obsolete. It vanished into the oblivion around them, leaving only a sweet happiness that was warm all over, like the touch of sun on his skin.

His mother leaned closer, lifting her hand to his shoulder. He closed his eyes, smelling the sweet scent of lavender, her favorite flower. "Look again," she said, her voice echoing around him.

He opened his eyes and flinched. In front of them was

their home so long ago. Ripped open and mostly destroyed by fire, it was blackened and dripping wet from the fire hoses. But what was it she wanted him to see? There was the fire crew with downturned faces, wrapping up hoses and locking gear away. The moment he spotted paramedics lifting gurneys into the ambulance, he turned his head, squeezing his eyes closed.

"Look again," she repeated, louder this time.

He turned back to the scene to see the ambulance pulling away. And then he was watching himself walking up to the house from his car. He was so young, and yet he remembered the fear pounding in his heart as if it were yesterday. The pain was unbearable, even now. But what was it he needed to see?

People stood about, watching. Everett had already disappeared, not to be seen again during the following weeks. His young self was frozen ten feet from the house, just staring. He didn't remember standing there for that long, nor did he remember the people who approached him, patting his back and giving soft words of encouragement. Slowly they were clearing out, heading home to spread the news until it would all suddenly change. The moment a few details hit the public, like the gas can in his car, or the fight they'd had the night before, then it would all begin to burn anew.

Still, he stood there.

"Young man."

Finally, his young self turned so slowly. He found himself facing the police chief, who held a gas can in one hand. He set it between them on the walk.

"This was found in your car," he said, sounding both shocked and angry. "Did you put it there?"

"No."

Lander was taken aback. Why did he say no?

"I took it out before I left," he told the police chief. "And set it right there." He pointed up the walk, by the front steps.

"You just left it by the steps all night? Why would you do that?"

Suddenly Lander remembered. He remembered taking the gas can out of his car before he left. His young self blinked, still in shock. If he'd been more alert, he might have understood that an investigation was taking place. But he didn't think anything of it. His parents were dead. What mattered besides that?

"I kept it in the back because I didn't want to run out of gas, but it had spilled so I took it out before I drove off." He turned back to the remnants of his house and tears began to trail down his cheeks.

Lander didn't remember crying that night. But obviously, he had.

"We fought, so I didn't want to go in."

He spoke so carelessly, so honestly. Couldn't they see the fire had been put out, but was somehow inside of him, burning his soul clean away? He remembered the hollowness. It persisted still as if he hadn't quite rebuilt everything that was destroyed.

"Now, look again," his mother repeated.

He turned to her, but she was gone. He only saw darkness and himself talking to Everett in the distance as if time were rewound. But directly in front of him was his small car. A man hid behind it. He wore a dark jacket with the hood pulled up. In the darkness of morning, he couldn't see who it was. But he held the gas can in his hand. Lander looked back toward the house, squinting to see the can he'd left at the steps, but it was gone. The trunk was lifted, and the can sloshed as the person placed it inside. He closed the back and pulled off a pair of gloves, revealing a tattoo on one hand. Black, carved roses trailed around his thumb in the shape of a ring. He turned his head, revealing black eyes and a familiar face. A face he knew. A face he hated.

And then everything vanished.

He gasped, opening his eyes. His cheeks were wet, and his heart pounded in his chest.

"Hal," he whispered, gritting his teeth until his jaw hurt. "I'm coming for you."

LANDER KNEW HE SHOULD HAVE SPOKEN TO HIS BOSS, BUT there would be time for that later. After he killed Hal. Something was awake inside of him, turning the wheels of his mind and leaving him nearly helpless to stop. He was rushing through the small airport with the one small bag of belongings he'd brought with him, thinking only of revenge.

Now and then, he would feel the presence of his parents. A kind, gentle pressure on his mind like a plea for reason. But he pushed it away. He couldn't resist the power surging through him, dragging him on so forcefully it hurt. He wanted to fight. He wanted revenge. His eyes stung with tears at the thought.

"Can I help you?"

The brunette woman at the ticket booth looked slightly terrified the moment he turned to her, and he tried harder to calm everything raging inside. Closing his eyes, he took a deep breath, feeling the shaking in his hands subside a little. It would have to be enough. He had to stop himself from running the last few steps to the counter. "I need a flight to Jackson Hole as soon as possible."

Her blue-gray eyes widened, and she swallowed, and he felt his hands begin to tremble again. Why wasn't she answering? What was she waiting for? He was nearly ready to jump over the counter and book the flight himself.

"I'm so sorry," she said in a soft, sweet voice. "But all outgoing flights are canceled for the next three hours at least." Her head tipped toward the window. "A blizzard is passing through the area. We're hoping it will swing north or east, but we won't know for at least two hours." She studied his face. "Maybe one."

He turned to the window, seeing a flurry of white zipping past the airport, obscuring the view. Still, the planes were lined up and looked ready to go. Planes flew in snowstorms all the time. Maybe it would only be a slight delay. Besides, it didn't look like too severe a blizzard to him. Just a skiff. He turned back to the woman. "Can I wait for the next available flight out? Anywhere near Jackson Hole is fine." He'd walk every frozen back road and highway clear to Ridgeville if he had to.

The woman looked immensely relieved. "Yes," she said. "Let me get some information from you."

"Great."

He rattled off his name and birthdate and handed over his credit card, finally settling down in a nearby seat. His hands were still shaking, and he knew he needed to calm down and think, but everything was hurting.

Leaning forward, he rested his elbows on his knees and dropped his head into his hands.

Relax. Just relax.

But the memory of his devastation and loss attacked, washing over him like the ocean. Drowning couldn't be any worse than this. He wanted to kill Hal. The thought overwhelmed his mind until it screamed inside of him. He sucked in a breath and scratched his fingernails through his hair, trying to find relief. It was too much for any one person to bear.

God, help me. I don't want to be this man.

Instantly, the warmth returned. But this time it was scorching with a power stronger than he'd ever felt. Whatever had trapped him in such misery and pain had been shaken. He could feel its presence growing further away until it was gone. There was still the knowledge of what Hal had done, but now he knew it wasn't going to destroy him. And with his head still in his hands, his heart swelled with gratitude. He didn't know what would happen with his future, but at least he was in control of his mind.

"Sir."

He started, looking up to see the flight attendant standing next to him. She knelt in front of him, and her hand rested on his arm. The kindness in her face had his eyes watering again. Would it never stop?

"Is there anything I can do for you?" She asked quietly, keeping her voice from those around them. Although, there weren't many. He was one of only three in the entire terminal. "Are you well? Do you need medical care?"

He couldn't help but smile, even through the turmoil. "No," he said quietly. "I've just learned of some tragic news back home and..." He glanced out the window again. The storm had strengthened so that he could barely see the planes anymore. "I really need to get back."

"I'm so sorry," she said, "Is there anyone you could call to help? Someone close to the family? Maybe they could step in for a moment until you arrive back."

Only one person came to his mind, but he didn't want to call her. Carmen might not even answer his calls anymore, and he wouldn't blame her. Still, he thanked the flight attendant, and she returned to the booth. He was left alone, staring down at the screen of his cell phone.

"Carmen," he said, trying her name out. It sent terror straight through him, but what choice did he have? He needed to do something, or Hal would just go on framing Lander for his parents' murder.

He selected her name, and the phone began to ring. Again and again, until he knew she wasn't going to answer. He wiped at the cold sweat on his forehead and listened to her cheerful voicemail message. After the beep, his mouth opened. He intended to leave a message. But the words were trapped in his throat. He ended the call, exhausted and breathing far too hard for someone just sitting still. He went to the window and watched. The storm wouldn't continue forever, and the second it began to ease, he would be on his way home.

⚜

CARMEN'S INSIDES ACHED LIKE THEY WOULD FALL APART AT any second. Maybe they already had; she wouldn't be surprised. She'd managed to keep her emotions in check for the remainder of the weekend after talking to Everett. But now, it was Monday. A new day, a new week. She needed a break, or she would never make it through. Forcing herself to appear calm and cheerful was going to drive her crazy.

She walked down the back roads of Ridgeville, taking in the wintery landscape. It was beautiful covered in snow. Pine trees and log homes everywhere. These were roads she'd never been on, and it was nice to feel a little lost.

A quaint corner market had a small group of people gathered out in front, and she walked cautiously closer, peering through the bodies until she spotted a litter of puppies. They tumbled around together inside a big cardboard box. Fluffy little balls of merle and red with striking blue eyes. She leaned in a little closer, admiring them. Two grown dogs sat beside the box, watchful and calm. Clearly well trained.

"Yes, Australian Shepherds," a woman said. She sat in a folding chair beside the box, holding a binder open on her lap. There were photographs of what looked like the puppies' parents herding cows and even one of a dead snake at the feet of the father. "They're excellent protectors, but very gentle with humans."

Carmen glanced at the puppies again, wishing they weren't so small. They were cute, but each one was a full-time job for two years before it became what the woman called a protector. She made her way around the crowd that surrounded the puppy box to approach the adult dogs. They noticed her attention immediately, but the only change was a shifting in their eyebrows and the swishing of their long tails against the snow.

"Hello," the woman said, after noticing the dog's distraction. "Are you interested in a puppy?"

Carmen held her hand out and let the dogs sniff her. The bigger red, white, and brown male began licking her hand, and she smiled. The smaller patchy white, gray, and brown female turned to her owner. "Actually, I'd be more interested in a closer-to-grown dog," Carmen said. "Do you have any older puppies, or maybe a trained dog that I could use on my ranch right away?"

"You're old Tagen's granddaughter, aren't you?" The woman's voice was full of tenderness, and when Carmen nodded, a full smile spread across her face. "It's been a long time, but I can still see the little girl I met so long ago. Your grandfather was always so proud of you." She sighed, looking down at the puppies. "I loved that man. He bought one of our first litters of Shepherd puppies. Back when my parents were breeding. Oh, it must've been forty years ago." She smiled again. "He never bought another one after Digger passed on. Do you remember that dog?"

"I do." Carmen's memories included long walks in the forest and playing in the creek. And just like his name, Digger would dig. "He was a fun dog."

"Saved you a time or two, if I remember it correctly." She glanced back when someone lifted a puppy from the box, then turned back to Carmen. "Wasn't there a wolf that gave him a few battle scars?"

"Yeah, he lost an ear that day." Carmen shook her head. "I don't know how dogs can be so brave. He's lucky he survived it."

"They don't know how else to be." She held her hand out. "I'm Tara, by the way. Nice to meet you, again." She winked.

"Carmen. Nice to meet you too." Carmen shook her hand but paused when Tara didn't let go. She only peered into Carmen's eyes as if searching for something.

"We do have another puppy," Tara said, finally releasing Carmen's hand. Her husband glanced over at them, seeming to catch what she'd said. He eyed Carmen thoughtfully and then turned to his wife. "You sure?" he asked.

Tara nodded. "It's Tagen's granddaughter." He smiled a bit and then nodded, returning his attention to the group around the new puppies.

"What is it?" Carmen asked, feeling a bit of intrigue pulling at her. Tara asked her to follow and led the way around the back of the market where an old Ford was parked. It had a solid cover over the bed and the tailgate was dropped.

Tara touched the side of the truck as they walked past, trailing her hand softly against the dirty blue metal. Carmen noticed the dirt caking her palm, but she didn't move her hand away. She walked carefully around the back of the truck and reached her hand in.

Carmen stepped around too, finally catching sight of a nearly grown Australian Shepherd. He still had gangly, young legs and scraggly hair that was just growing out of the puppy stage. His colors were striking, bold white flecked with layers of brown and gray. And his eyes were a pale, crystal blue. Carmen reached for him.

"Hold on," Tara said, rubbing the dog's head. "This one's special. He has the biggest heart of any dog I've seen come through our litters."

"But he never sold?" Carmen asked. She watched the way he crept to the edge of the truck but didn't jump off. Tara lifted him down, and she realized what she was watching. "He's blind, isn't he?"

"Yes, he was born blind." Tara let him go and stood, although her eyes were glued to him. "Good boy, Sam."

Carmen knelt in the snow. The puppy's fluffy ears perked up, and he reached his nose forward, sniffing her face. His body twisted as he wagged his tail, circling her. Coming in front of her again, he planted his two front feet on her shoulders and tucked his head beside hers.

She ran her hand through his soft fur, softer than any dog she'd felt before. Tara was right, he was special. "Hello, Sam," she whispered.

Chapter Twenty-Two

I t really wasn't the very best time to get a dog. She knew that. Decisions like the one she just made were usually preceded by months, or at least weeks, of preparation. Luckily, Tara had given her a small bag of dog food, a collar, and a leash.

Sam sat on the bench seat next to her with his ears perked up. He glanced this way and that at any sound they passed. His eyes were so beautiful and steady, it was hard to believe he couldn't see. A sting of nervousness tightened in her stomach at the worry that she'd acted too rashly. What if it was too difficult for this sweet puppy to navigate the ranch?

A cold nose touched her cheek, and Sam whined sharply. Carmen refocused on the road, catching a deer running alongside it. She took her foot off the gas quickly and began to slow, braking cautiously on the slick, snowy road. The deer glanced back and skirted across, narrowly missing her front bumper.

She released her breath and brought one arm around

Sam, rubbing his fluffy neck. "Wow," she whispered. "How'd you know?" Sam continued glancing back and forth as if keeping a lookout for more deer. Carmen brought her hand up and waved it across his view. He didn't move. "Hmm." She gave him a squeeze, and his tail swished against the truck seat. "Good boy, Sam."

Maybe he wouldn't have such a hard time after all.

By the time they turned down the long lane to Cedar Creek Lodge, Sam was curled up next to her, asleep. Her hand rested on his warm belly, and she found a substantial amount of peace in the way his body rose and fell with each breath. She pulled up to the lodge just as her phone rang.

Sam jolted to his feet, sniffing at her coat pocket where her phone was tucked away. She rubbed the side of his face. "I got it," she said. But when she glanced down at the screen, her face went cold. Lander's picture was something she hadn't looked at in a long time. It was her favorite, taken the night they'd ridden back to the lodge together on Dax. She'd fallen asleep in his arms then, so content. Their future together had seemed so solid. But now, as she looked into his gorgeous eyes and traced the expression on a face that once told her he loved her, she realized she should have picked a different photo.

Her heart was reeling as her finger hovered over the call button. She couldn't answer just yet. Not with how startled she was. Her throat felt so tight she could hardly breathe, and her pulse raced through her veins. Every perfect memory of him suddenly played in her mind, cutting like a knife in her chest.

His picture disappeared. She'd waited too long and now her eyes flickered to the small icon at the bottom of the screen, waiting to see if he'd leave a message. What could he possibly have to say to her anyway? He'd already said plenty. Still, there was one person he'd spoken to that she hadn't. Someone she could go to for answers. She'd thought about calling him before but never summoned up enough courage. She glanced once more at the icon to see he hadn't left a message, then began scrolling through her contacts. She'd give him a quick phone call and leave it at that. If he didn't answer, it would be the end of it.

"Hello?"

Pastor Evans answered on the first ring, leaving Carmen scrambling to decide how to start the conversation. "Hi," she said, looking back at Sam. His nose was pointed up at her as if he was watching. "This is Carmen."

"Yes, hello Carmen," he said, clearly already aware of who he was speaking to. "What can I do for you?"

"Well,"—Carmen swallowed through the tenseness in her throat—"I wanted to ask you about Lander."

There was a pause. "I see," he said, not sounding particularly pleased. "First, I need to remind you of the confidentiality involved in conversations between myself and my patrons."

"Yes, I understand." Carmen suddenly felt like a two-faced gossip. But that wasn't right. She wasn't looking to spread gossip; she was only trying to make sense of things. She trailed one hand through her hair. "It's just that, he tried to call me a moment ago and I missed the call." She hesitated, feeling like she might have just lied to a pastor. Because she hadn't technically missed the call. "Anyway." She took a quick breath. "I started wondering why he'd want to call me. Honestly, I haven't understood anything he's told me in the past month. I feel like there's so much he's holding back when he talks to me. I just want to shake him!" Her voice had risen with each word until she was very nearly shouting. She rubbed a hand across her forehead. "I'm sorry. I don't mean to get so upset."

"No, no." His voice, in contrast to hers, had quieted. "I completely understand, Carmen. I'm so sorry you're going through this. Both of you. And I believe there's a little information I can share with you that might help."

Carmen held her breath and pressed the phone to her ear.

"You see, I don't believe Lander planned on speaking with me that day," Pastor Evans began.

When Carmen's phone rang, she nearly cursed out loud. She pulled it from her ear and glanced at the screen. "It's him," she said, replacing the phone. "Lander's calling me right now."

"Then answer it," Pastor Evans said cheerfully as if he were smiling through the words. "Call me later."

Carmen nearly squeezed her eyes shut, trying not to look at Lander's picture as she accepted the call. "Hello?" she said. Her voice was shaking so hard, she worried he might not have heard her. There was a long enough pause that her lips parted as she prepared to answer a second time.

"Hello, Carmen."

She swallowed. Why did his voice have to have such an effect on her? Her hands immediately began to shake, making it hard to keep the phone steady. Sam climbed onto her lap, and she wrapped one arm around him, waiting for Lander to continue.

"I'm..." He cleared his throat. "Well, I've learned some things about, er..."

She listened to the audio flicker as if he was adjusting the phone on his end too. Was he as nervous as her? She doubted it.

"I'm flying back today if I can."

Her heart lodged in her throat. He was coming back?

"I learned that the fire wasn't an accident, Carmen. And I... I know who did it." His breath gusted into the phone. She could hear him working to control his emotions, and it set her own on fire.

Aside from how she felt about him, there was an entirely separate part of herself that ached for what he'd gone through in his youth. Apart from what their relationship might or might not be. This part of her was connected to him so intimately, there was no lessening in the height of emotions that coursed through her at the sound of his pain. She felt she knew completely what he was feeling, and that she might be the only person in the world he could turn to right now, and the news that his parents had been murdered was devastating.

With a sudden feeling of unease, she glanced up at the lodge. Her breath caught in her throat at the sight of Hal and Ernie. They stood on the front deck, watching her. Fear swelled inside of her. If they'd been there the whole time, they could be reading her like a book. Waiting for her to be at her weakest before they came at her. But what would they want? What were they doing here?

She bit her lip, wanting to tell Lander, but not wanting to at the same time. She couldn't just change the subject after he'd brought up something as life-shattering as that.

"I'm sorry," he mumbled. "I wasn't planning to tell you that. I just need a favor and don't know who else to call."

Her heart fell. He wasn't calling her because of a connection they had, or the closeness they'd shared in the past. It was only because he could think of no one else. But regardless of how she ached inside, she had to say something.

She ran her hand down Sam's soft coat. "You don't need to apologize, Lander," she said, her heart throbbing. "I'm just kind of shocked. Can I ask..." She hesitated, wishing he would have just told her instead of making her ask. It left her feeling nosy and shallow instead of the concerned friend she hoped to be. But there was no skirting around it. She had to know. "Who was it?"

He didn't hesitate, nearly answering on the tail end of her question.

"Hal."

His voice was rough and dangerous, sending a new shiver of fear through her. It wasn't the man she knew on the other end of the phone. And that terrified her. But as her eyes flickered back to Hal standing on the front porch, she wished she hadn't asked. How was she supposed to walk up to them now? One, a murderer.

She forced her eyes away from him and held Sam a little tighter. He tipped his nose up, licking her chin.

"Maybe it's why he stayed on at the lodge for so long. I don't know. It's like he's been watching me my whole life. But Carmen, I need something from you. If it's too much, just say it and I'll figure something else out."

Carmen had to force herself not to look back at Hal. Her entire body was tensing at the thought of leaving the truck and approaching them. She considered turning it around and going back to town. But she couldn't just leave her friends inside unaware. And besides that, she needed to see what it was Lander planned to do. Why he needed her.

"What is it?" she finally asked, although her voice caught with the question. She cleared her throat. "I just pulled up to the lodge if you maybe left something here?" She was grasping at nothing, only continuing on in order to sound stronger than she felt at the moment.

"I need you to find out where he is right now," Lander said, his voice strange and ringing with an edge she'd never heard from him. "I spoke with the sheriff, and he's willing to at least confront them, although I got the feeling he'd rather lock me up more than Hal. But I know Hal jumps around a lot from job to job. Is there any way you could maybe make some calls or talk to—"

"Lander," she interrupted, "it's okay. I know where he is." There was a pause and Carmen tried to stay calm through it. But oh, how she wished Lander was with her at that moment.

"You do?"

His voice was so tentative, she didn't know what he was thinking. But it didn't matter either way. Her answer was the same. "He's standing right in front of me."

"I thought you said you were at the lodge." His voice had risen, sounding panicked.

"I am. He got here first, along with Ernie."

"What?" he whispered. "Can you leave? Just leave and stay somewhere else tonight. I can be back soon—I hope. This storm just..." His words faded away as if his heart was pounding just as hard as hers. As if his thoughts were spinning in the same dizzying frenzy.

Voices reached her, and Carmen's gaze shot back to the deck to see Maddie waving her arm between them. "You need to leave, or I'm calling the police!" She shouted, her delicate voice ringing clearly.

"Oh no," Carmen said. "Maddie's out there now."

"Just get away from them, Carmen," Lander said. "Please. I'm waiting on a flight. There's a storm—"

"I can't!" Carmen turned off the truck, gaining the attention of everyone on the porch. "It'll be fine, Lander. They don't know that I know anything."

"But why are they there?" He was shouting now, his voice ringing in her ears.

"I don't know, but it's fine. I promise. I'll just get them out of here and away from my friends. Just..." She scooped Sam into her arms and pushed the door open. "Be careful."

"Me?" Lander's voice hadn't quieted any, and it somehow broke through the fear, making her smile.

"Yes, you." She glanced down at Sam, feeling a little braver with him in her arms. "Flying through a storm can be more dangerous than you might think."

"Flying is nothing," he practically growled. "If Hal even so much as looks at you wrong, I swear—"

"Pray for me, then," she said, cutting him off before he could finish his threat. She didn't want to hear it anyway. It wasn't him. He was obviously struggling with this news, and whomever he was becoming, it wasn't the man she knew before. "Promise me you will."

His sigh was long and heavy. "I will, Carmen. And I'll let you know as soon as the flight leaves. I'll be there as soon as I can. And Carmen?"

"Yeah." She was outside the truck now, standing alongside it with Sam content in her arms. He didn't struggle to get down and just snuggled deep in her coat.

"Don't tell them any of this. Not a word. Don't tell them it's me on the phone. Nothing."

"I know," Carmen said. "Goodbye."

She closed the squeaky truck door and tucked her phone

into her pocket. If she were alone, she would've let Sam down so he could explore his new home and get used to the stairs and the deck. But not now. The last thing she wanted was for them to realize her new dog was blind. She wanted to protect him, and also use him for protection. And telling them about his disability would negate both of those objectives.

By the time she reached the deck, she was trembling down to her core. But she managed to force an artificial calm through her body and stare down the two horrible men on her deck. She climbed the steps and held Sam tight, hoping nothing he did would give his blindness away.

"I believe Maddie told you two to leave," she said, standing so that she was in between the men and Maddie. "But I see you're still here."

"That's because," Hal said, glaring at Maddie and then turning the full force of his dark eyes to Carmen, "as delightful as our conversation has been, we didn't come here to speak with her. We came here to speak with you."

"What could you possibly have to say to me?" Carmen moved toward the door, encouraging Maddie farther away from them.

"We just came to warn ya," Ernie said, looking at her with less contempt than Hal. But just barely. "The way this investigation is going, Lander might be a more dangerous man than when he left." Ernie's eyes bored into hers. "Have you spoken to him lately?"

Carmen willed her eyes to stay steady. "No, I haven't," she said. She was a horrible liar, and they probably saw right through her. "We aren't exactly on speaking terms right now."

"That's unfortunate." Hal stepped closer, taking the lead

from Ernie. "Because we've been trying to reach him at the ranch he started working at. Turns out he jumped ship earlier today. No one knows where he went. Had some little accident out in the fields and then, bam! Gone."

He had an accident? Carmen suddenly wished she'd asked him more questions. Like how he knew Hal was the one at fault. What if he'd just gone and hit his head? What if the whole thing was just a case of a mild concussion?

"Anything else you want to tell us, Miss Carmen?"

Hal was studying her intensely, and she swept the thoughts away, shaking her head. "No. But I'll be sure to call the station if he shows up."

"Yeah." Ernie nodded. "Be sure you do that. They won't get off my back about that night, and I'm tired of explaining exactly where I was and what I was doing."

"It's exhausting," Hal added, giving her a tight-lipped smile.

"I'm sure it is." Carmen moved closer to the door again, practically trapping Maddie against it. "Well, he'll be back before too long, and everything will get sorted out."

"Lander?" Hal stepped in far too close, forcing Carmen to look up to stare into his eyes. "You're fairly sure he's coming back, are you?"

"Well." Carmen wanted to run, but she shook her head, trying to smile. It didn't work. "If he disappeared from his job out in Colorado, where else would he go? He's obviously heading home for a little while at least."

"Hmm." Hal rubbed his hands together. They were bright red in the late afternoon cold. "Let's hope you're right."

A truck pulled up and Carmen glanced over to see Jake and the Driscoll boys all crowded into the cab. The relief that coursed through her nearly had her passing out. But she held firm to Sam, reminding herself that the young dog was counting on her. She steadied her knees and managed a quick smile. "We'll see you both another time," she said, wishing she could be shouting at them to never come back again. But as it was, she wanted to leave things as civil as possible. Lander would be back soon, and then things would be okay.

"C'mon, Hal." Ernie pulled on Hal's arm, fairly dragging him down the steps. "We gotta go."

Hal didn't respond, he only allowed himself to be dragged along, all the while staring back at Carmen.

She felt the chill of fear spreading again, trembling in her arms and legs until she was exhausted.

Jake came first, glaring at Hal and Ernie as they drove off. "What did they want?" He said, meeting Carmen and Maddie at the door.

Carmen couldn't answer. She knew what would happen if she did, and breaking down into Jake's arms was something she just couldn't allow. Not again. Her weaknesses had already caused enough trouble. So, she only shook her head and pulled the door open.

"Maddie!" Everett came into view, jogging through the last bit of snow before he reached the house, and Carmen turned to Maddie, exasperated. "You didn't," she said, very nearly angry.

Maddie looked guilty, and her cheeks turned a pale shade of pink. She shrugged. "Well, I didn't know who else to call. And he's just right up the hill, so..." She let the explanation trail away, and Carmen realized she needed to speak with Maddie one on one. Alone. She needed to tell her how much trouble they might all be in.

But for now, she just needed some time. Her eyes were misty, but she hoped it wasn't obvious in the dim light of a cloudy winter evening. She turned to Everett first, then Jake and the Driscoll brothers. "I'm sorry, everyone." Her voice cracked, and she shook her head. "We just need a minute to ourselves, and then I'll try to explain." She scanned all five faces and her eyes lingered on Everett. "Just give us a minute."

Everett's strong jaw was hardened, and his expression didn't change. It was set in the firm, determined look that was so hard to argue with. His every movement seemed heroic. But Carmen reminded herself that he was working to prove Lander guilty.

For all she knew, Lander was mistaken, and Everett could've set the fire.

Chapter Twenty-Three

He felt nearly blind with emotion. Hate, fear, love. Everything. It crowded inside until he was reeling and half crazy. Sitting still was out of the question. He'd been pacing the halls steadily for an hour. What was Carmen doing? Why hadn't she called him yet?

He forced himself to return to the chair he'd claimed with his jacket. He sat down and took out his phone, something he'd done two dozen times now. And like every time before, his finger hovered over her name. But he couldn't do it. She was supposed to call him. He was determined to place his trust in her and await a reply. But what if she was in trouble?

He wiped at the cold sweat on his forehead. The flight attendant had gone off somewhere, but he was sure if she were around, she'd be overflowing with pity by now at the pathetic sight of him.

Pathetic was right. He couldn't even get back to Wyoming to protect the one thing in his life that meant something.

He pressed his fist to his forehead.

Dear God, please protect her.

The moment he felt his heart soften, the tears came. It hurt like his chest was caving in. He lifted his head from his hands and brushed the wetness from his cheeks. The flight attendant returned, watching him. But he didn't care anymore. Nothing mattered but getting back to Carmen.

Suddenly the airport brightened, and warmth flooded across his back. He glanced out the windows to see streams of sunlight breaking through the storm. Snow swirled and dumped all around it, but the light remained.

"Sir." The flight attendant waved him to her desk.

He stood and gathered his things, watching her type frantically on the keyboard as he approached.

She turned to him with a brightness on her face that had nothing to do with the sunlight. "I've got you on the next flight. It boards in ten minutes."

Suddenly he was so choked with emotion, he couldn't speak. He only stood with his mouth open, staring back at her. But she didn't seem to notice. There was no time anyway. He took the boarding pass she handed him and hurried to reach the gate in time, finding his voice enough to shout back his thanks as he went.

The flight was surprisingly full, with travelers hurrying to reach the gate right up to the last minute. Lander settled in his seat and pulled out his phone, but this time he selected a new number, and it only rang once before the line connected.

"Lander?" Pastor Evans answered.

It was no surprise his voice was so concerned. Lander had never given him reasons to feel at ease. All the while, he'd thrown any goodwill or help back in his face. And he regretted every moment of it. Now, all he could think of, all he wanted in life, was a way to create a future with Carmen. But he had no idea how, and it was terrifying.

"I want to believe that I can be the man she sees," he blurted out, watching the flight attendant come down the aisle. He was giving instructions and no doubt, Lander would have to end the call soon. "But I don't know how. I don't know if I can. And leaving would be easier than watching her realize she was wrong about me."

"Lander," Pastor Evans repeated, this time sounding like he was calming a child. "You're putting too much on your shoulders, son. Carmen is no starry-eyed teenager. She knows who you are, maybe better than you do."

"That's not possible," Lander argued, feeling the anger he so often clung to begin to rise up inside him. He took a deep breath, keeping it at bay. "I just... don't want to disappoint her."

"Well, to that I say, join the club." He laughed lightly. "Where are you right now? Can you stop by? I'd much rather talk in person."

"I'm on a plane, just making my way back." He nodded at the flight attendant who was gesturing to put his phone away. "I need to get off the phone, but I had to call you. I just wanted to tell you that I'm sorry. Your advice to me before was something I should have listened to and... I'm sorry I didn't."

"I understand, Lander. Come see me when you can."

"I will."

He hung up the phone and tucked it away, clutching the armrests as they accelerated and lifted from the asphalt. The ride was going to be rough, and more than a few passengers caught their breath as the plane tipped and shook.

But Lander wasn't worried. At least, not about the flight. He was more worried about what he might find back at home. If Hal and Ernie were out sniffing around at Carmen's place, what did it mean?

❧

"I UNDERSTAND, CARMEN, BUT I THINK YOU'RE WRONG." Maddie lifted her slender chin. "He's only trying to help."

"I don't know," Carmen replied, gazing across her friends' faces. Maddie was sitting closest to her, with Violet and Aries across from them. They had yet to let the boys in from outside, although the sun was beginning to set, and it had to be frigid out. Sam was curled up on her lap, having stayed close to her. "We need to be careful, is all I'm saying. Until everything is straightened out." She looked into Maddie's eyes cautiously. "Can we just please be careful until then? Maybe I'm completely wrong, but I just... I don't like not knowing. It would be safer just to trust the people we know we can trust."

"And where does that leave Lander?" Maddie asked coolly.

"What do you mean by that?" Carmen crossed her arms, angry. "What about Lander?" Sam's head lifted from his curled-up state, and he turned as if watching the group.

Aries lifted her hands. "Now hold on, you two. There's no point in fighting about this right now. There's a handful of men out there that we can't just ignore all night. What are we going to do?"

"My thoughts?" Violet raised her hand, garnering their attention. "We should call the sheriff."

"And tell him what?" Carmen asked. "Hal and Ernie left

and everyone else either works here or lives right over the hill."

Violet frowned, shrugging. "Okay, so let's just tell them all to leave."

The friends glanced back and forth at each other, but no one argued. It didn't seem like such a bad idea to Carmen. At least they'd be able to talk freely for the rest of the night if they did that.

"Okay," she said, standing. She smoothed her hand down Sam's back. "Stay," she said softly, touching his nose with her palm. "I'll tell them. Why don't you guys heat up some soup, and we can talk in a minute?"

They agreed although Maddie watched her closely as she left. Carmen was sure she wanted to talk to Everett before he was sent away but couldn't help feeling it was a bad idea. Besides, there would be time for that later.

The men were standing around quietly when she came outside, and they turned to her, Jake stamping his boots to shake the snow off. "I think we're just going to spend a quiet night at home tonight." Carmen glanced from face-to-face, but when she got to Everett, her eyes flickered away quickly. "It's been a rough day and we need some rest. We'll give you all a call tomorrow, or just come out in the morning. I'm sure there will be more to talk about then."

William stepped forward, his red hair escaping in a wild mess from underneath a wool beanie. "Well, I don't know what you thought we were doing here, Miss Carmen, but we've got chores to finish."

"That's right," Asher agreed, joining his younger brother. "In a snowstorm like this, it'll take some time to get it all done. So, count on us being out and about your place for a few hours at least." Chance smiled at her as he nodded, stepping up with his brothers.

Jake joined them, giving her a look that was deeper than the others, but at the moment she welcomed it. Having them nearby was going to be more comforting than she could say. She nodded back at them. "Thank you."

After a few seconds of silence, heads turned to Everett. He stood apart from the rest, looking on. He shifted his weight in the snow. "Need another hand?" he asked, pulling the hat tighter on his head. "I don't mind a little work."

"Sure thing," William said, leading the way toward the barn. "Come on."

Carmen watched them walking away like her own little army. She leaned against the door, smiling. Dax whinnied as they opened the barn door and the light flicked on. It streamed out of the barn, illuminating the snowfall beautifully. When it closed again, the darkness rushed in, and she turned quickly, going inside.

"Oh." She stopped suddenly, nearly running Sam over. "Hey there." She scratched under his ears and then stood. "C'mon," she encouraged, patting her hand on her leg as she went. He followed along, jumping up on the couch without hesitation.

"So, are they gone?" Maddie asked, although there was a bit of an edge to her voice.

Carmen's lips twisted a little. "Well, not exactly." She sighed. "They came to help with the chores, so everyone got to work. Even Everett."

Maddie's lips formed an O, and she glanced toward the window. "I see."

"Are you guys not hungry?" Carmen asked, glancing across their faces.

"Soup is warming on the stove," Aries said. She'd wrapped her dark, curly hair into a pretty messy bundle on top of her head. "But Carmen, I wanted to ask you..." She left her chair and sat down on the other side of Sam, petting him softly. "Are they sure the fire that killed his parents wasn't accidental?"

Carmen nodded. "They are."

"And you're absolutely certain he didn't do it?"

"Aries!" Violet scolded.

"No, it's okay," Carmen said. "I asked myself the same question not too long ago." She gazed slowly across their faces. Maddie's delicate concern, Violet's beautiful interest that was always filled with confidence, and Aries, with a fire in her eyes that only grew as the silence lingered. "Let's get some soup and I'll tell you everything."

LATER THAT EVENING, SOMETHING STARTLED CARMEN from sleep and she sat up with her heart pounding. Standing from the couch, she gazed over the room in the low light of the fire's last embers. Maddie had taken the smaller couch, and she stretched out on the larger one.

A whine came from across the room, and she glanced at the door just as Sam scratched it with one foot and whined a second time. No, it was the third time. Or maybe the fourth. No doubt it was what had woken her, and likely it was for a good reason. If she didn't want to be stuck cleaning up an accident, she needed to listen to him.

"Coming," she whispered, hurrying across the room. She pulled on her heavy coat and stepped into her winter boots. "I'm sorry, buddy." She opened the door, and wind blasted into her face, pelting her with snow. "*Brr.*" She shivered, pulling up her hood. "Let's hurry." She pulled the door closed behind them, careful not to slam it. But far from being timid, Sam bolted down the snowy steps.

"Sam!" She ran after him, although her snow boots slowed her down. He raced around the barn and disappeared from view. "Sam, no!" How could he tell where he was going? What if he got lost in the storm? She glanced back at the lodge, wishing she'd woken someone. But she hadn't planned on leaving the deck, let alone running out into the night. Where was he going, anyway? With another glance back, she realized the Driscoll's truck was gone, which meant they were no longer in the barn helping out.

Her running slowed to a walk, and she tried to fight off the fear that had crept up on her so suddenly. She didn't have her phone, or a flashlight, or even gloves. When she came around the back of the barn, she spotted him just sneaking inside. With a sigh, she followed, relieved that he hadn't run off into the mountains. The door was slid open just enough for her to follow. But the moment she stepped inside, she froze. Something was very wrong.

Sam was nowhere to be seen, but there were two familiar silhouettes at the other end of the barn. She could see the outline of a taller man and a shorter one, framed against the window and brightened by the barn lantern and white snow outside. Hal and Ernie. They hadn't noticed her, and she eased to one side, pressing against the stall door and hoping the shadows were deep enough. They were talking, but their voices were so low it was hard to make out. Wind whistled loudly through the small spaces between the barn door. It was likely what had masked Sam's entrance, and hers too. But where the young dog had gone, she didn't know. She prayed he would stay hidden, as she doubted the two men had a soft spot for animals.

What were they doing hiding out in her barn anyway? Were they lying in wait, or just biding their time until the sheriff came in the morning? Either way, it couldn't be good.

"I can tell when a woman's lying, and she was."

Hal's voice rose, and Carmen pressed herself harder against the stall.

"I'm telling you, we can't be here," Ernie argued. "Let's get off her property, or they'll have all the grounds they need to arrest us both."

"And what would you say if they were to arrest you?" Hal asked. His voice had twisted into a jeering threat, even Carmen could hear it clearly from across the room. It was a moment before Ernie replied.

"I've already agreed on your alibi, and I've held to it for all these years. So, if that's what you're worried about, you can quit with the threats. They'll have my word that you were with me that night working on the new hay barn south of town. No reason for them to suspect either one of us." He paused. "But..." His voice faded away.

"But what?" Hal challenged.

Carmen's gaze flickered to movement inside the tack room. Sam wandered into view, his tail swishing back and forth as he sniffed around.

"But where were you that night?"

She turned back to the two men, her breath held. Was Ernie really asking Hal if he was the murderer? Her hands tingled with anticipation as she awaited his response.

"I told you I was at my apartment alone. I went to bed early." Hal's voice was forced and rigid. "But I can't rightly tell them that, can I? They'll all but hang me."

Carmen could feel Ernie's suspicion as heavy as the low fog that often settled at the base of the mountain. Dax nickered behind her, breaking the silence. Perhaps Hal could tell when a woman was lying, but even the horses could see through his lies. Lander was right, and the truth of it only made Carmen sick, leaving her feet frozen to the concrete floor. All the pain Lander had endured from such a young age. The pain he still endured. Maybe their future together would have been an easy thing without his scars. A new wave of devastation settled heavily in her chest, aching. Just when she thought there was no more pain left to feel.

A sudden gust of wind beat against the barn, howling in a shrill whistle, and making the wood beams creak. Sam whined softly from the tack room, and Carmen looked back at the men, praying they didn't hear. If she could just get inside the tack room with him, they could hide behind the saddle mounts and sit out the night.

She watched them steadily as she dared to ease forward one inch at a time, awaiting her chance. If they spotted her, she'd scoop Sam up and run for it.

"I know he did it." Hal's voice rose. "It's why I've tried so hard to point them in his direction. All they need is to really look into him. His past. His personality. Everything."

There was something new rising in Hal's voice. Carmen could barely see them, but she noticed him take a step closer to Ernie, and Ernie backed one step away.

"But they didn't even spend more than a day on those cows."

Carmen's face went cold.

"Hal?" Ernie took another step back. "What are you saying?"

"You know what I'm saying," Hal spat, his ferocious voice

filling the barn. "Every single officer at the police station should have caught right on. Lander is dangerous and unhinged, everyone knows it. So why wouldn't they suspect him? What the hell are they waiting for?"

"You killed those cows?" Ernie's voice was careful and low.

"It's not like it made any difference," Hal said. "Even after the tip that reopened his parents' case. Idiots, all of them."

"But the tip wasn't anything," Ernie said. "It was just some anonymous claim that gave an old investigator the confidence that he could solve this thing before vanishing into retirement."

"Oh, it was anonymous all right," Hal said. "I made sure of that."

Ernie swore, and Carmen felt a new wave of sickness, realizing just how fully Hal had worked to have Lander take the fall for his crime. When they turned to the far door, she eased toward Sam. He'd taken to chewing on a strap of leather, and she hurried inside the tack room. Picking him up quickly, she took the piece of leather with them and sat down behind the saddles. Sam snuggled into her lap, happy to keep chewing. It was harder to hear their voices now, but luckily Hal was still angry, and the next words he spoke rang clearly through the barn.

"The tip was true enough, Ernie. You know that. Lander was seen that night returning to the house. He disappeared around the back for half an hour and then left again."

"And who was he seen by?" Ernie asked.

"Me." Hal laughed. The sound was eerie, like a ghost from the past as it echoed through the barn.

I need to get out of here. Carmen held Sam close, listening as Hal's laughter faded into silence.

"Well, lookie here."

Carmen froze, seeing Dax standing alert with his head high and ears perked, staring right at her.

"What do you suppose that horse is lookin' at?"

The wind howled, and with it came Maddie's voice calling Carmen's name from the lodge.

Hal laughed again, and Carmen held her breath. The wind calmed just long enough to hear footsteps on the concrete floor.

"Oh, Carmen," he said quietly. "Someone's lookin' for you."

Chapter Twenty-Four

✦❖✦

"Sir, your bag!" The flight attendant ran to catch up to him, huffing and puffing by the time he handed Lander the duffel bag. "Was this all you brought with you?"

Lander nodded. "Thanks," he said, turning toward the exit again. He'd been in such a hurry to get back to Cedar Creek Lodge, he hadn't even thought about his bag. Now he was looking out the window, thinking the same snowstorm he'd left had followed him back to Wyoming. But there had to be someone out there willing to drive in this weather. Someone brave enough, or perhaps crazy enough.

A semi-truck turned its lights on just past the exit doors. It was pulled up to the snowy curb, fitted with snow tires and chains. It was his ticket back. He raced out the door and waved down the driver just as the tires began to move. The truck stopped, and Lander climbed up the small ladder to the door, managing to pull it open even as snow swirled all around him.

"Where you headed?" he shouted over the wind.

"Goin' north," the driver said. "I got a place out there and need to get this rig home and parked. I can't take any detours."

"I need to get to the old Tagen Brooks place," Lander said, catching a change in the man's expression. "You know it?"

"Sure, I know it," he nodded, grabbing a bag of chips from the seat and tossing it onto the dash. "Hop in."

CARMEN'S HANDS WERE SHAKING, AND SAM HAD LOST interest in chewing. He squirmed to get out of her arms, but she held him close. Suddenly, he whined in protest, and she released him quickly, praying Hal and Ernie hadn't heard. Dax had stopped staring into the tack room, thank goodness, and the wind was howling again. She crossed her fingers that they'd take one look at the tack room and then head outside. Sam had his nose to the ground, sniffing. He bumbled over some brushes and ropes and into the back corner, thankfully out of sight again. Now he just needed to stay there.

There was only one small space between the saddle mounts that gave her a view of the doorway, and Dax beyond it. Now, she stared unmoving with wide eyes, waiting. When Ernie's head came into view, she cut off the sharp inhale that wanted to come. She knew she should tuck her head down, but moving was out of the question.

Suddenly, his dark, mean eyes met with hers. There was a chance he was just looking at the saddles, but she could feel it in his gaze. He saw her.

"Nothin'," he said, changing direction. He leaned out the barn door, peering outside.

Hal's head came into view, but he was looking at Ernie.

Ernie tucked back into the barn, and his expression charged. "She's out here, let's go," he rushed, stepping outside.

"Wait," Hal said, "What..." His gaze scanned the tack room, and then he swore sharply, following Ernie. "What did you see?" he shouted.

Carmen didn't waste a second. She scooped Sam from the floor and ran for it. If she could make it out the other side of the barn before they came around the back, there was no way they could catch her before she was back inside and behind a locked door. And if they returned the same way they left, the only thing they'd find was an empty barn.

She slipped and slid in her snow boots and Sam struggled to get away, probably afraid she was going to fall on him. And she might. All she knew was they only had seconds before Hal and Ernie would see them. She caught sight of Maddie stepping out of the lodge again, squinting her eyes against the snow as she looked into the darkness from the porch.

"Maddie!" Carmen yelled.

"Gotcha." Hal grabbed her by the elbow and spun her around, knocking Sam from her arms. Carmen screamed, fighting to get out of his grip. "Let go!" She shouted, turning back to see Maddie with a terrified face, shouting into her phone.

Sam growled and barked, biting at Hal's leg. With a strong swipe of his heel, Hal kicked Sam away. The puppy yelped, then spun in the snow, and raced back. He lunged for Hal several times before finding success.

"No, Sam!" Carmen shouted, fearing Hal would get a worse kick in this time. She reached for Hal's neck, hoping to pull him to the ground. But he caught her by the wrist, holding both her arms down.

"Sam!" Maddie shouted, running down the steps in her sweats and jacket. "Sam, come!" Lights shone across the drive, illuminating Maddie until she was shielding her face against it. A semi-truck rumbled up the driveway and stopped at the steps of the lodge. Someone jumped out and Carmen didn't even care who it was. By the way they were shouting, they weren't friends of Hal, and that was enough.

"Let her go, Hal."

It was Lander, although she couldn't see him behind the blaring headlights. Hal held her wrist and elbow painfully tight. And at the sight of Lander, his grip had only tightened. Sam tore at his pant leg again, but he ignored it.

"Let 'er go, son," a man called from the semi. Carmen could see the driver leaning out of the cab, resting a rifle atop the hood. She remembered him. An old neighbor of her grandfather's who had always brought them goat cheese and milk. Now, he was staring down Hal with the business end of his rifle. "Muzzle's pointed at you," he warned.

Hal smashed her wrists together, pinning them with one hand. When something cold and sharp pressed against her neck, Carmen gasped. She didn't need to see it to know he had a knife to her throat.

"Back up, Lander!" Hal shouted, his voice echoing through the storm.

Snow was piling up, but Lander took a few steps to the side. She could finally see him clearly. He was frozen not far from the semi, leaning forward, and looking like he didn't much care for the command he'd just been given.

Hal stepped back, and Carmen shuffled her feet with him. Every inch of movement shifted the pressure of the sharpened steel at her neck. She worried it would cut through if she didn't stay on her toes. Hal's attention was clearly distracted. He looked from Lander to the man with the rifle, and then back at Maddie, who had managed to coax Sam away. She held him in her arms and stared back at Carmen with frightened eyes.

"Keep coming, Miss Carmen," Hal warned, pulling her wrists as he backed farther away.

She stumbled over uneven snow and gasped, settling her feet again. "You don't need the knife," she said, angry. "I'll go with you."

"No." He tightened his arm around her, keeping the knife pressed too close. "I think this knife is the only thing keeping them away right now. But I knew you were lying. I knew Lander was coming. You gave it away in your eyes."

His mouth rested against her ear, and she tried to shy away, repulsed by him.

"It's in your best interest to stay still," he warned. The knife slid against her skin, and she swallowed, clenching her jaw.

"What do you want me for?" she said. "I don't have anything to do with this."

"You have everything to do with it," Hal said. "But now that you mention it, things definitely haven't gone as planned, have they? I was to go free while Lander took the blame. But now, this doesn't exactly fit with that scenario. No doubt they'll want to take me in for questioning."

"No doubt," Carmen said. "But if you let me go right now, you can just tell them what you did last time. They won't have anything new to go on and the case will go cold, just like before."

For the first time, Hal relaxed slightly. She felt the loosening of his hand on her wrists, and the knife moved away from her skin just a fraction. Hope burst into her chest. She leaned forward, eager to take a step away from him. "Just let me go and you can leave. Get out of here before the police arrive."

Of all the horrible timing, red and blue lights lit up the snow around them. There were no sirens, just a cruiser SUV that slid to a stop next to the semi.

"Hal!"

Carmen turned to see Ernie hunched down in the trees next to them, beckoning.

"Too late," Hal said. The knife vanished from her throat, and he ran, dragging her with him. Carmen slid in the snow, trying to get out of his grip. A shot rang out, and she watched with wide eyes as Hal cried out, reaching for his shoulder.

He dropped to the snow next to her, grabbing her by the throat. "Move or I'll kill you."

"I'm trying," she said, scrambling to her feet. Hal was up again and dashed ahead, his hand still clamped tight to her wrist. Carmen ran hard, afraid he might not give her another chance if she slowed him down again. Scanning the trees and snowbanks and barn, she looked for any opportunity to get away. A trail of blood dripped on the snow as they ran, gushing from the gunshot wound in his shoulder. Maybe he would pass out. Maybe all she had to do was wait.

He dove into the trees, clawing at her wrist continually while Ernie took up the rear. The branches scratched and whipped at her face and hands, but she kept running, stumbling along in the dark.

"Hurry up," he whispered in a graveled voice. "Now get down." He shoved her behind a tree trunk. She watched him study his arm, turning it over to see his hand was covered in blood. Below him and trailing back the way they'd come, blood was spattered through the snow.

Shouts rang out continuously from all around them. A few sounded like they were still back at the lodge, but one was close. Lander's. Carmen looked back down the trail to spot Ernie. He stood holding his hands up.

"Tell me now, Ernie." Lander's voice rang through the trees, a haunting threat that sent chills up Carmen's spine. Suddenly, Hal replaced the knife at her neck. She gasped, but his voice whispered in her ear low and dangerous.

"Don't make a sound," he growled.

Carmen didn't respond. How could she when the sharpened steel was pressed so tightly to her skin?

"I lied for him." Ernie's voice was lowered, but not enough to escape their ears. "He had no alibi, and I didn't believe he started the fire that night. But he's admitted it. The fire, the cows, everything."

Hal cursed under his breath. He lowered down next to Carmen, peering into her gaze with eyes that were more lucid than she'd expected. "It looks to me," he whispered, "that this is the end of the line for both of us." He laughed in one breath, and then it was gone. "Who knew it would be this hard to pin a nobody for the crime of killing his parents." He shook his head. "If I would've realized for one second it would take this long, I never would've tried it. Would have left the mystery to go cold until the world ends."

Carmen took a careful breath. "But why?" She whispered, swallowing against the knife that pressed her throat. For a moment, he didn't move. Then slowly, the knife eased away from her.

"Why'd I do it?"

He took her arm and squeezed hard. She could no longer hear Lander or Ernie speaking, and she was afraid Hal would become angry if she were to turn and look back where they'd been. She hoped they hadn't gone in the wrong direction. It sounded like there was no one but herself and Hal for miles and miles. She prayed that if she got him talking, she could buy enough time for Lander to comb back through the area.

She imagined he was debating on giving his motive away or not, and when he started talking, she feared she knew the reason why.

He didn't expect her to live.

"I worked for old Tagen a long time. He was old-fashioned in the way he handled money. Wasn't long until I found a drawer in the library loaded with cash."

Carmen's cheeks warmed, feeling hot against the cold snowy night. She hated the thought of someone like this man working for her grandfather. Such polar opposites in every way. Still, she tried to keep her rising anger hidden, sneaking an occasional glance into the trees in search of Lander.

"I didn't take it right away. Just watched it. He'd take a stack to the bank every month. Load up portions into envelopes for the staff every few months and write their names on the front." He sighed, looking lost in the memory now. "So, after watching a bit, I began loading more cash in my envelope every time. Started with a thousand and then five thousand. Soon I was loading twenty thousand in cash into that envelope. He had larger bills at the bottom of the drawer, so it wasn't impossible."

Carmen couldn't speak. She wanted to—she probably should have by now. But she was shaking with rage, remembering her grandfather's bankruptcy worries that had led to a heart attack. Was this why? Had he been a responsible accountant for his business, but then he got swindled by Hal? It was infuriating beyond anything she'd ever felt in her life before.

Hal just glanced at her and then shrugged. "Would've gotten away with it just fine if Lander's father hadn't been so up in everyone's business. He'd barely lived in Ridgeville a month when he met a few of us in town one day. Got to talking with Tagen about his ranch. The old man was too honest, spilling his financial worries to a stranger like that. But it wasn't long before Mr. Casey came snooping around the ranch. He took an interest in old Tagen's woeful stories for some reason. Mighta lived longer if he'd just kept to himself though. Fool." Hal glared as he looked out into the night. "He suspected me after that day. Not sure why, but I knew it was gonna be bad if I didn't do something."

"So, you burned their place down," Carmen said, hardly able to muster more than a whisper. Hal's eyes were mean when he turned back to her. Cold and unfeeling. A murderer. Carmen shivered all over, terrified anew of this man. She needed to get away from him. Maybe he was hindered enough by the loss of blood that she could tear out of his grip before he could use the knife in his hand.

Where was Lander?

"That's right," he said. "I set the place on fire as they slept in their beds. Thought that was the end of the story. I'd collect the rest of the cash from that drawer before anyone knew any better, and Lander would take the fall. It was sheer luck that he'd been arguing with them that night. Thought I got away with it for sure."

"But you didn't get away with it," Carmen said, her voice rising from a whisper. "Ernie was your alibi, but only because he believed you were innocent. He didn't know he was assisting a criminal."

"If you think Ernie's an honest man, you're mistaken." Hal leaned closer, his hot breath in her face. "He's done plenty of bad, believe that. He's no one to cheer for. If my guilt rests on him telling the truth, I'm already a free man."

Carmen could see an edge of fear in his eyes, and she knew she should keep quiet. But she couldn't resist the firm smile that tightened on her lips and the strength of her gaze as she looked back at him. "What if you're wrong?" She peered back at him, waiting.

It took a second for him to react. No doubt the loss of blood was getting to him. One of his hands was still clutched tightly to her arm, and the other held the knife. So, she stayed put, aching to hear anything in the woods around them. Broken twigs, boots in the snow, even the startled sounds of animals and birds would bring her hope. But there was nothing. Only silence.

She could see something changing in Hal. His eyes moved slowly back to her. His hand twisted her arm like the coiling of a snake. She took a quick breath. "Ernie's been making excuses for you, hasn't he? That's why he chased me off Lander's property that day. He was keeping me away from you. He was afraid of what you might do."

"He doesn't like getting into fights," Hal growled, keeping his glassy stare locked on her. It was as if his thoughts dwelled on something entirely different. Something dangerous. "That's all," he finished.

She caught the change of his hand as he adjusted the angle of the knife. "Are you sure about that?" She said, her head spinning, desperately trying to get him talking again. "Ernie's been your friend a long time, but maybe he's had enough. Maybe he's the one turning you in."

"I see what you're trying to do," Hal said. "You're right, but it doesn't matter. I only have so much time left before I eventually run out of strength, so I'd better do this now. I've been imagining this moment for a long time."

His grip tightened painfully, and she winced, gasping.

"Time to end the Brooks line for good," he whispered. In the darkness, his silhouette moved as his arm lifted in the air. The razor-edged knife glinted in the moonlight.

And then it fell.

Chapter Twenty-Five

❧

"Hal!"

Carmen heard Ernie shouting before she realized what was happening. Suddenly, the knife was in front of her. She pulled away, shielding her face. But Hal was no longer holding her. Someone pulled her from the ground, and she struggled to get away.

"Carmen," he said quietly.

Finally, she paused, breathing hard, and focused on Lander.

Hal and Ernie fought in the snow, shouting and grunting. Slowly, Lander's expression hardened, and he turned to them. Carmen turned too, seeing Ernie holding Hal face-down with his arms pinned behind him. His knee was pressed down hard into Hal's back. The knife lay in the snow near Carmen's feet, and she reached down, taking it in her hand.

In one quick movement, Lander shot forward, ripping Hal from the ground. His fist landed hard, cutting the skin under his eye. Blood quickly began to streak down his face, but Hal only smiled. Lander grabbed his coat with both hands and slammed him against a tree, bringing his fist back again.

"Lander." Carmen grabbed his arm. "We've got him," she said. "It's over." Hal's eyes rolled back, and his head sagged forward. His hands held Lander's wrists and Carmen's eyes caught a trail of roses tattooed around the base of Hal's thumb. But Lander wasn't letting go. She could feel the strength in his arm constrict as if he was going to hit him again. But the last thing they needed was another murder, and Hal was hurt. "Please," she said, gripping his shoulder. Touching his back. Even with the terrifying circumstances, she wanted to hold him. She wanted his arms around her. But first, she needed to stop him from killing Hal.

She stepped around so that he could see her face. His gaze seemed to flicker unwillingly to her. She sank into it. Her emotions swelled inside, but she locked them away. Her hand at his face, she set it gently along the firm edge of his jaw. His shoulders lowered, and after a moment, he dropped his arm. He took a deep breath and then glared back at Ernie.

"Take him," he said, dropping Hal. Ernie caught him under the arms and held him up from the ground, struggling. But Lander didn't move. He only tilted his head toward the lodge. "You lead. We'll follow. And you'd better hurry, or he's not going to make it."

Ernie didn't respond. He just started pulling, dragging his friend through the snow. Carmen walked alongside Lander, watching Ernie. She couldn't imagine what Lander must be thinking. What he must be feeling having his parents' killer and accomplice right in front of him. She couldn't decide if she should speak or not. But after one look at Lander's stony gaze, she decided against it. Let him be the one to break the silence.

Carmen wasn't prepared for any length of time in this weather, and now she felt it. Her body shivered relentlessly, and her toes hurt so bad she wished they'd go numb like her fingers. It was a long, silent walk back to the cabin. Carmen glanced at Lander often, wishing she could hear his thoughts. But his eyes never left Hal and Ernie, and she couldn't help noticing the muscles in his jaw twitching from time to time.

Finally, she saw bits and pieces of Cedar Creek Lodge through the trees and spotted the lantern at the front porch. The forest opened up, and they emerged not far from the barn. Police called to them from both sides. One group appeared to have finished a search of the surrounding forest. Their flashlights trailed along the snowy ground and illuminated the flakes still falling. A few officers stood together next to the semi and police cruiser, their jackets and hats topped with snow. Puffs of frozen breath trailed up from their conversation.

The minute they were spotted, everyone seemed to converge at once. Carmen backed out of the way as officers surrounded Lander, Hal, and Ernie. They asked questions and gave orders, quickly deciding to transport Hal themselves. He was loaded into the back of the cruiser and Ernie joined him, charged with holding him still while they drove. Hal hadn't regained consciousness, and Carmen was glad. It felt like his waking up would be reason enough for Lander to attack him. And something told her once he did, he wouldn't be able to stop.

Carmen caught sight of Maddie on the front porch, struggling to hold on to Sam as he wriggled and barked.

Finally, he leapt from her arms and scrambled across the snow. He stopped after a few feet, and his head turned side to side.

"Sam." Carmen knelt as he sprang into action again, tumbling towards her in a clumsy puppy-run. He plowed into her, and she lifted him into her arms, hugging his soft body. "You're so brave, Sam," she said, letting him climb up so his front legs hung off the back of her shoulder. He tucked his nose into her hair and whined quietly as she stroked him.

She glanced back to see Lander watching from the group of officers.

"Don't leave the area," an officer warned, pointing at Lander. Lander nodded quietly and watched with a somber gaze as the cruiser drove away.

"Are you okay?" Carmen pulled her eyes from the scene just as Maddie wrapped her arms around her. "Sorry, I couldn't hold on to Sam." Closing her eyes, she hugged her back, so drained. But at least her toes had finally gone numb.

"It's okay," she mumbled the words into Maddie sleek, silky hair. "Thank you."

"You should get inside."

Lander's strong voice behind them had Carmen and Maddie turning around quietly. He seemed taller than Carmen remembered. But the smile she loved never showed. He only nodded his head as if he expected a hat should be there instead of simply the wavy dark hair that hung alongside his face.

"Frostbite settles in quickly," he continued, taking a single step closer. "I noticed you were walking a little stiff." He glanced down at the boots she was wearing and nodded again. "Your feet should be okay in those. How are your hands?" He held out his hand, and Carmen kept hold of Sam and stretched the other hand out of her coat, where she'd tucked it away for warmth. Her fingers were cramped into a fist, and she slowly straightened them.

Lander frowned and took off his gloves, pressing her hands between his. "C'mon, let's go inside," he said, keeping her hands sandwiched in his as they went. His eyes glanced at Sam, but he didn't ask about the puppy. Likely, there was too much on his mind already.

Carmen vaguely noticed Maddie standing aside as Lander walked with her up the steps to the lodge. The warmth of the cabin was heavenly, making her cold nose sting. It was likely bright red, but she didn't care. Her fingers were slowly regaining some feeling, and Lander's touch was something she wanted to feel. His hand was constantly moving, adjusting, and covering the coldest parts of her hand.

They stood in the entryway, but Carmen wasn't sure what to do next. It didn't feel like there should be a next. She'd made it to a moment she never thought would happen again in her life, and the idea of moving on to something else was impossible. She could hardly breathe—forget moving on.

Lander took a sudden breath and looked into her eyes. Pain showed in his face briefly. His eyebrows pressed together, and he shook his head. "Thank you," he whispered. He paused and glanced at Maddie.

Carmen looked over to see her friend with wide, mesmerized eyes. But her attention turned back to Lander as he squeezed her hand, and then his hands slid away, releasing her. "For stopping me." He looked back at the door, then his gaze returned to her. "I don't think I can make it back to my cabin tonight..." His statement hung in the air for a moment.

"Oh." Carmen set Sam on the floor, and he trotted back

to the couch. Thankfully, she was able to find her voice. "No, of course not. There's a pullout bed in the library if you're okay with that?"

"That would be wonderful, thank you."

His voice was rich and deep, and everything her dreams were made of. But was he only staying because the storm made leaving physically impossible? If so, she really needed to control her emotions before they got away from her. However, the stabbing pain in her chest told her it was already too late. She'd given herself fully to him in those two minutes when her hands were in his, and now the grief was unbearable. But all she had to do was assure he was comfortable and then escape to her room. She needed a place to fall apart.

"I'll just grab you some blankets," she said, turning around before their eyes could meet.

"Thank you."

His voice came quietly behind her. Torturously so. Why couldn't he just treat her like dirt? Yell at her and drive her away? That would make everything so much easier.

"Do you need any help?" Maddie asked, giving her the compassionate look that meant she knew Carmen was struggling.

"No, it's fine." Carmen shook her head and shrugged out of her coat. She draped it on a hook by the door and hurried down the hall. "You guys grab some food if you're hungry. I'll just be a minute." Her voice shook, but she hoped they didn't notice.

In her room, she paused in the quiet and privacy, wanting so badly to never come out. Just bury herself under the covers and say tonight never happened. She hadn't looked into his eyes and he never held her hands in his. Never gazed so tenderly across her face. But memories quickly flooded her mind, memories of more than just holding his hands. She closed her eyes, wrapping her arms around herself before her emotions could take over. She rubbed one hand soothingly across her neck and tilted her head, trying so hard not to remember his kiss.

Something tapped the floor behind her, and she caught her breath, spinning around. Lander stood just inside the doorway. He'd removed his coat and wore jeans and a flannel loosely buttoned at the neck. It was a look that most would call casual, but not on Lander. He managed to stretch the fabric in all the right places, looking utterly tempting. Carmen's eyes wandered over his shirt before she forced them back to his eyes. But that was no better. Nothing was more excruciating than looking into his eyes. She could feel that her face was flushed, but hopefully in the dark bedroom it wasn't noticeable.

"I never asked if you were all right." Lander hesitated, and his chest lifted in a deep intake of breath. He took a step closer. "Hal didn't hurt you, did he?"

She shook her head, but he reached for her hands, lifting them. She looked down with him to see cuts littered across her arms from the tree branches. She hadn't noticed before. With her heavy coat on, most of it had been covered. Now they were on full display as she stood there in her pajama shirt and sweats. And she had to admit, it looked a little gruesome. Some of the cuts had bled and dried, leaving dark stains on her skin. Others had swelled and were left a bright red from the cold and trauma together.

He touched her skin, and she flinched. But his fingertips continued to trail lightly along her arms and the tops of her hands. Her heart was racing, ready to explode. But after only a moment, she couldn't stand it. Anger burst to life inside of her. What was he doing? It was just a few scratches. She managed a ranch in the Bridger-Teton for heaven's sake. This was nothing. If he was just going to leave, why did he insist on making it harder?

"Stop," she said, pulling her hands away briskly and turning around. She took a deep breath, crossing her arms even though it made the cuts sting. "I'm fine, as you can see." Something about the feel of the air in the room had her imagining him right behind her. Just like the night of the banquet, she wanted to lean back and close her eyes, if just to imagine he was holding her.

"I never meant to break your heart," he whispered.

His breath brushed against her neck, telling her she was right. He stood very close. But if he was just trying to smooth things over, he was wasting his time. She clearly couldn't be friends with him. It was too difficult when everything inside of her wanted more.

She swallowed hard, and her lip trembled. "If you're going to leave, just do it," she said, surprised at how calm the words sounded when her insides were crumbling.

"Carmen." He said her name like it was his last breath of air. Like he was struggling just as hard. "I... only meant to save you the pain of being with someone like me." His hands touched her arms, but he didn't hold her. She could tell he wanted her to turn around, but he only waited with his touch so light on her skin. Luckily, her anger was enough to keep the tears at bay.

She turned around quickly, if only to show him his touch didn't affect her. "And what does that mean?" she asked, looking steadily into his gaze and trying to hold her emotions in. Her eyelids flickered only once before she forced her expression to be still. "What pain?"

For once, his gaze faltered. She saw him swallow and take a breath that looked heavier than all the snowfall outside. A tear escaped his eye, and he brushed it away quickly. "I don't know if I can be the man you deserve. I'm still full of so much anger and hatred. And now, finding out Hal had been the one to take my parents away." He shook his head, still avoiding her eyes. "It's going to take some time for me to be who you deserve. I know it. You might not see it, but it's there. This poisonous venom I feel when I look at people who made life hell for me when all I needed was a single person to reach out. Show a little compassion. I just... I don't know if I can forgive them."

His gaze lifted to hers suddenly and another tear fell. "And then I look into your incredible eyes..." He paused and his gaze wandered slowly across her face. "And I've never felt more fear in my life that you'll end up resenting me for not becoming the man you think I am. And... I don't know if I can. That's the problem. I don't know myself well enough to promise I could be a good companion. That I could find a way to overcome this trauma I feel inside."

His gaze dropped to the floor as if he was defeated already. "How can I give you a future I'm not even sure of? Make promises I don't know if I can keep?"

Carmen was stunned. Her lips had parted in the revelation that he was only struggling to know himself. But nothing had ever brought more hope into her heart. Her chest warmed and her anger vanished. She brought her hands to his arms, feeling the soft flannel of his shirt and the warmth of his skin underneath. "Lander Casey," she said. A thrill trailed up her spine when his eyes met hers again. "The only problem I see here is that you don't know who you are. But I promise you, I do."

She moved in closer. "You've already proven yourself to me. Maybe others have their ideas and opinions, but that's none of our concern. You can prove yourself to them with time. But listen to me—"

He dropped his head, but she brought her hands to his face, tilting his gaze upward until it returned to hers. The sadness she saw was so honest, it melted her heart. "I told you I loved you, and I meant it," she whispered, finally losing grip on her emotions. Tears gathered in her eyes, and she blinked them away quickly. "Why didn't you believe me? Because I do, Lander Casey." Her voice caught. "I love you so much it hurts."

His hands came around her back, but the sadness hadn't left his face. He shook his head. "You love me now, but what about in six months? What about in a year? What about when strangers whisper and store owners shun you for being with me?" He shook his head. "What then?"

This was all he was worried about all this time? Nothing had ever encouraged her more. She could face a thousand wild horses for him, stand up against the entire wolf pack along the north pasture. What were a few rumors to that? Her heart was racing like it never had before, because suddenly she knew they were meant to be together. If only she could get him to see it.

She leaned against him, trailing her hands deeper so that her fingers tangled into his hair. "In one year, yes," she whispered, lifting on her toes. She touched her lips to his softly. "In ten years. In twenty." Her eyes clouded again, but she didn't fight it. She let the emotions swallow her up, making her head dizzy, her thoughts swimming. "In fifty." A tear trailed down her cheek, then another. She brushed her lips against his and waited, hovering so close. Asking. Her breath was impossible to catch, so she only inhaled each shaky one and waited. Whatever his answer was, it would be forever. This moment she'd laid everything out for him to have. Her now, her future. A family, a lifetime. Everything was his if he wanted it.

Slowly, his hands moved across her back. She could feel his heart pounding in his chest. He wrapped her in his arms, holding her tightly. His head tilted and one hand brushed her jawline, trailing up to rest at the side of her face. His lips trailed over hers. "Carmen Amelia Rivera," he whispered, his voice reverberating in his strong chest. "My body... my life... my soul." His fingers slid into her hair. "It belongs to you. And has since the day we met." He took a slow breath, and his voice came rough and broken. "I love you."

His lips finally pressed to hers, and she inhaled, happiness exploding in her chest. She didn't need to hear another word or ask a single question. She kissed him with a passion she'd never felt before. A promise of their lifetime together. An unbreakable, everlasting love. His arms held her; his hands caressed her like they would never part again.

He pulled her with him, sitting on the bed, and lifted her across his legs. She wrapped her arms tightly around his neck, her eyes closed while she kissed him through the brilliant smile on her lips. Again and again, as the minutes ticked by. Maddie was likely glancing back at her room, wondering if she should check on her. But let her wonder. This moment was what her entire life had led to. The meaning behind every decision she'd ever made.

This moment. This kiss. Was everything.

Chapter Twenty-Six

Carmen slid her toes through the soft sheets, smiling before she'd even opened her eyes. She inhaled, finally taking a glimpse of the world to see Sam fast asleep on the pillow next to her. She smiled. It was her favorite time to wake. Just before the sun. And today was going to be a good day. She could feel it. Every day for the rest of her life would be good. The way her chest was still warm with the memory of the night before when she was in Lander's arms. It was like heaven had fallen from the sky and settled around her.

Her head turned at the sound of voices, and she buried her face into the pillow. Closing her eyes again, she entertained the idea of falling back to sleep. But the thought of Lander a short distance away had her eyes opening again. She stared out the window with her heart beating faster, suddenly wide awake.

She recognized Maddie's voice, although it was too softly spoken to make out exactly what she'd said. A deeper voice answered just as softly, and Carmen sat up, listening. She slid her toes to the floor and took her robe from where it hung on the back of a chair. Sliding her arms through the silky material, she tied it around her waist as she walked out into the hall.

"I know it must've seemed that way, but I never suspected it was Ernie." Everett gave a sigh. "Back when all this happened, I trailed a stranger for months. Nearly a year of watching and tracking this man who ended up being only a vagabond, who took a dishonest opportunity when it came to him. But he was no murderer."

Carmen came out into the living room to see Maddie wrapped in a blanket and Everett leaning against the armrest of the couch. They both looked very comfortable in each other's company. But when Everett's gaze lifted to Carmen, he straightened suddenly.

"Carmen," he said, crossing the room. He looked intently into her eyes. "How are you?" He only waited a second or two and then continued, "I'm sorry I wasn't here for you both last night." He shook his head. "I should've been, but my supervisor came out and wanted a meeting. He's the one who opened the case up again, and it's..." He hesitated, glancing across her face.

Carmen's eyebrows lifted. "It's why you came out here."

"It is." He released a breath, sounding disappointed in himself. "I'm sorry I couldn't be honest with you. I came here this morning to check on you both, but also to speak with Lander. To, uh"—he shrugged—"sell him his cabin back."

Carmen glanced at the library door, already quite sure Lander was awake. She was an early riser, but he was even more so. Turning back to Everett, she took in his worried expression. "I understand," she finally said, watching his shoulders fall a small bit as if it was just what he'd been waiting to hear. "So, all that talk about you escaping from a bunch of political drama?"

"Well, no, that part was true." Everett smoothed one hand over his hair. It was tied at the back of his head in a knot. "Although it isn't something that would have me running away. We just used it as a good excuse as to why I came back here after all this time."

"I see." Carmen's thoughts were elsewhere. She started toward the library. "Just a moment," she said, not giving any reason as to why she was abandoning their conversation and checking in on Lander. It just wouldn't leave her mind that he should have been up already. Was he just overly tired from all the events that had happened, or had he been hurt and didn't let anyone know?

Everett returned to chat with Maddie as Carmen tapped softly on the door, leaning in to listen for an answer. "Lander?" she said quietly.

If there was an answer, she couldn't hear it. She turned the handle slowly and opened the door just enough to see in a small bit. Tapping it again, she stepped through to find Lander sitting on the pull-out bed with his jeans on, shirtless, leaning against the wall. He didn't look up and only twisted what looked like a piece of leather in his hands.

Carmen stepped inside and closed the door behind her. She turned back to him, but still, he didn't look up. His bare chest, firm and built, she could hardly keep from noticing. It had her hesitating to come closer. "Are you okay?" She asked quietly.

He took a heavy breath, giving an impressive display of strength that she tried to overlook. "I'm sorry, I just..." Finally, his gaze found its way to her and Carmen was instantly breathless. But the sadness in his eyes pulled her from any thoughts of his well-toned body.

He shook his head, his eyes returning to whatever was in his hands. "I just can't be part of that conversation right now. Not yet. Maybe that makes me weak, but I feel twelve years old again. Missing my mom and dad."

The silence that followed was both devastating and rejuvenating. After all, their deaths had been wiped from his name. He was cleared, one hundred percent. Carmen couldn't help feeling so much hope for his future, and hers as well.

Suddenly he adjusted his position, sitting up taller. He gave her a quick smile through watery eyes. "Would you, um... do you want to sit with me for a little while?"

She walked around a few couch cushions that had been stacked to one side and climbed up on the bed, trying to focus on Lander's pain. But she was ashamed how difficult it was when her arm rested against his bare skin. Finally, she pulled her attention to the strips of leather in his hands. He twirled them through his fingers. "What's that?" She asked, settling into the mattress, and leaning against him comfortably.

He held it up to show a men's bracelet. "It was my dad's," he said. "There's no real significance to it or anything. He didn't even give it to me, but he used to wear it all the time. I don't know if there was a reason or if he just liked it. I wish I could've asked him."

She watched him twist it in his fingers. Then, she reached her hand out cautiously, and he glanced over. His hand moved toward hers, and he dropped it in her palm. He watched her turn it in her hands, and then he leaned to one side, snatching his shirt from the floor. He slipped it over his head and pulled it down. "Sorry, should've done that first, I'm sure." He laughed. "No one wants to be squished next to me before I've had a shower."

Carmen managed a quick laugh, although she couldn't disagree more. He smelled pretty amazing. Still, it was nice that she had better control of her thoughts now that he was dressed. She handed the bracelet back, and he slipped it over his hand. Carmen set her hand on his shoulder, waiting only until he'd turned to her.

"No one expects you to go through all this without feeling anything," she assured. "It's only human to relive the past, especially with such extreme circumstances." She ran her hand along his back. "It doesn't make you weak." She took a deep breath as her emotions tried to surface. "I admire you even more for the way you loved your parents."

He turned, a pleasant smile settling peacefully across his face. She was relieved to see his tears had dried, and he seemed mostly recovered from his struggles, at least for now.

"I appreciate that," he said. But then, instead of continuing, he leaned in and kissed her. His hand touched her face gently, and her heart throbbed. When he leaned away, his fingers tangled with hers, and he stood, bringing her with him.

Her head spun for a few seconds while she tried to shake off the euphoria, proud that she managed to make it into the living room without toppling over. A smile tugged at her lips incessantly, but she didn't mind. Let everyone think she was a fool in love because it was true.

Finally, her gaze wandered back to Maddie and Everett. They both stood next to the couch with amused expressions.

Carmen couldn't think of a great explanation, so she decided on the next best thing. Distraction.

"Who's hungry?" She asked, making her way into the kitchen. She slipped an apron over her head and gathered ingredients for pancakes, setting them along the countertop. But when Lander plunked a carton of buttermilk down next to everything, she stopped, eyeing him curiously.

A smile lingered on his lips as well. "Do you mind if I handle this?" He leaned in close, smiling wider as if he knew how it sent her heart rate out of control. "I have a secret recipe you've never tried."

Carmen tipped her head, impressed. "Wow, a secret recipe." She sidestepped to keep from falling over. "By all means." She removed the apron and lifted it over his head, giving him a hug as she tied it around his waist. His hands ran gently across her back at the same time, and she couldn't help laughing.

"You won't be disappointed," he said, tugging a little on the apron to straighten it.

"I don't doubt it." She caught the grin on his face and then turned to the griddle. "Let's see what we can do here," she said, placing a spot of butter on the hot surface. It sizzled and melted, and she pushed it around with a spatula. "What kind of secret pancakes are these?"

"Buttermilk," Lander said, scooping out the first portion.

"My favorite," they said in unison. Carmen paused and looked back at Lander, and he looked back at her. A drip of batter landed on the griddle. He grinned and sidestepped, bumping her with his hip. "You're reading my mind, Carmen Rivera," he said quietly. He poured the pancakes one by one.

"And you're reading mine, Lander Casey."

They laughed as Maddie and Everett wandered over,

looking curious. Carmen set some plates and forks out and had a cheerful conversation with them about why buttermilk were the very best pancakes. She helped Lander as much as he would allow and couldn't have enjoyed it more. Especially when she took every chance she could to show him she was thinking of him. When she walked around him, she touched his back. When she stood beside him, her fingertips grazed his arm. It was a thrilling victory every time she caught his eye. If there was any doubt just how deep her feelings ran, she wanted it wiped clean away. And she was happy to do the work to make that happen.

When he handed over her plate, his fingers grazed hers, and her heart raced delightfully. The look in his eyes was too aware as if he knew the way her pulse soared, and her knees went weak. It was a delicious sort of dance; one she would never tire of. Even the hot syrup and fluffy pancakes couldn't distract her from his face. She managed to keep up a conversation even as her attention was completely absorbed in Lander. Every adjustment in his chair or movement of his eyes. She noticed. It was excruciating and wonderful and dizzying all at once.

Every once in a while, she caught a look from Maddie. A hesitation where she could see her friend was trying to make sense of this wild shift in her and Lander's relationship. Even Everett appeared a little caught off guard. But they'd get the idea soon enough. Everyone would. The whole town. The whole state of Wyoming. That Carmen Rivera was madly in love with Lander Casey.

His hand settled on her back, and she glanced over to see him wipe his mouth with a napkin. He gave her a wink and turned to the others, starting up a story about the ranch he'd been working on. She heard it and yet, she didn't. Her mind was too completely lost in the way he spoke. In the comfortable, confident sound of his voice. His expressions and each tiny movement.

Lander Casey was perhaps the best kept secret in the world, and he was all hers. Happiness swelled in her chest until it hurt. But she didn't mind. Nothing could ever bother her again, it seemed. There was only her and Lander, and the most beautiful future imaginable.

Chapter Twenty-Seven

"All I know is, they didn't know who we were and yet everyone said the same things. Everyone." Her father's voice was distraught, but soft. He didn't have the kind of temper that allowed anger to flare. It only existed, at bay until resolved.

Carmen sat on the couch with the phone to her ear, eyeing Lander. He stood with his back to her, gazing out the front window of the lodge.

"I'm worried about her, Alejo," her mother's voice chimed in from the background, sweet and strong. "She's been out there for so little time. And to hear about that boy, Lander."

Carmen cringed, pressing the phone tighter to her ear, worried Lander would catch their voices through the phone. But she didn't get a chance to defend him before her father replied.

"If you'll remember, Jasmine, I only visited Cedar Creek for one weekend before we knew there was something deep between us." Her father sighed. His voice returned in full

269

volume, speaking into the phone again. "But to be honest Carmen, I'm worried too. It sounds bad."

"Very bad," her mother said. "Maybe you should come home, just for a while. You could be in danger."

"But—" Carmen tried to argue but her father joined in, cutting her off a second time. "Lander may have some things to work out on his own before committing to anything as far as a relationship goes. His background is violent and isolated and, well, full of red flags."

"That's only what you've heard," Carmen rushed, before they could continue. "But I promise you, it's not true. The ones responsible for his parents' deaths were locked up last night."

Now Lander turned from the front window, facing her. Suddenly, her words were caught in her throat. She wanted so desperately to prove to him that people would give him a second chance. They'd found the one who had murdered his parents, for goodness' sake. How could anyone hold onto a grudge after that?

Lander gave a gentle smile, walking forward. He stopped beside Carmen and took her hand, lacing his fingers through hers. His gaze settled on her face, and for a moment, he only looked at her. Then he held his hand out. "May I?"

Carmen hesitated. Not because of what Lander might say, but more because of what he might hear. Her parents were kind and loving, but they were also protective. She swallowed hard and handed the phone over.

Lander looked deep into her eyes as he brought the phone to his ear. "I love your daughter, Mr. and Mrs. Rivera," he said quietly.

Carmen's eyes watered, and she blinked back the sudden sting of tears as he continued.

"She's the most important thing in my life." He took her hand and pressed it to his lips with a kiss. "And I hope to prove that every single day."

Carmen's eyes remained misty as she looked back at him. He set the phone to speaker and sat next to her on the couch. It was silent for long enough that Carmen glanced at the screen, hoping they hadn't gotten disconnected.

"There was a time," Carmen's father said, "when I said something similar about Carmen's mother. We hadn't known each other for long, and her father thought he knew me." He paused, and a quiet sigh could be heard. "But he was wrong. Jasmine and I have been happy together every day since the day we married. It didn't stop her father from hating me. He never welcomed me back to the lodge. Well, not until a few years ago. At that point, too much time had gone by to heal all that had been hurt. At least, not that quickly."

Carmen replied to her father as she gazed back at Lander. "I didn't know it was that bad," she said quietly. "I just thought you were always too busy."

Again, her father sighed. "No, I wasn't too busy. It would've been nice to spend time out there where your mother had grown up and enjoy coming to know a place she loved so dearly."

He paused, and Lander took the moment to settle a soft kiss on her cheek. Carmen tucked her knees up. Snuggling closer, she rested her head against his warm chest.

"I refuse to repeat a mistake that was so harmful in my daughter's life. Especially when I can clearly hear, Lander, that you mean every word you speak about her. But..." His tone darkened. "Should you go back on those promises, let me make you a promise. A promise that I'm powerful enough to chase you out of at least one state. So, you think long and hard about what you've decided."

"Yes sir," Lander said, holding Carmen in his arms, knees and all. "I'd expect nothing less from a good father."

A pause settled in, and Carmen couldn't help the apprehension that twisted in her middle. Her mother's words had yet to come, and she feared they would be less inviting. Finally, a sweeter-pitched voice rang through the phone.

"I appreciate your loving words about my daughter," she said. But the pause that followed was uncomfortably long. When she spoke again, her voice was slightly hardened. "Can you explain to me what happened that night with your parents? Were you absolutely, one hundred percent uninvolved with such a tragedy?" She stopped for a quick breath. "I'm sorry to be so blunt, but after the things we've heard, and out of concern for our only daughter, I just have to know."

"I can understand that," Lander said. His chest lifted and fell, and Carmen slid her arms around his torso. "I know the rumors, Mrs. Rivera," he said, his deep voice filling the room. "All of them. They started the morning after my parents died and have continued to this day. I nearly ended my life because of them. If it wasn't for Tagen bringing me on at Cedar Creek those years ago, I wouldn't have made it through." He paused, and shadows crossed his face before he continued. "But let me assure you, as emphatically and earnestly as I can, that they aren't true. Money was stolen from Tagen and my father figured it out. The truth very nearly died with him and my mother those many years ago. But thankfully the truth has finally been revealed. Their deaths have finally received justice."

Lander glanced out the window. The sun reflected off the

snow, giving a brightness to the room. "But whether the truth will stop the rumors, I don't know. Will people finally see me differently after all this time?" He paused, finally shrugging. "Honestly, it seems like more than I should hope for. But then..."

A smile slowly made its way across his face, and he leaned in quickly, kissing Carmen with a surprising amount of passion. She held him tightly to keep from falling over, giggling lightly when he released her. He was still so tantalizingly close. She needed only to lean an inch or two, and he would kiss her again. But she didn't. She only remained dizzyingly close, drinking in the sight of him and the feel of his arms around her. His head tilted ever so slightly, and her eyes brushed closed.

"Miracles do happen," he finally finished, although more breathless than before.

She opened her eyes.

He smiled and settled back into the couch, keeping his arms around her. "But if the two of you were able to see me as I am, it wouldn't matter. Everyone else can think what they want. Your faith in me would mean more than—" His voice caught, and he cleared his throat, his next words coming rough. "More than anything."

There was silence on the other end as they waited for an answer. Carmen hoped beyond anything that they would accept him. She could easily see how hard that would be for them when they were so far away, but she hoped with everything inside that they would.

Finally, Carmen's mother spoke. "Carmen," she said softly, "my opinion will be coupled with yours. I can't very well say with any certainty that I know every word spoken has been truthful. But you, my dearest Carmen." She sighed.

"You know him well. So, tell me, what kind of man is Lander Casey?"

Nerves coiled in Carmen's stomach. But when her gaze shifted to Lander, everything stilled like the lake on a summer day. Her mind, her heart, her soul. She couldn't help taking in his face for a time, and a smile touched her lips. "He's the kind of man I'd trust with my life. The kind I want to know better every single day for the rest of my life."

Sam jumped up on the couch and snuggled up to them. A smile settled on Lander's face and he rested his hand on the small dog before turning back to her.

"He has a soft touch with animals, and a humility I admire," Carmen continued, "He makes me feel capable of anything." He smiled, and she paused again, her pulse racing. "I love him more than I ever thought I could love any man."

A smile tensed on his lips, and he reached for her, touching her face gently. "I love you," he whispered.

"Well then."

Carmen's mother spoke considerably louder, and Sam lifted his head, looking toward the sound.

"It looks like we've misjudged him, along with a few others. And if this is the case, I want you to know that we support you both." She paused briefly. "I'm still going to fly out and meet you properly. I hope you know that."

"I'm looking forward to it." Lander smiled. "I'd love to see you both again. And... *thank you*." His words were deep and sincere.

"We'll give you a call again later, Carmen," her father called from the background now as if he'd become distracted. Carmen didn't doubt her clothing-designer father was patching a new design together while he listened.

"Okay," she said. "I love you both."

"Love you, Carmen."

They hung up the phone and Carmen set it aside on the couch, wrapping up with Lander again. It was getting late in the afternoon, but thankfully, there was still plenty of time for being together.

They'd gone about their work that day with a strangeness in the air. Everything had changed, and yet they fixed fences and cared for the animals. The Driscoll boys came and plowed the roads. Jake offered a small apology for suspecting Lander at one time, which he'd brushed off and forgave easily. Then Jake had, seemingly spontaneously, asked Maddie to go riding together sometime. It caught the whole room off guard. But she'd accepted, and the day wound down. Everyone went home. Maddie went to her room to finish a book.

And here they were. She snuggled deeper into his arms, enjoying the pure euphoria of it all.

"Miss Rivera?" He asked, grinning a little as she looked up at him.

"Yes, Mr. Casey?"

His head tipped, gesturing to one side. "It appears we'll be neighbors again in a week."

She smiled. "You bought your cabin back?" It was something she'd wished all along, to have the cabin that her grandfather had worked with him to build. It belonged in the... well, the family. Her cheeks felt a little warm as she imagined marrying him. Starting a family. Being together day and night, and day and night again. She closed her eyes, and the memory swam and warped as sleep pulled at her mind, and she sank a little heavier against his chest.

"I bought it back," he answered, lightly touching her neck as he brushed her hair back. The comfort and safety of his arms had her drifting off quicker than she usually would. She hardly noticed when he slid one arm under her legs and lifted her from the couch. Holding her to his chest, he carried her down the hall. She settled gently on her bed, and he pulled the comforter over her.

"Wait." She caught his hand before he could walk away. With her eyes drifting closed and her breathing deep, she still couldn't stand the thought of him leaving. Her dreams had twisted in that short time, becoming her worst fears again. Fears of him leaving her alone. "Can you stay just for a minute? Please." Her voice caught, and she pulled his hand to her. "Please don't leave."

For a moment he didn't move, and then she heard the sitting chair being dragged closer. His hand still in hers, he settled beside her. He cleared his throat, and the rough way he breathed had her waking a little more. She still had his hand pinned to her chest, hugging it tightly as if she'd never let him go. But when she opened her eyes, she saw there were tears trailing down his face.

She lifted up on her elbow suddenly, alarmed.

"I'm so sorry, Carmen," he whispered. He came closer, resting his face beside hers. His free hand touched her face gently, combing through her hair. "I'm never leaving you again. Never."

Carmen was overcome with a wave of relief. She sunk back into her pillow. His hand touched her cheek and traced her jaw. Her eyes heavy, she finally relented and drifted to sleep.

When he managed to free his hand and get some sleep, she didn't know. Once, her bad dreams returned, and she startled herself awake only to find him as before, leaning in close. Soothing her. Again, there were tears on his face, and again, he apologized, but she tried to stop him. Tried to tell him it was okay. That she loved him and was so very happy. But sleep dragged her back to her nightmares as if toying with her. Didn't her mind know this was her happily ever after?

When she woke, it was later than usual. She could remember waking more than once during the night, frightened from her dreams, and each time Lander was there. Now, as the strong sunshine filtered through the edges of her curtains, she scanned the room. Sam was lying next to her, alert with his head lifted as if he'd been waiting for her to wake for quite some time. She petted his smooth coat, and his tail whipped across the bed happily.

"Where's Lander, boy?" She asked, stretching. "Where'd he go?"

Sam jumped to his feet and leapt off the bed.

Suddenly a groan came from below. Carmen slid quickly out of bed to find Lander lying on the floor next to the sitting chair, his coat wadded up and used as a pillow. A wave of embarrassment washed over her at the fears that had seemed so real in the night. Now they felt childish and ridiculous, and here he'd gone and stayed up all night trying to comfort her.

She sank to her knees beside him as he opened his eyes, looking groggy. "You didn't have to stay with me," she whispered, not wanting Maddie to hear from the other room. "I don't know why I—"

"No, no," He shook his head and sat up quickly, "Please don't apologize." He took her in his arms, holding her close. "I'm going to be here for you when you need me." His lips touched her cheek before he leaned away, speaking tenderly. "And last night you needed me."

Carmen's heart throbbed with emotions and tears stung her eyes. But she held them back. She still felt foolish, but couldn't deny the fact that she'd been so afraid. Despite it all, she was so very grateful he'd stayed. "Thank you," she whispered.

His eyes glimmered with something beautiful; a hopeful, incredible gaze lingered there. "This is forever," he whispered, staying so close. "Me and you; one day at a time."

A smile grew on Carmen's face, and her love for him swelled in her chest. "This is forever," she repeated. "And so far, it's beautiful. It's perfect."

His smile softened, and his gaze wandered her face adoringly.

"It is."

❦

SIX MONTHS LATER...

A SMALL DELUGE SPLASHED OVER THE TOES OF HER BOOTS. Carmen woke from her thoughts and pushed the pump lever closed, stopping the water. She'd been so absorbed in memories of Lander, she hadn't noticed the flood gathering around her feet. Now she stood in a puddle large enough to tell her she'd been lost in her thoughts for far too long.

But the early summer sun would dry it up in no time. It would be fine. Still, she glanced around in case he was watching. Lander seemed much too aware of her thoughts sometimes. She fought back a grin as she remembered the late night ride they'd taken. The moonlight was just getting good this time of year, and it had been completely magical.

"The, uh... "

She quickly recognized Lander's voice, and turned around with her lips pursed. "Yes?" She tried to challenge him, sinking into one hip and crossing her arms. But she could see him fighting back a grin as well.

He held a hay bale in one arm, tucked to his side. But he took a step closer, and then another. Soon he was toe to toe with her, gazing into her eyes in the most scintillating way. "The trough's full," he said. But his smile won over and stretched across his face. He let the bale of hay fall to the ground and took her into his arms, lifting her boots off the ground. "What were you thinking about?" He laughed.

Carmen squealed as he tickled her. His lips found her neck and she squirmed until her feet were on the ground again. But he didn't stop. His arms bound her close and he twisted, dipping her back. Finally, she had a fighting chance. She grabbed his face and kissed him before he could say another word. Her breath was nearly gone when their lips finally parted, but somehow it wasn't enough.

The smile returned on his face and he brought her back to standing. "I've been a little distracted today too." he said, straightening his hat with a wink. He gripped the twine from the hay bale and lifted it up again. "Lot to think about."

He continued to the barn, glancing back at her frequently. Every time Carmen's legs felt like jelly, until finally he ducked inside the barn. She took a deep breath, trying to remember what she'd meant to do that morning. There was a chore she'd been planning to get to...

"Nevermind, I got it,"

Carmen spun around to find Maddie lugging a bucket full of tools.

"Oh, that's right," Carmen went to take it from her. "I don't mind taking the tools up to Lander's place—"

"No, really," Maddie had a cute weaved western hat on with teal flowers along the brim. She wore a beautiful worn linen sundress. The maroon color really complimented her milky skin tones, and her short leather boots were picture perfect.

Again Maddie shook her head, "Really," she said, fighting a smile. "I want to. I, uh... need a walk." This time Carmen noticed her dark hair, which had grown nearly to her shoulders, was formed into silky loose waves.

A smile stretched across Carmen's face. "Hey," she called after Maddie as she loaded the bucket of tools onto a four wheeler. "Is Everett back? I heard Lander say something like that..."

Maddie grinned before managing to squelch her obvious delight. "I don't know," she said, keeping her eyes from Carmen's. "He might be. Anyway, I'll see ya!"

"Yeah," Carmen couldn't help laughing. "See you soon." She watched Maddie ride down the trail that crossed the creek and curved through the trees to Lander's house. She drove fast and confident, which was a big change from her first wobbly, terrified, stop-and-go attempt at driving a four wheeler.

Jake came from the barn and quickly caught sight of Maddie driving down the trail. He watched for a long time, until she was lost from view among the trees. Something pricked at Carmen's suspicion, and she wondered if perhaps Maddie was a little hasty in chasing after Everett. At least, if that was indeed what she was up to.

But then, Maddie was the type who liked getting the

work done quickly so she had time to sit and read. Maybe it was as simple as that.

Carmen returned to the lodge, but stopped on the porch. The sun was so warm and inviting, she sat in one of the wooden rocking chairs and tipped her head back. Warmth flooded her face and neck, sinking into her skin.

There was a conversation inside the lodge and she recognized Annette's voice and one other. It sounded like one of the Driscoll boys. She didn't necessarily mean to listen in, but it was a fun sort of challenge to try and interpret the words. However, in the end, she failed. The cabin walls were too thick.

The door swung open.

"I can keep her busy—" Annette's voice cut off like she'd just suddenly vanished.

Carmen opened her eyes and twisted in the rocking chair. Annette and Lander looked back at her with almost identical smiles. But Lander's drew her attention more. She couldn't help letting her eyes linger on him, warming her much more than the sun ever could.

"What's going on?" Carmen asked, standing from her chair. "Keep who busy?"

Annette's smile widened. "Maddie," She swiped one hand through the air. "She's been a little sullen lately and I think keeping her busy is just the medicine she needs. "

"Oh," Carmen couldn't remember Maddie being sullen. It immediately had her feeling a little guilty that she'd been so distracted lately. "Is that why you sent her up to Lander's place?"

Annette hesitated only a second or two. "Yeah," she said, heading down the steps. "I'd better go meet up with her. We're helping fix a few things and get some cleaning done."

Carmen gave Lander a teasing grin. "You'd think you could manage all that on your own."

He held his hands up, laughing. "Hey, they practically forced me to let them help. But I will admit, it might've been a little selfish of me."

"How's that?"

"Well," Lander came closer, touching her cheek and neck gently as he brushed her hair back from her shoulder. "I wanted to go on a quick ride." He leaned in, kissing her. When he moved back, he smiled again. "With you."

"Ah. With me," Carmen grinned. "I was wondering."

They set off down the trail soon after, with Carmen on Dax, and Lander on a white gelding quarter horse named Dusty. He was fairly new horse at the ranch, but as a retired cattle roper, he'd been trained beautifully. The sounds of the horses was relaxing all on its own. The gentle rhythm of their feet as they tromped over dry grass and leaves was as natural as the sound of wind through the pines. A stick snapped under their hooves occasionally, and their tails swished often.

Side by side, they took the first twenty minutes of their ride in silence, although they found each other's gaze continually. Finally, Lander sat back in the saddle a little. His gaze grew deep and tender. "I don't know if I've ever truly expressed my gratitude for you, Carmen."

"I'm grateful for you too," She replied, a soft smile drifting across her face as calm as the wilderness around them.

"No, not like that," He smiled suddenly. "I mean, thank you, but..." He brought Dusty to a stop and the big gelding dipped his head, pulling at a few blades of grass.

Carmen stopped as well, waiting for his explanation. He

gazed across their surroundings a moment before continuing.

"I never felt part of this life," He shrugged. "It's so hard to explain. Until I met you, I was on the outside just watching people live their lives. I worked, but only as an escape. There were no goals, no tomorrow, no... *purpose*. There was just trying to find cover and exist because," He turned away, scanning the area again as if searching for the words. "I was lost."

He tugged on the reins and came close alongside her. "But now I'm found." His voice was rough and his eyes shone. "And it's thanks to you that I ever bothered to try. I don't know how you managed to give me so many chances, but I'm forever glad that you did."

His eyes simmered back at her and Carmen's throat felt increasingly tight with emotion. There were a lot of struggles getting to this point in her life, but now that she was looking back at him, it had all been more than worth it.

"Let's go down the trail a bit farther," Lander said, his voice remaining gentle. "There's something I wanted to show you."

Carmen gave him a questioning look but he only winked and led Dusty ahead of her. She followed, observing their surroundings more carefully. The thought that he'd had something in mind when he suggested a ride was intriguing.

They followed a trail she'd ridden many times, in so many different situations. The very first time she'd ridden out to his cabin in the high country was to say thank you; because he'd paid off all her grandfather's debt. The second reason was to give him a piece of her mind... because he never even said goodbye.

She'd ridden out to look for him more times than she

wanted to admit, and then there'd been the storm. She wished she could forget that one. But since then, each time had been with Lander by her side. And it was becoming her favorite place in the Bridger Teton.

They passed his first rickety cabin, which had been remodeled to be neat and useful. But when they kept going, Carmen's pulse began to race. She followed him past the shed and over a wide hill to finally catch sight of his new cabin.

She caught her breath.

Lander finally turned Dusty around, facing her. His face was radiating happiness. "It's finished." He said, giving a shrug. "If you want to take a look at it."

"Take a look? Lander!" Carmen laughed. "I can't believe this! It's incredible," She urged Dax on, who'd finally gotten a good mouthful of mountain grass. He plodded on with half a bush sticking out on either side of his mouth as he went.

They explored and toured and Carmen couldn't get enough of Lander's eye for design. And yet, it was still empty. She could picture the furniture that would look best in each room and corner, and she hoped he would let her have at least a little say in decorating.

But something else caught her attention and she began to feel suspicious. Lander seemed distracted. He glanced out the window often and checked the time on his phone. Finally, after they'd spent a good hour and a half wandering through his place and sitting and talking, he suggested they head back.

Maybe she was just imagining things, because it was getting dark and it was a perfectly reasonable time to head back. But then she saw him check his phone again. Something was definitely up.

"It's a nice night," Carmen said. Although, she wished she didn't have to resort to small talk. Clearly something was on his mind, so he should just tell her what it was.

But the more she caught glances at him, the more she realized how tense he looked. And his skin was a little plaid, and he was sweating too. But that cold be nothing. It had been a hot day, after all.

The sun had just dipped beyond the trees when they made it to the overlook. A steep cliff with a view that looked out on Cedar Lodge and all the wilderness beyond. It was breathtaking.

Lander stepped down from his horse and walked over to Carmen's. "May I?" He asked, taking the reins. Carmen dismounted Dax and watched as Lander tied them to a tree.

When he returned, he threaded his fingers through hers gently. They gazed over the lookout to the lodge. The sky was growing dim quicker than she'd expected. But then, it wouldn't really matter if they rode back in the dark. The horses knew the trail well.

Suddenly, lights flickered to life all around them. Tiny white lights like stars were strung throughout the pine trees that bordered her land.

And Cedar Lodge!

It was framed by a blanket of electric stars. The lights were so uniform and so plentiful! Carmen couldn't imagine what kind of work that would have taken to get them wound so intricately around each beam, eave, and tree branch. Her breath was stalled in her chest, awaiting exhale.

"Carmen Amelia Rivera,"

Carmen pulled her gaze from the glimmering scene to find Lander lowered down on one knee next to her. She gasped, turning to him. Her heart pounded with shock.

"I never dared to dream that I would find someone like you," he said quietly. His voice was rough and he took in a deep breath, one side of his mouth lifting in a quick smile.

His hand was shaking in hers and tears quickly stung her eyes.

"But this life would be more than a dream come true if I have you to share it with." He reached in his pocket and when he brought his hand out, a glittering ring was pinched between his fingers. "Carmen, I love you," His lip shook and his eyes shone. "And I promise to love you every single day for the rest of my life. Please say you'll marry me,"

His voice was so rough he could hardly get the words out. And Carmen worried she'd fall apart before he had the chance. Her vision was so blurred, she could hardly even see the ring. She blinked quickly, trying to clear her vision and keep herself together at the same time.

It felt like all the time in the universe passed by as she took a single breath. She brought both hands to his and smiled through the tears trailing down her cheeks. "Yes, Lander," she said, unable to hold back her thrilled laughter. "With my heart and soul."

He slipped the ring on her finger and scooped her in his arms, swinging her in a circle. The entire world spun with them. Far beyond, back at the lodge, she could hear voices shouting.

How many people had been in on this little secret? She was immediately sure Maddie, Annette, and Jake were all involved. And of course the Driscoll brothers. The lot of them. Maybe even Everett. She could hardly wait to ask them when they ever had time to plan it all.

But when her feet finally touched the ground, Lander pulled her close and kissed her. Every other thought floated away and she settled into his strong, capable arms. When she felt him begin to pull away, she reached for his face and kissed him harder... and he didn't need any additional persuading. Her heart raced and her head spun delightfully. If this moment was how he wanted to spend the rest of their lives together, she would be perfectly content.

Never mind that now they had to plan a wedding, or that they found themselves in the strange circumstance of having three houses to choose from... those problems could take care of themselves. All that really mattered was keeping this man in her arms. Starting a life with him. A family. Their future together couldn't possibly be brighter.

It was nearly an hour later that they arrived back at Cedar Lodge, walking hand in hand and leading their horses behind them. But even after the long wait, everyone was there to greet them. Maddie ran out to meet them and wrapped her slender arms tightly around Carmen.

"I'm so happy for you," she whispered, "Don't worry about anything else." She leaned back and looked knowingly into Carmen's eyes. "Just start here."

The smile had never left Carmen's face, but it widened at Maddie's advice. It was perfect. She nodded back at her incredible friend and her eyes roamed the lodge and the glittering pine trees beyond. A beautiful canvas for painting her happily ever after.

She caught Lander's gaze and couldn't look away again. His smile matched hers. "That's what I plan to do," she said, stepping into his embrace. He wrapped her in both arms while still chatting with Jake, rocking her gently.

The sound of his voice was so familiar, it was practically part of her. She kept her ear to his chest and listened, falling in love with him all over again. Lander Casey was hers. Their life together had just begun. And there was nothing in the world she wanted more.

THE END.

NOTE FROM SAVANNAH:

Thank you so much for your interest in my books! I hope you really enjoyed the deepening and finalizing of Lander and Carmen's story. Please consider leaving a review! If you'd like to keep in touch with me, you'll need to join my newsletter here...

https://sendfox.com/lp/1w9yz6

Right now, I only release one small-town western romance per year and I'm already at work on 2024's edition. Can't wait for you to return to Cedar Lodge and see what's happening with Maddie. Her story will be beautiful and fun, but also a challenge. Let's see if she's tough enough to live out in the Bridger-Teton.

UNTIL THEN, ALL MY LOVE,

Savannah

Made in the USA
Las Vegas, NV
26 November 2024

12732271R00173